The Insolence and the Free-Heroes

By Crimetest

The Insolence and the Free-Heroes

By Crimetest

Cover picture inset:
From Hironimus Bosch, Visions of the Hereafter

The Insolence and the Free-Heroes

Copyright © 2016 Crimetest
All rights reserved.

Author's note:

The characters and criminal events in this book are fictitious, and any resemblance to any event or actual person, living or dead, is purely coincidental.

Dedication

To all who have helped me, regardless of whether you knew it or not.

The Insolence … and the Free-Heroes.

Chapter 1- The baptism of David Bell

"At the very centre of every wrongful intention, there lurks a lie, which becomes our cellmate for as long as the truth is shut out."

Approaching the 18th century, Italian, whitewashed, Roman Catholic, church, on the outskirts of a quiet, sun baked, Italian village, David Bell recalls the above quote in his mind. It is true that he had committed wrongdoings in his life. He had even gone to prison, after he and his wife Claire, had tragically broken the law when trying to gain justice for their daughter Lucy; who had died at the at the uncaring hands of drug dealers.

However, as David mounts the first of five stone steps; in his own mind, he is now about to oppose something far more ancient, and far more corrupting than any drug cartel; for he is hoping to stand toe to toe (or at least word to word) against the cartels of religion.

Continuing up the well-worn steps, there is little doubt in David Bell's mind; that although his intentions might not be legally criminal in the heavily Roman Catholic country of Italy, his protest would undoubtedly be a definite social no-no, teetering on blasphemy.

To his credit, since committing his last crimes with, his then, wife, Claire, David Bell had given up crime; although he had not given up on criminals. He had even managed to create, and establish the successful, Crimetest's Crime Advice Line; a legally confidential, crime advice line for potential criminals who wanted to, at least, question the pros and cons of their intended crime. Indeed, the "lurking lie" quote, had come from the Crimetest Advice handbook.

Since creating Crimetest, the nearest David Bell had come to committing a wrongdoing, had been when he had 'bent the rules' (his own rules) of Crimetest; by deliberately initiating unofficial contact with a caller to the centre; one Steven

Chadwick, who happened to be threatening the very existence of the Crimetest's help-line. Steven Chadwick had been eventually jailed for kidnapping Elizabeth, a Crimetest employee, and for the non-fatal shooting of "A bunch of Goody-goodies!" as Steven Chadwick called them, namely, Sandra Lott and Andy Jones, and police sergeant Tom Vanner; who were at the time, trying to rescue Elizabeth, another Crimetest's Adviser/Negotiator.

What is more, it was his own rule bending that prompted David to resign his Crimetest directorship. After his resignation, he had moved to Southern Italy, and settled in a comfortable, modest villa; situated on the outskirts of Catanzaro, tucked under the arch of Italy's foot. Nevertheless, the problem of religion had been progressively taunting at his senses of right and wrong, for some years now.

As the creator and now ex-director of Crimetest, he had, of course, heard about many religiously motivated crimes. Yet, such experienced based knowledge is not the only source of his displeasure with religion. What taunts him, are what he calls the *"Leech-pooh-promises,"* of an after-life, with a ready-made paradise." To David Bell, all religions used such promises to ensnare and suck their victims dry, or at least drain them until they became zombified followers. Indeed, To David, such lies, are an insolence against humanity and morality, not to mention God … if God should exist. Therefore, regardless of whether God exists or not; by the time David had seen the sole lemon tree in his garden, bear fruit, he had decided on a campaign of non-violent, direct action, against all religions. However, seeing that he now lived in Italy, the Roman Catholic Church would be his main target.

Standing on the top step and cautiously, looking into the unattended interior of the church, he feels a sudden and strong desire; to go back to his modest Italian villa, make himself a pitcher of chilled, freshly squeezed, lemonade, and attend to the needs of his garden. Before he can stop it, the urge for some chilled, scrumptious, lemonade becomes so strong, he cannot help but look around - for any pressing excuse to turn away from the church and leave it far behind him.

However, after looking at the church's modest even stark furnishings and decorations, he initially feels disappointment, that no such pressing excuse to leave, exists. What is more, as he continues to look, he also begins to feel rather proud, that he has planned his intended crime (or social-amiss) so well. For a start, having heard many first-hand versions of failed crimes, during his time at Crimetest, David has chosen his timing and venue well. The village sits more than a four-hour drive away from his home; there is no one stirring from their traditional, mid-day siesta, and apart from the main square, and what serves as a high street (both of which he had bypassed on this occasion) there are no CCTV cameras to avoid. Even a nearby mongrel dog, seems to be far more interested in scratching her own backend, than in noticing David presence. So, having no other excuses, David Bell, the Goody-goody, begins to pass between the open, simply carved, wooden doors of the church.

But, as he enters the church, immediately, his legs begin shaking so uncontrollably, that he places his hand against a white stone column, for support. Nevertheless, although his sweating palm feels alien-like, upon the dry, weathered pitted column; his fearful reactions are not entirely new to him. He had reacted and felt similar feelings when he and Claire had taken actions against the local drug baron. Yet that was with the emotional and moral support of Claire – but now, he is acting alone.

Nevertheless, he can hardly stay immobile forever; as if he were some modern version of the wife of the biblical Lot, frozen in time; as a permanent warning to all potential, sinners. So, pushing away from the stone support, David finally steps, cautiously, right into the church's interior, which immediately becomes - as silent, as a spider's web.

Looking around, David notices that nothing has changed from his previous resonance trips. The faded red pigments of the saintly wall frescos are still more faded than the faded blues. The black and white floor tiles, leading to the simple altar, still bear the chafed channels of the ever hopeful. The simple bunches of local flowers, placed around the church interior, are still fresh enough to smell from an arm's length away. Taking a few more steps inside, David finds the familiarity of what he has predicted, reassuring. His legs become more supportive and his breathing less tense - only for his symptoms to instantly increase again; as the church briefly fills with the rasping din of a passing moped. As soon the moped passes on by, David continues his deliberate steps toward the threadbare, red carpeted alter, until suddenly - he is looking up (almost pilgrim like) at the life-size marble statue, of Jesus Christ upon the cross.

On other occasions, the symbol of the crucifixion would have prompted David to feel taunted once more, and even angered. However, today, as he looks up into the marble face of Christ, he feels fearful, and even guilty. Was this, how first-time believers in religion felt? Or were such reactions prompted by the imminent loss of salvation; which might be felt by any returning habitual, criminal, or at least, wrongdoer?

The sound of a passing car distracts David's thoughts, and twists them towards the need for urgency. Looking around at the sunlit entrance, he quickly puts on his gloves, delves into his rucksack and withdraws a rolled up, laminated placard. Stepping up to the Christ statue, and holding onto Jesus's outstretched right arm for support, David Bell pulls himself up, and loops the placard's chord over the Christ head. He then begins to, at first frantically, and then delicately, pulling the protective film off the double sided, sticky tape on the back of the placard. Uncovering the sticky side of the tape, he firmly presses the lower end of the placard against the cool, stone stomach muscles, of God's only son; so that the placard hangs and stays flat.

Stepping back to check that all is as he intends, David imagines that the hollowed-out centres of the Christ figure's, half-upraised eyes, are filling with an impotent sadness. Looking behind him yet again, he gets out his unregistered mobile phone, quickly takes a picture of the placarded statue, and after returning the phone to his thigh pocket, he turns around and strides out into the welcomed sunlight; where he lets out a short sigh of relief, and then, at last, feels grounded again.

Yet, it isn't until he reaches near the outskirts of the village (unobserved), that David realises with a rising dread, that although he had taken a still photo shot of the placarded statue, he had not taken his intended video shot; which he would have zoomed in and out, so that the wording on the placard could be read. What's more, he had also totally forgotten all about taking a photo of church's exterior; so that it could be identified by viewers on the main social sites, on which he had intended to post his "*Curch of Free-Heroes*" grand plan, and "*The Ten Quests.*"

Despite his normal reluctance to use swear words, the only initial reaction that David comes out with is, '*Bollocks!*' He then keeps repeating the word, until reaching the road bypassing the village, at which point he adds, '*Fucking bollocks!*'

However, it was only as he arrived at his second-hand car; bought solely for the propose of the placard campaign, that David finally admits to himself, that when added together, his mistakes are glaring and embarrassing examples of his amateur, fumbling's, as a practicing, hands on, criminal. Getting into the car, he throws his rucksack onto the rear passenger seat; for he has no intention of risking a recovery expedition to the scene of his failures - goodness knows what would happen if he tried.

Five days later, David is still feeling despondent as he sips cold, freshly squeezed lemonade, made with lemons picked from his lemon tree. He is sitting on the veranda of his modestly sized, but well-constructed villa. He hasn't even bothered to post his photo of the placarded statue, onto any of the social sites. What is more, he has increasing doubts, that he has what it takes to risk even further outings to more churches. He might well possess a wide knowledge of crime, criminals, and their modus operandi, but when it came to practice, particularly when it was without the moral boosting support of a partner, he just couldn't find the … *balls*! David Bell's grand plan had been to mount a series of propaganda stunts, by placarding 10 churches, and even finishing off the campaign - at the 'Big one,' the Vatican itself. He had already designed draught placards, on his campaign-computer, which is permanently unconnected from the Internet. Nevertheless, after his first shambles of an outing, he knew that he would be caught before he had visited even half that number of churches. It was simply unachievable.

Ten minutes after he had finished his drink, he wanders off into his garden to do some needed weeding; at least that campaign would be more achievable.

As David Bell pondered the future of this garden, Cardinal Luigi Padovano sits at the wide 18th century solid rosewood table, which serves as his office desk in the Vatican. As the Cardinal looks at the placard, retrieved from around the statue of Christ, he ponders on what to do about it. Turning to his assistant, Anthony, Cardinal Luigi states, 'It appears to be some sort of protest, but we have had worse. And there is no record of a live or past website called the Church of Free-Heroes …'

'Curch!' his assistant, Anthony, politely corrects.

'What?'

Bowing his head in reverence, Anthony repeats, '*Curch*. It's pronounced, Curch, an obvious play on the word Church.'

'Thank you, Antony, thank you. But for the present, I think that we will let sleeping … Curches … lie.' With that decided, the poster is handed to Anthony, who then carefully

places it on the bottom shelf of the 17th century cabinet,
which sits in the corner of the outer office; and there it would
have probably remained, until it had been moved to one of the
many basements, or to the recycling bin.
However, as it happens, David Bell's so-called unachievable
campaign, is about to receive a helping hand from an
unexpected "friend," or more to the point, from someone who
he would have expected to be, a total enemy.
The placard that now lay in the cabinet stated:

The Curch of Free Heroes

Curch: A feeling or a place, from which a person's or a community's Secular-Spirit can pursue; the unattainable, yet increasingly rewarding pursuit of creating a fair and just way of life (moral-paradise) upon the Earth (and any other planets that we may yet settle upon). A Curch evolves alongside the verifiable truths; that bad leads to bad, and good leads to good - just like you knew they both would.

Free: Being free, by accepting that both good and bad have equal strengths - until you stop holding either's hand.

Free-Hero: Any man woman or child, who pursues the call to reach kindness and beyond; by pursuing the Ten Quests of a Free-Hero.
The Ten Quests
By the powerful grace of all that is noble about humanity, the daily, weekly and lifetime quests of a Free-Hero are to explore, gain, and share the freedoms of: Forgiveness of self and others. Responsibility. Empathy. Emotional Ecology. Honesty. Equality (of opportunity). Reality. Orderliness. Everlasting life and Support.
www.curchoffreeheroes.info

Chapter 2 - Making a break

Strictly speaking, although the phrase "doing bird" applies to the serving of a prison sentence of four years or more; amongst the general British prison population, "doing bird" usually refers any prison sentence, during which a prisoner is caged, like a tame bird. However, being caged or being tamed, did not come easily to Steven Chadwick. Nevertheless, it took Steven just over three and a half years to escape from the medium to a high-security prison in England. He was due to serve a 22-year prison term; for the (non-fatal) shooting of Detective Sergeant Vanner, and two Crimetest's Crime Advisers, Sandra, and Andy, who were trying to rescue Lizzie. Steven had kidnapped Lizzie, so he could humiliate and destroy the Crimetest's reputation as a trustworthy confidential crime advice service.

The first major step of Steven's escape plan was to gain more freedom than the allotted 1 hour a day exercise, which (weather permitting) all prisoners are allowed. To achieve more freedom Steven (ideally) needed to get a job as a wing cleaner, which in turn would allow him almost eight hours of mostly unsupervised access; to the whole of his prison wing. Being a manipulator, Steven soon made it known to the warders that he was a suitable candidate for the job of wing cleaner. Steven also made his "CV" for the job more attractive, by supplying the odd bit of information (to the prison officer who was responsible for detailing the position of wing cleaner), about the petty illegal activities of the other prisoners. Steven had little affinity with the other prisoners, as far as he was concerned they were like the prison staff, who were all there for his use.

It took Steven two attempts at creating a vacancy for the wing cleaner position. The first attempt was only partially successful. He managed to convince a particularly paranoid, thug of a man, called Chinese John, that the current wing cleaner, Robert Sands, had put it about that he (Chinese John) was a 'grass' (an informer) for the 'screws' (prison officers).

The name 'screw' originates from the duties of prison officers in the late 19th century. As a part of the then hard labour regime, prisoners were required to perform repetitive, and often useless labour; including the turning of a large handle, connected to a series of gears, which were hidden on one side of a wall. It was the job of the 'screw' officer to tighten a screw, so that the handle was increasingly more difficult to turn throughout the prisoner's increasingly hard labour. Fortunately, for Steven, such hard labour no longer existed. In fact, most inmates considered the wing cleaner's job as being a 'cushy number.' Three days after telling Chinese John about the 'libellous' cleaner, the cleaner was found badly beaten. Unfortunately, for Sands and Steven, somebody else got the job of cleaner and Steven had to wait a while longer. Nevertheless, four months later, after Steven had repeated a similar exercise (using a different, but equally gullible thug), the wing officer responsible for choosing the wing cleaner, popped his obviously bewigged head around Steven's cell door, and offered him the wing cleaner position.

With his new semi-freedom, Steven set about the next stage of his escape plan. Although he had not yet bought any contraband, he had soon made friends with the two main suppliers of the most popular prison contraband, namely drugs and cell phones. However, as wing cleaner, and with far more accessible hiding places up for his use, he ordered and received 2 cell phones (one as a spare) and three pneumatic syringe kits; which upon pressing the release button, the syringes would rapidly release its contents into a patient's, or victim's, bloodstream.

The first phone call Steven made on his newly acquired phone, was to his faithful little helper, Freddy Grace. Grace was an ex-prisoner who Steven had befriended before he (Grace) was released. Grace was of average intelligence and had an emotional need for having someone to look up to and follow. Steven planned to use him as an assistant, both before, during and after his escape.

As wing cleaner, Steven had various duties, including; cleaning the prisoner's toilet sluice room, the wing landings, stairwells, and most importantly, the Wing Officer's office, which is in constant use during the day. Steven also made an occasional habit of polishing the office windows, inside and out. To clean the outside, he had to stand on a chair, which also allowed him access to the office flat roof, and an electrical junction box; under which, Steven hid his phone. Thus, either confusing or frustrating the sniffer dogs who were trained to sniff out, amongst other things, mobile phones - just like those that most of the Wing Officers carried around all the time, including such times as when any sniffer dogs happened to be sniffing around the office.

Two weeks after he obtained his phone, Steven received a visit from Grace, who passed him a small, sealed, plastic sachet of a highly effective liquid sedative. However, the next step of his escape plan, which was to gain a uniform of a prison officer, would take more time and a lot more risk. Having chosen the uniform (which was normally worn by the prison officer responsible for plumbing maintenance and repairs), Steven began setting up the ambush.

After getting official permission to change his appearance by growing a beard, Steven styled it in the general fashion of the maintenance officer. He also had his eyes tested (during which he faked short sightedness) and ordered and paid for a pair of glasses similar to those worn by the plumbing officer. In his single cell, at night, he also practiced the mannerisms, walk and the voice of his target.

Amongst the plumbing officer's (and his civilian assistant's) duties, the task of unblocking any blocked toilets turned out to be an almost a daily task. Amongst Steven's duties, the ordering of cleaning materials for the ex-cell, now storeroom, became an essential part of his escape plan; mainly because the storeroom still had a toilet and washbasin.

On the chosen weekend day, when the number of wing officers on duty in the wing office had, as per normal, been reduced to three, Steven deliberately blocked the prisoner's sluice room sluice, and the toilet in the cleaning storeroom/cell. He then reported the blockages to the wing officers. Just over one hour later, the plumber and his assistant came to unblock the sluice and toilet.

As soon as the plumbers entered the main sluice room, Steven apologised to them, for blocking the cleaning storeroom, toilet, 'I was emptying a bucket of dirty water down it, to save having to come all the way over here to do it, and I bleeding forgot to take the floor cloth out, bloody idiot! Anyway, it went straight down and got stuck. I tried to fish it out with a toilet brush, but it was too far down.'

The plumbing officer acknowledged Steven, with an 'Ok! We'll see to it when we've finished up here,' whilst his civilian assistant mumbled on about the stupidity of trying to flush a floor cloth down a toilet.

A short while later Steven saw the two men go into the cleaning store/cell. A minute later, as Steven casually entered, both men faced away from the open cell door. The plumber handed a flexible rod to his assistant kneeling in front of the toilet. From that point on, Steven moved swiftly and smoothly. Stepping fully inside the cell, and casually taking two sedative primed syringes from a shelf piled with cloths, he immediately stabbed the men in the neck; thereby injecting them with the rapidly acting, powerful sedative. By the time either man had worked out what was happening, they were becoming far too sedated to even try to call out for help. As soon as the officers were unconscious, Steven closed the cell door as much as possible (whenever a prison officer entered any cell, it was standard procedure to flip the lock, so that the door could not be fully closed – with the officer inside).

Just over ten minutes later, Steven, wearing the uniform of plumbing officer uniform, used the plumbing officer's keys to lock both the heavily sedated men inside the cell. Keeping his head down whilst reading the notes in the plumber's notebook, and walking casually past the wing office, Steven did not bother about the security cameras, which cover all wings and outside areas. Dressed, acting and moving as he was, someone else would have to be within three metres, before noticing anything worthy of a second look.

Standing in front of the gate which led out into the outside areas that lay between the prison and outer walls, and leaning against the bars as if bored, Steven slid the key into the lock, then without ceremony, he turned it. Although it would have been very strange if the key had not unlocked the gate, when he heard the lock opening, it sounded like the "*snick*" of a bird-cage door, springing open.

Nevertheless, although he may be out of the aviary, he had yet not made it out of the zoo.

Even under the dripping pace of the prison's regime, each stage of his plan seemed so slow to Steven that for a moment, when he had still been inside the main prison block, it all began to feel like some cruelly staged, surreal daydream. Nevertheless, on finally exiting the main wing altogether, and feeling gentle rain on his face, he *knew* it to be real rain.

Next, came the locked gate to the fenced off maintenance area. Temporally thwarted by needing a different key from the wing keys, he became aware that searching for the right key meant delay, a behaviour that could potentially be seen as suspicious by the eyes behind the eyes in the sky. To play for time Steven drew his phone out and pretended to make a call, whilst absentmindedly trying what turned out to be the wrong key, in the lock.

Four minutes later, Steven casually entered the plumber's workshop itself. It being a Saturday morning, when (barring emergency callouts) most other Maintenance departments were closed, he found he had the place to himself. Opening several unlocked lockers, he found a virtual treasure trove of tools, including various wire cutters; which were more than able to cut through the razor wire that ran along the top of the, much less escape-proof, outer wall at the rear of the workshops. Just to the left of a variety of ladders which were padlocked to a sturdy wall frame, Steven also found a wall rack of wrenches, wire cutters and bolt cutters, and lots of rope (to tie to the top rung of the ladder so that he could then hang the rope over the downside of the wall). On a workbench lay, several types of thick work gloves, plus a greased-smeared copy of a DIY maintenance book, and several equally greased-smeared copies of various Men's magazines.

Having previously phoned Freddy Grace, to make sure that he is already parking in the right place, there was nothing more for to do than to, 'Go for it!'

The brazen hooting and shrill ringing of alarms; sending the prison into 'Lockdown' mode, filled the air as Steven steadily cut through the razor-wire on top of the outer wall.

Nevertheless, as soon as his feet landed on the pavement, Steven became almost overjoyed to see Grace pulling up to the kerbside, and before there was even a sign of any pursuing prison staff … the "*bird*" had already flown!

Chapter 3 - Warmer climes

Steven had formulated the next stage of his escape plan, even before he had any sure plan of escape. He knew too well, that the chances of staying in Britain and staying free, were almost non-existent. Although the news of his escape would quickly die down as far as the public were concerned, his face (and criminal record) would be at the recall of just about every police officer's memory, for years to come.

However, on the European mainland, the news of his escape would hardly cause any concern. By going to the continent, it would provide him with a comparative haven … until he could organise a safe journey to far safer lands. What he needed in Europe; was an out of the way place to stay, for a month or two, and where any request to see, let alone scrutinize his current false identity documents, would be unlikely.

However, good fortune and good preparation favour the bad as well as the good. Since his incarceration, Steven had followed the news about Crimetest and David Bell. Well before his escape plans had finalised, he knew that Bell had moved to Italy, and was now resident on the outskirts of an out of the way village. Therefore, Steven long ago decided that after escaping from prison, he would migrate, to safer and warmer climes.

As soon as he was free from the claustrophobia of prison, Steven noticed several things about the "outside world," which of course, had now become his "normal world." Everything seemed to take some re-adjusting to; everything and everyone seemed to flow at a far speedier pace than the drag of the prison's regime. Everything seemed fresher than he remembered. Half-forgotten smells, such as freshly ground coffee beans seemed to almost assault his senses, colours seemed almost frantic, and old sights seemed to be almost brand new. Sounds seemed louder, sharper and more imposing than the muffled drones of prison. It wasn't so much that the normal world seemed strange; it felt more like as if he were a stranger, in the normal world.

Notwithstanding the growing distance between himself and the prison, Steven felt that people were looking at him; as if he had a sign hovering above his head, proclaiming, *"I am an escaped prisoner!"*

However, having spoken to other prisoners about their past official releases, he knew that such paranoia was par for the course. Nevertheless, after parking their getaway car and appearing more normal than either of them felt, Steven and Grace, made their way without undue incident to Hounslow and the pre-arraigned safe-house.

The house stood opposite an abandoned office building, which once housed a council funded, computer college. Behind a grubby windowpane of a long abandoned second story office, a vase of yellow plastic flowers still seemed to be trying to exude an aura of obstinate optimism.

Once inside the safe house, Steven began opening the various packages that Grace had obtained for him. Inside the parcels were various, genuine looking false documents, required for his travel and temporary residence in Italy? The forgeries were good, but not expert proof, though they should at least gain enough time for Steven to acquire more reliable and permanent identification, once he had chosen his final destination.

After a meal, Grace gave his judgements on the various facial disguises that Steven tried out and might use during his travels. Steven had used such disguises before, during his time as 'The Body Part Murderer,' so using disguises was of no great concern to him. However, what with the ever-growing pace of technological change; the possibility of one of one his disguises being 'unmasked' by some automated facial recognition program, attuned to spotting wanted criminals, was not as unlikely as it may seem. Yet hopefully, the false documents and disguises should get him past the borders of Italy - and straight to the front door of David Bell's abode.

Chapter 4 - Old enemies, new 'friendships'
When David Bell, dressed in shorts and t-shirt, answers his ornate Italian front door he felt curious, then astonished, and finally frightened.
Steven, however, is in high spirits, 'Hello David. I've come for my, giving up crime, residential course. The one that you offered to me if I let our dear friend Lizzie go free and unharmed, remember?'
David Bell did indeed remember. Out of all his dealings with Crimetest, his ones with Steven Chadwick were the most memorable. 'Yes … I do recall such an offer, Steven, but that was some time ago, and the course is a residential one, and it is meant to be taken at the school, in Hertfordshire, which is a long way … what the hell are you doing out of prison?'
'Royal pardon!' Steven grins, 'It was thought that my imprisonment caused such a loss to the greater cause of humanity, The Home office, astutely decided to release me early. However, as a sure-fire precaution, they insisted that I take up your offer of the Crimetest's crime prevention course. After all, we, that is, the Royal We, don't want a recurrence of my past mistakes.'
Looking past Bell's shoulder and into the open space of the entrance and beyond, Steven asks, 'So, where shall I be sleeping, do you have a guest room, or do I have to make do with the couch, not that such minor sacrifices are not worth the greater cause!'
'You have escaped … from prison ... haven't you?'
Grinning broadly and raising his hands in mock surrender, Steven admits, 'I never could get a fib past you, could I. Ok! You've got me.'
'To be quite honest with you,' David states, whilst purposely not opening the door wider, 'I don't really want you. Nor do I want anything else to do with you, not after last time. Not until you have served your prison sentence, anyway.'
'That's not very magnanimous of you David, didn't think you were the sour grapes type.'

'It is not a matter of sour grapes, it is a matter of obeying the law. You know I should be reporting you to the police, don't you?'

'Of course, you can, and I am sure that you will ... in good time. That is when the time is no longer so … bad!' At that moment, and although there was no apparent change in Steven's body language, the aura around him seems to alter into one of imminent menace, as Steven emphasises, 'And, I assure you, David, the time is so close to being … bad.'

With that, Steven again looks past David Bell's shoulder and into the open space of the entrance and beyond. Then returning his attention to his past adversary, he adds, 'But for the moment, you still owe me two weeks of crime prevention advice, and as I remember it, that will still come under the Crimetest's Anonymity Code of confidentiality. That is … unless you don't believe in that sort of thing anymore?'

The one certain thing that David Bell knew about Steven Chadwick, is that he is not to be trusted on an inch. Chadwick was and would probably remain a highly intelligent, highly manipulative and highly dangerous psychopath. What is more, he knows that Steven had not come all this way on a whim. Nevertheless, it was unlikely that he had made the journey, let alone taken all the risks it entailed, just to kill him on his doorstep. He guesses that his old enemy wants a safe place to stay, for at least a day or two, probably longer. After that, all options would be open - including murder. So, on the basis that a growling dog is safer than a biting one, David Bell presumes that he is safe, at least for the present.

Opening the door more fully, David says, 'Come in Steven, after coming all this way I guess you deserve a coffee. You can stay until tomorrow, midday, after that all options are open, do you agree?'

'Understood and agreed.' Steven humbly acquiesces, as he holds out his hand, which David Bell accepted and shakes. On entering the villa, Steven feels a great relief. The main thing that he knew about Bell, and is relying upon, is that the "goody-goody," would always try his uppermost to keep his word. Whether Steven could further persuade him to go further (using force would be a last resort), was yet to be seen. David Bell was no fool ... but then again, neither was Steven. So, as the sun set on the horizon, both men eat a simple, well-cooked evening meal, then went to their respective bedrooms, and sleep as soundly as the three hens in the chicken coop, at the far end of the Eco-friendly(ish), garden.

There is a particular light, in the southern part of Italy, a certain hue brushes the landscape, the water, the skin and the mind. It is a light that has beckoned many a great artist of the world to make the pilgrimage to this part of Italy. At first light, Steven is looking out from the veranda of the guest room, He gazes for some time at the near and distant landscape; which is so more expansive than the allocated view through the wire mesh window of his old prison cell. However, even the panorama stretching before him, suddenly seems dwarfed, by the … silence.

To Steven, as he leans over the wood railing of the small veranda, this silence, stretches beyond the visible horizon; for it brushes the yet unpainted canvases of his future. A quiet, before the storm perhaps … or a silence … to silence his past. As to whether his future would be all-enveloping enough to silence, or at least muffle, his long-established urges to commit crimes against those whom he judged as having achieved some undeserved successes in life, is yet unknown to Steven. Nevertheless, at least this silent homage to his future, feels far more acceptable, than the mocking silence of a prison cell.

A short time later both men sit at the kitchen table, enjoying freshly squeezed lemonade, and free-range poached eggs, on locally produced wholemeal bread. As both men enjoy their after-breakfast coffee, Steven decides to try his hand at negotiating a deal. He is fully aware that Bell is a very adept negotiator; having dealt with the likes of countless politicians and establishment figures whilst he had been in the process of establishing Crimetest. Bell had also many hours of verbal negotiations, with the vast variety of criminals who used the Crime Advice Line. Nevertheless, Steven opens his negotiation with a plea to David Bell's sense of duty, his sense of rightness.

'I know you offered me the giving up crime course, at a different time and place. But in prison, I truly did have a lot of time to think and to re-evaluate,' looking straight into the eyes of Bell, Steven emphasizes, 'I *need* to change, by changing my needs … and that's for sure! If not, I'll end up dying in some prison, and for what, the sake of fulfilling a bloody stupid and selfish fantasy!' Looking down into his coffee and then back to Bell, Steven adds, 'But I am not sure if I can do it on my own, and to be frank with you … you are the only person I trust!'

Steven's plea is believable, yet David Bell is no fool, 'I'm sure, that if someone really wants to change, they can, particularly when they have support to do so. I am also sure, that you are conceited enough to know all about the traits of a psychopath. So, you won't be that surprised or hurt, when I tell you that I don't trust you further than I could throw you. Now tell me, what you really want?'

Smiling at David, Steven gives his answer, 'Two weeks, four at the outside. That will be enough time to arrange and get all the papers and documents I need to get me to, another continent.'

Steven's gaze holds David's, though this time Steven's face bears an expression of trust. It is the same face that appealed to most of the people he had manipulated, but now, there is an unusual twist to his mouth, as he adds, 'But I still want to take the course! If you agree that I can do it, David.'

The two men hold each other's regard, without speaking, for what seems to Steven an embarrassing amount of time.

Finally, David Bell states, 'I will make you a firm promise. If you are still here at the end four weeks, from today, I will be calling the police to let them know who and where you are. If

you are genuine about taking the course, I will let you know what you need to know, if only for the sake of the people that you would otherwise hurt sooner or later.'
With that, the two men nod to each other, and then clear away the breakfast things.

Chapter 5 - SIDS

SID: A Seemingly Irrelevant Decision. Everyone (not just criminals) make such decisions; so that he or she may simultaneously follow a course of action toward a temporally parallel, but in the end, a different aim, other than that of their conscious aims. It's sort of like getting a wolf whistle … from a real wolf.

For example, an almost reformed criminal might innocently decide to go for a stroll in an area, which by "chance" just happens to be one that can trigger an urge to commit his or her sort of crime. Alternatively, a perfectly law-abiding citizen, on a diet, might innocently choose to take a route that although slightly longer than a shorter one, but just happens to pass the bakery that sells his or her favourite fresh cream cake. Of course, either the criminal or the dieter may eventually choose against committing their "crime." On the other hand, he or she might take advantage of the apparent "unforeseen" lucky situation.

The first stage of David Bell's Seemingly Irrelevant Decision begins the following morning, in his study; whilst he is sitting in front of his computer and strolling through his past entries about the Curch placarding campaign. Even though by then, he apparently looks upon the campaign as being a bit of a lost cause, he could not quite let go of it. So, before Steven is up and about, David decides to fiddle around with the plan. The next step of the SID happens, when he suddenly gets an apparently impulsive urge for another cup of coffee, despite just having drunk one. The next step is taken when he decides that as long he is in the kitchen, and still in view of his study, then he would be aware if Steven is about to enter the study. Next, after leaving his study door wide open, he goes down to the kitchen to make his coffee; whilst leaving his computer screen on; at the page displaying the Curch of Free-Heroes placard, left hanging from the statue of Christ on the cross.

Ten or so minutes later, David is still innocently engrossed in the distant cloud formation, when Steven enters the kitchen, looks at Bell and casually announces, 'I didn't know you were so anti-religious!'

'What?'

'I was passing your study, the door was wide open, and I saw the picture of that statue of Christ, with the poster around its neck.' As he spoke, Steven enters the kitchen, goes over to worktop (made from a locally sourced marble), and pours himself a coffee, then continues, 'Naturally, I went in and had a closer look and I couldn't help but scroll down the page. *My*, you do have a *thing* about the Roman Catholic church don't you just.'

Bringing his coffee to the breakfast table, Steven comments, 'Not that I condemn you, far from it. As far as I'm concerned, all the religions can all go to hell, if there were such a place. In fact, in a way, it makes me rather sad there isn't. It could be worth going there, just to see the entire priesthood there too. Can you imagine their horror, when their stuck-up noses begin to smell their own over-cooking, flesh?'

Looking rather horrified himself, David answers is just a little too desperate, 'It's just an idea I was playing around with, nothing serious really.'

Taking a seat opposite, Steven asks, 'Do you usually *play* around in real churches? By the way, I also read your point-by-point plan to target more churches, even the Vatican. So … do tell me more.'

After seeing that Steven is not going to let the matter go, David relents, and then to his own surprise, as he makes breakfast, he recounts, without any self-editing, his tale of the disastrous placarding attempt at the church. When he has finished his story, he sits down and shrugs his shoulders in an almost apologetic fashion and concludes, 'Whether the evolution of human goodness will be found in the openness of empathy, education and freedom of expression, or whether it will be found, superstitiously squatting, amongst the caves and caverns of religion, is a matter for every individual to dwell upon, or dwell in. Personally, I favour the first lot.' He then dismissively flicks his hand as if to be finished with the whole conversation, and subject matter.

Nevertheless, Steven had not quite finished with the subject by a long shot, 'You know, David, I'm rather surprised you're just going to give up. Whatever else happened at the church, I know from your history, that you've faced far more dangerous opponents than a load of guys running around in cassocks. You even took on the drugs trade for God's sake … sorry … for Goodness's sake. Besides, what are they going to do if you do get caught, make you say three Hail Marys a day, for a month?'

Letting out a sigh, Bell informs, 'Admittedly, Italian laws on blasphemy do not carry the death penalty any longer, like some of the more fanatical branches of Islam, but the church is still very powerful here. Besides, to be honest, I'm not that scared of prison, anymore.'

'What then? Are you even going to post that picture of the crucifix and placard somewhere, other than your study? I also looked on my phone for your website, The Curch of Free-Heroes, but there is no sign of it. Why not? From what I saw on your computer, you have some decent ideas. I'm almost tempted to join the cause myself. So, what are you frightened of my friend?'

'I'm scared … of being caught before the quest to establish The Curch of Free-Heroes, has had a decent chance to succeed, to be completed, I'm scared that the quest will fail, because I will fail it.'

Looking at the cloud formation in the distance, Steven states, 'I saw in the Crimetest's monthly magazine, about a year ago,' then turning, he adds, 'By the way, I ordered a standing delivery when I was in prison, but please, there's no need for any thanks.'

When David Bell showed no sign of thanking him, Steven continued, 'I also read that the crime advice line had tried to establish an Italian branch. The article also strongly suggested that the failure to establish any branch was due to a great deal of anti-lobbying, by the Roman Catholic Church. Something about the proposed service would have been in direct competition with their confessional box service, confessing one's sins to a priest and all that.'

Nodding his gratitude as he took the offered breakfast, Steven added, 'I also know that although the crime advice line doesn't condemn religion outright, it advices against it being relied upon as a motivation for giving up crime.'

Dipping a torn piece of bread into his egg, Steven proffered, 'I don't suppose the Roman Catholic Church's opposition to the crime advice service, has anything to do with *your* Curch of Free Heroes campaign. I mean you wouldn't be a party to anything as reasonable, as good old-fashioned revenge … would you David?'

Before answering, David picks up his lemonade and his own breakfast and then gestures to the patio, 'Let's go outside, I love the feel of the sun on my face.' Settling themselves on the patio, he looks at the horizon and replies, 'Acts of revenge are acts of bravado, and not acts of true bravery. True acts of bravery …' at that point he gives Steven a look of challenge, '… as in setting out to reclaim and regain your lost or damaged life qualities, are far more gratifying than merely gaining revenge for the loss or damage of those life qualities.' Looking at his old adversary, David gently smiles, 'So believe me, Steven, revenge is the last motivation I would use to try and achieve justice.'

Giving a genuine smile back, Steven replies, 'I believe you. Yet I know from when you faced up to that drug baron, Lenny something or other … that you are well capable of stepping over the line between crime and the law. So, there must be something missing, between now and then … and I believe that I know what it is.'

David Bell raises one eyebrow in surprise, and perhaps even a little hope, and asks, 'Really, and what would be?'

'Not what, but *who.*'

'Who then?'

'You're missing your wife, Claire … or to be more exact her moral support ... you're missing a partner in crime. I read in your blog of the whole business, how reliant you both were on each other.'

For a moment, David considered Steven's uncannily accurate, diagnosis; indeed, the same, had crossed his mind on more than one occasion since the failure of the first placarding. However, now that it was in the open, and although it renewed his sense of loss, he also feels that Steven's answer has more than a touch of truth in it. Nevertheless, before he could reply, Steven, put forward a solution himself.

'You know, what you and I both need David, old chum, is a partner. I need help to give crime up, and you need support to help you commit, your so-called crimes. At least as far as your placarding of the churches goes, including all the way to the Vatican. We both need someone who could help to get to the places, where we *each* may fear to tread, my friend.'

For a brief while, David Bell looks as if he had just been offered a £20 note by a destitute street beggar, then he answers, 'Go on,'

'I'm quite sure, you have the know-how to commit, shall we say any dodgy actions, such as placarding the churches, and maybe even the Vatican building itself. What with all your experience from Crimetest you could hardly not have. But turning know-how into practice isn't always so straightforward.'

Seeing the look of growing interest on David's face, Steven explains, 'What I am suggesting is an ongoing skills exchange. You can take me through the course, on giving up crime, and living a just life … whilst I can take you to your goal, right to the steps of the Vatican itself, without getting caught.'

Sitting back, Steven smiles and suggests, 'It'll be just like a buddy road trip. Like the Blues Brothers, or Robert De Niro and Charles Grodin … in … Midnight Run, or …'
Whilst Steven searches for another example, David suggests, 'Or like the ending of Thelma and Louise?'
In reply, Steven gives a wide-open grin, and concludes, 'The choice is ours … Buddy.'
The trouble with making a SID, is that once you suddenly find yourself standing before an array of, "*deliciously tempting cream cakes,*" it is not that easy to turn your back on them. Nevertheless, David Bell is not a fool.
'You know, all religions claim that moral salvation can only be achieved through them. They claim this, to stop people from realising that each of us already has the total power and freedom to choose to do right or wrong, without religion. However, to totally recognise and feel such power requires accepting total responsibility for, *all,* of our personal choices, desires, and actions … Steven. Whether they have been good, indifferent or bad. Such total recognition, becomes all powerful, because it means that you must also recognise … that you are equally free in the future, regardless of any past influences, desires or indeed loyalties to religion … or crime … Buddy.'
Shrugging his shoulders, David adds, '*In short,* you can be and *feel* all-powerful, Steven … without having to commit crimes … that is, if you really want to take on such a road trip?'
For a moment, the two men eye each other as if they are a pair of duellist, each unsure of each other's next move … or even their own.
Smiling, Steven answers, 'Naturally, if we agree to the trip, then the same anonymity rules apply as they do in Crimetest,' then as he raises his cup of coffee, Steven salutes, 'Agreed?'
Let's say,' David confirms, as he gestures with his glass of lemonade, 'that we don't completely disagree.'
'To fresh lemonade and fresh horizons!' Steven acclaims.

As each man brings his drink to his lips, both men think that they had come away with a comparatively better part of the deal.

David Bell knew that a short-term residential course was certainly no guarantee of completely giving up crime. To reach that sort of certainty, normally required many follow up parallel supports. Nevertheless, the course could be very powerful in the short term and might well go some way in achieving his own safety for the near future, or at least until Steven could get his travelling visas and documents for fresh horizons. Moreover, if Steven's horizons were less cluttered by his old criminal urges, then so much the better for Steven, himself and the world.

Steven is also happy, that taking part in the course could be very useful in the short term; by allaying Bell's fears and potential to call the police because he (Steven) might do him some harm or even kill him. What is more, Steven concludes to himself, "If my old urges become less of a hazard to me, then so much the better for me in the longer term."

Putting down his empty glass, Steven asks, 'So, where is your … sorry, I mean our … next church to be?'

Chapter 6 - Skills exchange

The afternoon following their new partnership, David and Steven sit beneath a large, lime green and white beach umbrella, on the veranda. On the table, beside them, sits a glass jug almost full of cold, freshly squeezed, lemonade. The first lesson for Steven is to try to get him to start from square one.

'Working with what you have,' David informs, 'is a lot more effective than trying to use something that you hope you will have.'

In response, Steven acknowledges the point, with a nod and asks, 'So what do you think I have already. And if you answer that it is up to me to decide, I'll pour that jug of juice all over you.'

Taking the jug, and pouring Steven and himself a drink, David asks, 'Are you sure you want the full answer?'
'Why not?
'I suspect that a greater part of your motivation for committing your crimes, originates from a desire for revenge against a perpetrator or perpetrators, who you feel, have committed a wrongdoing against you in your past. Your hope, is that this revenge, will regain you some your feelings of lost power, lost at the time of the wrongdoing.'
'What wrongdoing what perpetrator?'
'It doesn't matter. It could be a person, persons or the world. As for the wrongdoing, all you need to recognise is that you believe it damaged or stole some life qualities from you, and your life.
'What life qualities?'
'That is for you to recognize as you go along, but things such as self-respect, respect for other people's situation, in short, the ability to empathize. Nevertheless, don't worry about them for now, they are all things that we can pick up along your way. So, let us return to the things you have now. Besides a bloody cheek in turning up here in the first place, you also have several other things going for you. You have the ability to step over distinct moral boundaries. That ability will be useful when it comes to, permanently crossing back over … into to a law-abiding world. Of course, wanting to stay in such a world, by leading a lawful life, will depend on what you *allow* yourself to find there. Which in turn, will depend on what you allow yourself to find, rather on what your old habitual ways of thinking allow you.'
When there are no obvious objections from Steven, David continues, 'So, if it is alright with you, we can start thinking about doing some daily exercises, in new ways of looking at the world, and yourself. To get your insight muscles limbered up and getting accustomed to the idea of looking at things differently, you could try the Surprise Exercise, by looking out for the … unexpected.'

Steven cocks his head to one side and David Bell continues, 'By surprises, I mean, you simply look for unexpected, small, surprises in your environment. There is no great mystery to it. It is simply a matter of exercising the adage of, we see what we look for, rather than what is merely there.' Sweeping his arm around the immediate surroundings, he suggests, 'Try it. Take your time, and just look for something that you had not expected to see.'

After looking suspiciously at David Bell for a few seconds, Steven says, 'I used to exercise in prison, press ups, sit ups and the like,' then looking sharply at Bell, he states, 'If you're to get fit for your purposes, you could do with some daily exercises too.'

'Fair enough,' David agrees, as he looks over his own body, 'I think you are right. And if you have any in mind …'

However, having already begun to regard his surroundings, Steven almost immediately he spots that the cacti plant in the corner of the veranda, has several small, bright red flowers on it. Obviously, they had been there before, but he just hadn't noticed them. For a while, he regards them, and then their honeycomb yellow, delicate centres.

As David sees Steven's interest in the plant, he suggests, 'If you spot something, interesting, there is no need to dwell on it just for the sake of trying to give it more importance, or to attach some kind of, kudos, to it. Just move on whenever you feel like it.'

Steven then notices that the weathered, ceramic pot that holds the cacti, is intricately carved. For a while longer, he follows the lines of the carving and, inwardly, he has to give credit to the carver.

Suddenly David diverts Steven's attention, 'Would it surprise you, that perfectly ordinary law-abiding people, get an equal, if not a greater sense of excitement, achievement, and wonder from their ordinary law abiding, daily challenges, than people who go around committing crimes?'

Giving David a challenging look, Steven quips, 'Maybe they just have lower expectations for themselves.'
'No! They just have lower expectations of crime. Which then allows them to throw their criminal desires to where they belong, which is … *way out!* That in turn, leaves more room in their lives for being grateful, not only for the little things, but big things, such as love, respect, shared responsibility, and other things that crime leaves little or no room for.'
For a moment, Steven seems unsettled, and then breathing in deeply, he asks, 'So are you saying that I should apply these surprise exercises to my moral way of looking at things?'
'In a nutshell, yes! Particularly when it comes to looking at people more closely. Being an ordinary person does not mean that *Life* is boring. If you care to look, an ordinary life is as fascinating as is Life itself. Your attempts to liven your life up, and make it more meaningful by using crime, lacks vision.'
Looking closely at Steven, he states, 'You have little to no idea of where someone has come from, or where they are trying to get to in life. You need to read in-between the lines, Steven. You need to understand the meanings of the words, the sentences, and storylines of people's lives, instead of scrawling crime-graffiti all over them. Develop empathy, and let it show you how alike they are to you, with your struggles, disappointments, and successes, except of course they choose not to go around killing people.'
After looking thoughtfully at David, Steven becomes inwardly thoughtful, then after a moment, a sudden look of optimism spreads across his face as he asks, 'I don't suppose Boots the chemist sell it, do they?'
'Sell what?' David asks, almost dreading the reply.
'This empathy … in tablet or cream form, I don't mind.'
'No! Empathy can be an instinctive quality, or you can learn it, but Boots don't sell it. Which is a shame. Because it can simultaneously act as both a magnifying glass and mirror. Empathy can also place a telling question mark, between an

otherwise unstoppable desire and an immovable consequence.'

Holding his hand up, David concludes, 'Although empathy is something I hope you will gain more of, it is not one of your most plentiful qualities yet.'

'What about Superdrug, do they sell it?'

'No, but there are exercises, such as M. E.'

Answering Steven's quizzical look, he continues, 'M.E stands for Motivational Empathy. The advantage of M.E is that the *tools* of the exercise can be found and used during any real-time fantasy or even a real-time situation. You can, for instance, ask yourself questions about a potential victim's clothing and everyday possessions, such as who bought them and why. From there you can move on to questions about their life, their friends, and enemies. You can also ask yourself about a potential victim's hopes, fears, and vulnerabilities … to gain some empathy, and even comparisons with your own hopes, fears, and vulnerabilities. But as I mentioned before, it's best to work with the qualities and abilities that you have.'

Steven accepts the point in good grace and then asks, 'Any other of my qualities that you think might be useful?'

'It's good that you are used to the discipline of regular physical exercise, you'll need that inner discipline,' David emphasises the point with a knowing smile, and continues, 'Tomorrow we can look deeper at other forms of exercises, we can build up a collection of distraction techniques, which can be used when a criminal thought or so-called urge appears.'

Opening his arms out, David Bell continues, 'Such as resolving the cases of one's own mistaken-self-identity. To use a Crimetest's quote. Our prisons are full to the brim with cases of mistaken *self*-identity.'

Steven smiles at the quote, and David continues, 'Then there is using the immense power to be gained by ignorance, just as you would have ignored a victim's pleadings … except that now, you can start to ignore the whining's of any of your wrongful urges.'

Raising his own eyebrows in reply to Steven's raised eyebrow, he continues, 'You can also have a law-abiding, hero figure, or more than one, so that you can automatically ask yourself, what his or her, reaction would be to a particular crime? You can also replace the image of your intended victim, with one of you as a child, and ask yourself the same question about the crime, as if it were to be committed upon you.'

Taking a sip of lemonade, David continues, 'But for now, it's probably best if we end this session with one very useful tip. Which is …' and at that point, he leans forward to emphasise his point, 'That all crime fantasies, are based on a lie, and that the point of this whole course, is for you to gain the ability to recognise those lies and use that knowledge … to mistrust crime!'

With that said, he raises his lemonade in a toast to Steven and then sits back. Steven looks at David for about a half minute, and then towards the distance, and then back to David, and states, 'Ok! I get that.'

'Good. Because there will vulnerable times ahead.'

'I'm sure there will be.' Steven replies, with a smile.

After a break, the men returned to the proposal of David's Free Heroes campaign, and Steven starts David Bell off in his training, 'I've downloaded a daily physical exercise workout routine, and I'd like you to practice it each day. We aren't talking Royal Marine levels of fitness here, but it will get you into a reasonable level of physical alertness and readiness. You will also, find that it will give you a sense of self-confidence, which will be important when it comes to dealing with stress. You can start tomorrow, before breakfast. If you do it after breakfast then you are likely to spew up, particularly if you do the exercises in earnest.'

David takes the sheets of instructions, and after briefly scanning through them, he lays them aside and declares, 'Thanks, I'll start first thing tomorrow.'

 'Like most things in life,' Steven asserts, 'preparation is essential. We will approach every mission, by being prepared. That way we can face any assignment, with a feeling of cautious optimism backed up by thorough research and practice. We will reconnoitre every target and the available surrounding routes both in and out, because just one may not always provide the same availability as it did at the start. We will have a plan A, a plan B and a plan C.'

Suddenly, David Bell remembers Steven firing a gun at Sergeant Vanner, at the Highgate Cemetery, 'You realise that if we attempt any mission, then using any form of violence is strictly off limits.' Before Steven could answer, David asks, 'Do you have a gun?'

'The answer is yes, to your first question and no to the second. Carrying a gun can is likely to cause a lot more trouble, than it can get you out of.'

Then smiling at David, Steven states, 'Besides, I escaped from prison before, and I can escape from prison again.'

'I just thought I'd ask.'

'As far as being randomly stopped by the police, we will be dressed as, and be acting as tourist, and innocent tourist don't carry guns. I have enough good quality identification to get past any casual police inspection. If we are caught in the act of placarding a church, then I will make a run for it, you can either stay or run too. Though as we agreed beforehand, my identity comes under the confidentiality code … right?'

'Right.'

'If I am physically held, I will fight, if somebody gets a bloody nose, then you can offer them … empathy … and a handkerchief or whatever. But if you expect me to meekly go back to prison, then think again.'

'I just don't want any sort of violence used for the sake of the mission.'

'If we prepare as we should do, then there won't be any use for any sort of violence, as you put it.'
'Ok!'
'As for changes of clothes, we can get them from any shop. After we have used the clothing, in action as it were, we destroy it. Forensics can place you at a crime scene even if you have just passed through it.'
Steven then sat back and said, 'I know that this placarding business wouldn't be classed as anywhere near a serious crime, in England, but we are in Italy. And you're right, there are many high placed people here, with a highly-placed interest in the industry of Roman Catholicism. If you are caught, then it may be you who ends up serving a prison sentence, so pay close attention.'
'You are right, and I will.'
'All purchases that we make from now on, including things like snacks, meals, and petrol etcetera, will be paid for in cash, with no exceptions.' Steven pauses to let David take that information in, and then, giving his protégé a knowing look, he continues, 'I'm sure that from all the listening to the tales of the failed crimes of your callers at Crimetest, you will be well aware that even with the best of well-laid plans, you cannot prepare for the unpredictable.'
Without having to recall any of the stories, David nods, and Steven carries on, 'When the unprepared for happens, you will require a large set of *balls* to deal with the consequences. And the best way to acquire those balls, is to practice in the field of battle. So, our next lesson will take place at your next chosen church on your list.'
'It was meant to be just outside Bari.'
'Then to Bari we will go.'
The next day of training started with Steven undertaking a meditation on gratitude. He learned how to count each breath, from one to ten and repeat the process once ten breaths had gone by. On each count of breath, he either had to call up an image of anything that came to mind and find some reason to

be grateful for that thing to exist in the world; he would then let the image go and move on to the next breath and repeat the exercise.

At first, even when he found a reason to be grateful, Steven also found that he kept fighting it with inner arguments. Nevertheless, after a while, and with occasional inputs from David Bell, he began to stop the arguments, and to enjoy the experience of being appreciative for its own sake. Both during and after the gratitude exercise he felt progressively, calmer, and it had to be said, albeit rather grudgingly, more gratitude for life in general.

In the meantime, David Bell was thankful for every breath he could manage to take during his strenuous physical workout, which he performed whilst and alongside Steven as he, in turn, continued his Gratefulness meditation.

During breakfast, David asks Steven to choose five things to be grateful about, which might also distract him from any wrongful temptations. To his surprise, Steven found it quite difficult choosing just five.

After breakfast, David enquires how he feels, and was not too surprised when Steven answered, 'Good,' then after a pause, added, 'in both senses of the word.'

David was not surprised at Steven's initial reactions; the program had been devised by much hard-edged research. However, he also knew that without daily practice, Steven's, feel-good state would probably fade sooner rather than later.

By the mid-afternoon, both men are heading toward a village outside Bari. As they travell, Steven once again runs through a list of requirements; designed to prevent suspicion by any busybodies who happen to be in the area and evade capture by the police.

Arriving at the pre-chosen Church, they took 'tourist' photos; of the main entrance and side doors, the surrounding streets, and alleyways in between, with particular reference to any CCTV camera positions. They also study the surrounding escape routes that they might have to use, needing a car, public transport or on foot.

By the time, they had returned home and had eaten an evening meal, both men felt as exhausted as any tourist, and they thankfully retired to their beds and slept soundly.

In the morning, after their respective good night's rest, they completed their allotted exercises. David Bell did his physical workout, and Steven practiced some 'Surprise' exercises, and some "Nice fantasy-but dumb thought!" exercises; in which he had to find reasons for committing a crime (any crime he could think of) and then find reasons to not commit the crime. As soon as they had showered and breakfasted, the duo did the Being Grateful meditation, together; with Steven relating his thought processes to David Bell, who then added useful alternative ways of looking at things. By mid-morning, Steven was left alone to create an extended a favourites list of his reasons for not trusting any crime. David, on the other hand, was sent on a shopping spree; to buy some of the things that would be required to commit the next placarding successfully.

After David left, Steven used the time to create his list, by going off to explore the surrounding countryside. As expected, he saw few people and encountered only one local; who waved a greeting to him and then went on her way. During his walk, Steven practiced a few "surprise" distraction exercises (not that he was in the mood to commit any crime); and once again he found that things, even so-called ordinary things, seemed to take on a more meaningful presence than he usually experienced. However, the biggest surprise that he found was that, he, was turning out to be a more surprising person than he once thought himself to be – or might ever be. Ironically, if he had known it, Steven would have also been surprised to find out that; whilst on his shopping expedition and in order to both hide his nervousness from the shop assistants, and to distract himself from his own nervousness, David Bell was also doing the "surprise" exercise. The fact that he was doing the exercise in the process of preparing for a crime, or at least a social wrongdoing, rather than to distract himself from wanting to commit a crime did not escape David Bell's attention.

When David returned from his trip, both he and Steven recounted their day's events to each other, with both men genuinely congratulating one another on their individual achievements. Nevertheless, as the two of them jointly prepared the evening meal, Steven senses an uneasiness in the air. Yet, it was not until halfway through eating their evening meal that Steven identifies the nature of the spectre, and it is one of ... loss.

As when a newly re-housed tenant misses their old slum neighbours, Steven presumes he might be subconsciously mourning the potential loss of his old criminal ways, and although there might some element of truth to such sentimentality, he knew that is not the whole story. Suddenly, as he looks at David Bell, the feeling of loss finally solidifies, and Steven finds himself with a new experience, for he feels sympathy, for David Bell.

Beginning to wonder about keeping his part of the deal, which includes training Bell to be a "criminal" or at least a vandal; a fleeting vision of David Bell as an old man, rotting away in some Italian prison cell, flips through Steven's mind. However, as he helps himself to a second helping of homemade beef pie, he does not say anything of his doubts or vision; mainly because of his desire to maintain a mutual tie to Bell for many reasons, and not merely for the secondary pursuit of moral improvement.

Ironically, if he had told David of his concerns, then he too might have also paused to reconsider their deal. He also might have recalled the edict; "If you start being pulled in by the person you are trying to pull out ... then it's time to let go!"

Chapter 7 - The first outing

By the following morning, all previous night's doubts had been barged aside by the rush of adrenaline; which surges through both men even before they had completed their exercises.

As they prepare for the forthcoming trip, David Bell insists, 'Of course, I'll reimburse you for all the expenditure.'

'You'll reimburse me, in cash, when the whole campaign comes to a successful end.'

Just over two hours later, and driving the hire car, rented with one of Steven's false identification documents, the villains of the Holy peace arrive at the outskirts of the target village. David parks up at an unmonitored free car park, and both men change into their outer clothing disguises. As they leave the car, each man has a complete set of outer clothes; including sunglasses, a low brimmed hat for Steven, and a hooded, lightweight sports top for David Bell. The tools of their trade, include two placards, hidden in the ruck sack, which David carries. Taking a route that by-passes all obvious CCTV cameras, the men stroll to the small square in front of the church. By the time, they reach the steps of the church, David's heart is pounding; as if he had just run all the way from his home.

After completing a casual inside reconnaissance, Steven comes out again, comes over to Bell and asks, 'It's all clear …are you ready for this?'

'As ready as I'll ever be!'

'If you want to wait outside, I can do this on my own, if you prefer?'

Pausing for a moment, and looking into Steven's eyes, Bell answers, 'So can I.'

Smiling at Bell, Steven suggests, 'Let's do it together, partner!'

As expected, no one else is present inside the church. Nevertheless, David Bell feels his legs trembling as soon as he enters the church, and they continue to tremble as he ventures further in.

Standing at the main doors, posing as a tourist holding up a phone, Steven begins videoing the rear view of David, walking onto and up the steps of the altar.

Quickly removing the two placards from the rucksack, David Bell, Blue-tacks one placard along the outstretched right arm of the crucified Christ, and the second placard along the left arm. Getting a phone from his pocket, and taking a much-needed deep breath, he takes one photo of the placarded statue, took two more zoom shots of each placard, then lowering his head, he turns around and begins walking out of the church. As he passes Steven, Steven exclaims, '*Well done!*'

As soon as he is out into the bright Italian sunlight, and away from the scene of his, "social no-no", David feels an exhilarating rush of achievement; so much so, that Steven must increase his own pace just to catch up to him.

'Slow down, walk at a normal pace, just as if you are a tourist.'

'Ok! But we've done it! We did it!' David exclaimes as he slows his pace.

Fifteen minutes later, the pair pull into a secluded side-track, and David again checks that the images of the statue and placards are as they should be. Satisfied that all is well, and looking at Steven, he states, 'I guess this is it, the point of no return?'

Steven, just nods, three times.

Seconds later the images; of the statue of the crucified Christ with the two placards hanging along its arms, the zoom image of each placard and the church's interior and exterior, its location and the 'Curch of Free-Heroes' website address, are buzzing around various news media offices and the worldwide internet and pollinating all that they touch.

The placard left along the right arm of the statue replicated the original first placard; which lays rolled up in the bottom drawer of Cardinal Padovano's outer office desk - it was not to remain rolled up for much longer.

The second placard displayed, "The 1st Quest."

The Curch of Free-Heroes
The 1st Quest: Freedom through forgiveness:
 A Free-Hero's quest for forgiveness can be enriched by creating a personal recovery space; for re-claiming any Life-qualities, such as self-respect, empathy, love etc. which have been lost or damaged during a crime or wrongdoing; committed either against one's self - or by one's self. The potential of a recovery space is independent of whether the Life-Qualities, are being reclaimed by a victim or a victimiser. However, any recovery achieved within and beyond the space, is vastly enhanced by actively mistrusting the wrongdoing, rather than one's self.

The 1st Question:
Some religions claim that, Life, is in essence, a boot-camp for kicking any unhealed moral down and outs, out and down, from a totally-crime-free, after-death paradise. What is more, because such unhealed down and outs have already had their Life-Qualities severely marred (by being sexual, physical and emotional abused or neglected - even to point of becoming victimisers themselves), then after they die, they will be denied God's forgiveness, and (*spoiler alert!*) will be further damaged with even more abuse, in an after-death-Hell.

Alternatively, does your religion have a version of a god; whose crime prevention plan is just a tad more realistic, rehabilitating, and down to Earth?

www.curchoffreeheroes.info

Chapter 8 - Road-trip rage
Six and half hours after the emergence of news reports about the placarding in the church near Bari, David and Steven drove six kilometres south of Bell's villa and Googled the Curch of Free-Heroes website.

'Look! We have one thousand and fifty-two hits, and sixty-three posts!' David exclaims. Scrolling through the posts, he enthuses, 'There is a variety of responses, but most seem positive. Look here is one, unsurprisingly, telling us that we will be condemned to everlasting hell. Scrolling down he adds, 'There is another one calling for a sit-in, at various churches, so they can be used for more uses, other than religious ones.' Searching through more responses, he states, 'Look, there are lots more likes on Facebook than there are dislikes.'

Steven congratulates David and slaps him on the thigh. In truth, Steven felt quite elated as well; it is almost like the feelings that he used to get, after achieving some measure of success during one of his crimes … almost … but not quite. After another few minutes, Steven advises to stop viewing, 'If you stay connected too long to the website, or view it too often, it can seem to anyone who cares to look, that you may have more than a passing interest.'

'Right, you're right. It is a shame though, I could learn a lot from the post. But you're right!' With Steven's warning agreed to, David is about to switch to some other website, when he asks, 'Do you think I should leave some sort of negative post? As if it was sent from someone who is furious with the placarding?'

Raising one eyebrow, Steven looks stony-faced, and replies, 'On advice from my legal counsel, your Honour, I make no fucking comment, text or post, what-so-ever, and that's the way it's going to stay!'

David agrees, reads two more posts, and then switches to Amazon, looks at the gardening tools section, buys nothing and switches the phone off. After wiping any fingerprints off and driving for a few minutes, he throws the phone out of the car window. A short time later, a well-meaning citizen picked up the discarded phone. The well-meaning citizen found no practical way to trace the phone's owner; judged that the phone is too cheap to bother handing it into the police, so he took it home and forgot all about it, until he took it, and other various unwanted electrical pieces of electrical equipment, to the recycling depot.

A short while after David threw the phone out of the car window; the two men were still feeling pleased about the growing internet interest in the Curch website. They are driving along a quiet, narrow countryside road that runs between two villages, when they arrive at a crossroad. Thinking quite rightly, that he has the right of way, David has to quickly swerve to avoid a green car, which had suddenly tried to pull out in front of him.

Recovering his proper course, David Bell, who is normally a polite and careful road user, toots his horn several times to admonish the reckless driver of the green car that is now tailgating him.

In an effort, to pass the car in front of him, the driver of the open top, green convertible impatiently sounds his horn. David, however, is not feeling in a polite mood as he sticks to the middle to nearside of the road. Two bends and much hooting of his horn later, the driver of the green car tries passing on the nearside. When the driver of the green car could not fully get by, he spits at the annoying car - which turned out to be an unwise manoeuvre; as the offending spit hit the partially closed passenger side window.

'Slow down and stop!' Steven orders Bell.

Knowing Steven as he does, David keeps his speed constant and replies, 'Don't worry about it, we do not need any trouble, remember!'

'I won't worry, and he or we won't be any *trouble*!' Steven replies, whilst firmly holding and jolting the steering wheel; to get David to stop the car.

Reacting instinctively; David Bell tries to keep a true course; estimates what Steven might do if he did not get his way, then he slows the car to a stop, applies the handbrake, sighs heavily, and then waits.

Taking a box of tissues from the lower shelf of the dashboard and getting out of the car; Steven smiles as he walks toward the offending driver - who having been forced to pull in behind, is now looking slightly apprehensive as he speaks, in Italian, into his phone.

Reaching the driver, Steven grabs the phone, drops it on the ground and then lifts his right foot, as if threatening to stamp on the man's phone. Offering the man, the box of tissues, Steven points to the passenger side window of the hired car, and using English he instructs, 'I am going to count from ten, which gives you ten seconds to start wiping your fucking spit, of my window! After the phone, I start stamping on your fucking head!' He then starts to count backward, in Italian, and with his fingers.

By the time, Steven has reached four, and after looking at Steven, and considering some options, the man has run out of realistic ones; grabbing the box of tissues, he gets out and heads off toward the car, and wipes his offence off of the window. When the man returns, Steven throws the phone over the roadside hedging and into the undergrowth beyond, then he returns to his car, gets in, and David Bell drives on.

Five minutes later, David half turns to Steven and says, 'You really must try to stop holding people and things as hostages, Steven. It only leads to trouble.' David was not only referring to bad drivers, but to Stevens' last true hostage, Elizabeth, who Steven had kidnapped and held hostage, in order to get Crimetest to renege on their promise of confidentiality for all callers.

Turning sideways, Steven replies, in a rather hurt tone, 'Give me a break David, I've only started doing the rehabilitation course, you can't expect bloody miracles!'

The next day, having packed the night before, the men made an early start, for they had agreed that the next placarding would be well away from David's home. After double checking that they had all that need for the near future, David Bell secured his home, and they started off.

For ten kilometres or two, David and Steven occasionally pondered about the potential outcomes of the journey ahead; until they returned their attention to the road ahead as they approach and then passed beneath the large sign for *Florence*.

Chapter 9 - Florence, Hanna, and Rita

As a mixture of devotees and tourist pass into and out of the main entrance to Florence's Cathedral of Saint Mary of the Flowers, an elderly priest, and his apprentice greet them. The 21-year-old apprentice priest, named Mario, pays great attention to the comings and goings, and to the mentoring words of the elderly priest who handles the various questions of the visitors. "One day," Mario thought, "I may be here answering the needs of these people by leading a mass … Our Lord willing."

Just then, a shadow flits across the sunlit threshold of the main entrance, as a small gathering of startled pigeons burst into flight. When Mario turns his head to look, he sees ... *beholds* … a woman ... an attractive woman ... *a Belle Donna*, walking ... pacing ... *gracing* … back and forth across the entrance.

Mario could tell from her dress style, that the woman is Italian, she seems to be in her early thirties. She also seems to be waiting for someone, "Or perhaps," Mario thought ... imagines ... hopes, "she is deciding to enter the cathedral to seek temporary solace from a confusing world ... or to seek comfort from prayer ... or even to seek protection from an abusive lover or husband. A husband who would be cast into the deepest pits of Hell as soon as he met his *much-deserved,* death! Not that anyone should be wishing such a thing …," Mario quickly reminds himself, "… for such justice would rest in the just hands of The Lord."

Mario also reminds himself that he should be concentrating on his duties and not on any outside temptation, however distracting ... sensual ... stunningly beautiful … *she* … may be!"

As praiseworthy as Mario attempts to distract himself from the sort of temptations - which had driven the likes of Anthony and Cleopatra, Romeo and Juliet and Fred and Colie Ramshaw of New Malden, England, to the brink of mutual self-destruction - Mario's efforts began to waver. His attempts to out-manoeuvre epochs of human sexual instinct fell somewhat short, of what Catholic religious edicts on sexual temptation, demanded.

To give him his fair due, Mario did try his best to overcome the guilt that was rising as rapidly as his blushes. Not that he had any natural reason to feel so un-naturally unworthy. Indeed, if he were to run out to the woman and beg her for her forgiveness, she would smile and give her forgiveness immediately and totally, along with her gratitude for his implied compliment.

However, with the predictable demise of the tower of Babel, Mario's guilt crumples and collapses, as yet, *another* "God created Bella-Donna!" joins the first. Next, and to Mario's stricken heart, mind and loins the women started to depart. Nevertheless, before they disappeared completely, and to Mario's everlasting bliss, the first woman quickly steps into the cathedral interior, then she gives the traditional bow and sign of crucifix, sees Mario gazing at her, and gives him the most radiant, and most irresistible smile, that he had ever seen, or indeed would ever would ever behold (this side of heaven), and then she left his sight forever!

To the stricken Mario, the departure of the woman felt as if Death itself had cast its shadow across his soul. Yet, it was that very feeling that prompted the young priest to slowly but surely, return to his first, ecclesiastical, love. And so, it passed, that Mario stayed true to his first, 'beloved' Mary the Holy Mother of God. However, as he watched the returning pigeons flutter back to the very place where the women had departed, he felt that the final chance for his bottled-up Italian manhood had forever been swept far beyond his reach, or salvation.

The two women's names are Hanna (who had turned many a head, besides that of Mario's), and her best friend, Rita, who had on more than one occasion, prompted the inevitable collision betwixt a captivated mind and a solid lamp post.

The two best friends are on a four-week holiday, which would include a stay at Hanna's home village; to see her sister and her newly born son. Hanna works as a shop assistant in small, yet popular clothes shop in Florence. Rita, who is also from Florence, works as an outreach worker for a zoo. As the women head away from the cathedral, they make their way to the restaurant at the far corner of the piazza. As they walk, Hanna, impulsively lifts the hand stitched hem of her second-hand bought Giovanni dress, to above her knees (but below the level of social indecency), she then takes off her shoes, politely hands them to Rita, and then she splashes barefooted, through several recently made rain puddles.

As Hanna runs through the last puddle, her shoe holding best friend, Rita, realises; that it was already *far* too late to prevent a passing, distracted male cyclist from cycling straight into the iron railings surrounding the Giotto's Campanile 85-metre-high, square, bell tower. Unfortunately for the distracted cyclist, the Campanile's first stone works had been laid on the 19th of July 1334, which gave the Campanile as such, the far greater claim to the right of way. Consequently, it was he (the cyclist), rather than the Campanile, which ended up somersaulting over the protective railings before collapsing into a sprawling heap on the ground.

Fortunately, neither the cyclist, bike, nor railings received any injury more serious than a few minor chips, scratches, or bruises. So it was that everyone involved, soon carried on their respective journeys.

Five minutes later, as the two women are enjoying freshly served coffee and liberally buttered croissants, the arrival of two men stop Hanna in mid-sip, as she announces to Rita, 'Ah! Such a handsome man!'

Looking at the newly arrived men, Rita asks, 'Which one?'

Indicating to Steven, Hanna confirms, 'The taller one!'

'Really? I think the other one is far more attractive.'

Not having noticed their two admirers, who by now had continued to eat their own holiday treats; Steven and David go to the counter, order two cappuccinos and two muffins, and then sit at a table two tables away from the two women, in the front of the café's outside frontage.

After the waiter had brought the men their order, Steven and David begin talking in a slightly conspiratorial manner. However, two minutes later, Steven rose and went towards the gent's bathroom, meanwhile, David; wishing to find out if their placarding of the church had made the latest editions of the Italian national press, walked over to a nearby news kiosk to buy a newspaper.

By the time both men almost simultaneously arrive back at their table, they are mildly surprised, to find a small pile of white linen napkins neatly placed over each of their muffins. Seeing each other's surprise and curiosity, both of them look around.

'It is against the pigeons!' Hanna informs them. 'If you leave any food on show, they will *swoop* it all up!' With that she makes a swooping motion, and then adds with a highly infectious grin, 'They are especially fond of chocolate muffins … bought by English tourists!'

David and Steven just look at each other, and then at the women, as Rita apologises, 'I hope you didn't mind two strangers interfering, but as Hanna said, the pigeons have small table manners, even towards guest in our country. As you must think the same of us, by not first introducing ourselves,' Rita then announces, 'This is my good friend Hanna, and I am Rita!'

'How did you know that we are English?' David asks, returning the infectious smiles of both women.

'Because we heard your friend orders the muffins, in English.' Hanna replies.

Just then, Rita leans forwards and further explains, with a mischievous smile, 'Besides, only an English man would try to pay for his meal, before it has been served, let alone eaten!'

The two men look at each other, shrug their shoulders, and in a token of submission, Steven lifts and then waves one of the white napkins, as he says, 'I think we have been uncovered!'

After a round of further introductions, and quickly discovering that they are all on vacation, the group begin talking about the places they each wish to see.

'I must see the Donatello's bronze, the David!' Hanna exclaims.

'I wish to see two places.' Rita insists, 'One is the Uffizi gallery,' she then explains to David and Steven, 'It used to be an Ufficio, an office for magistrates and judges, but now it is home to works of art by Giotto, Paolo Uccello, Leonardo, Michelangelo, Raffaello, and Tiziano and there is the Birth of Venus, by Botticelli.'

'Sounds brilliant,' David agrees.

'We are going there in the morning,' Rita informs, 'and then we must visit The Mall, in Leccio. It is about an hour journey, but they have every famous fashion house name from Prada to Gucci there. Everything will be unbelievably expensive, but it is a must-see place to visit.'

Although the men are not overly enthusiastic about visiting a fashion mall, it is obvious that they are attracted to the women. 'Very well …' Steven suggests, '… if you both would like to, we can all go together, and make a day of it.' However, before the women have agreed, David adds, 'But what about the Museo Galileo, the Institute and Museum of the History of Science! There is the Medici gallery, which has telescopes of Galileo, the father of modern physics, as well as the Lorraine collections, which charts the progress of fundamental laws of physics'

At that point, the other three give each other a mixture of quizzical looks, and burst out in gentle laughter, as they resign their fate into David's hands; for it is apparent to all four, that they have decided to form a tour party together. As if to confirm their unspoken pact, Hanna asks Steven, 'And where will you take us to Steven?'

'I am new to Italy, so for the moment I will follow your
wisdom and decide later.'
It was not that long before the conversation turned to learning
a bit more about each other. And after some encouragement
from Rita, David spoke about his involvement of the
Crimetest's crime advice line. In answer to Rita's question
about how Crime Advisers dealt with callers, David
answered, 'I guess you could say that we try to get them to
mistrust crime, before we ask them to trust themselves.'
'So, what do you actually offer when someone calls you?'
Rita insists.
Giving Rita a long look and a warm smile, David suggests,'
Well let's pretend that you are a caller, and let us say that you
want to kill your cheating lover, not that you would ever
dream of being a murderess.'
Giving David a long look and a warm smile, Rita quips, 'I
should wait until the end of the call before you believe that. I
can get both highly competitive … and jealous.'
'Even so … I would suggest,' David answers, 'that there is as
much chance of you committing such a murder, as there is a
lover of yours ever wanting to cheat on you.' At that point, all
three of his companions look at David Bell a bit more closely,
as he continues, 'In short, we try to get a caller who is
thinking of committing a crime to mistrust the crime … by
uncovering the lies that lay behind their criminal urge. We
also try to get them to forgive themselves for wanting to fall
for those lies in the first place. After that, we help them to
`start looking at the power and freedoms that can be gained
from, consciously, taking *total* responsibility for all their *past*
choices and behaviour, so they can in turn, use that freedom
to change their *future* choices, no matter what they have been
in the past. We also advise on finding and using non-criminal
ways of expressing their freedom and power.'
After turning to each other, Hanna and Rita look at David
with an air of admiration, as he raises his arms and adds,

'Though, in the case of your cheating lover, I would say that he would be … totally … unforgivable.'

Once again, his three companions look at him more closely, then Hanna and Steven cheer and applauded him, whilst Rita bowed her head in acceptance of his compliment.

'*I have only cheated once in my life,*' Hanna exclaims, as she gives everyone a huge grin (that included the waiter who had just brought their bill), and then she concludes, 'It was on, a lover … *who cheated on me!*'

With that said, the company (including the waiter) laughed with Hanna, the four companions paid for their drinks and snacks, and then left for the beginning of their joint tour … and beyond.

Chapter 10 - Caravaggio, shopping, and friendships
The first place that the companions had decided to visit is the Museo Nazionale dell Bargello. The building once used as a prison, but now the walls are adorned with prestigious artworks; which would have bemused the former prison's inmates. As soon as they arrived, Hanna makes straight for the famous Donatello's bronze statue of David. The statue's academic fame is partly due, because it is the first unsupported standing work of bronze cast during the Renaissance, and dates to the 1430s or later; and it is the first freestanding nude male sculpture made since antiquity. Strictly speaking, the David is not completely nude, yet the statue earns public fame and even infamy, from the unsettling aura of its presence. The bronze figure depicts an almost feminine looking young David; whose lips bear an enigmatic smile as he rests his foot on Goliath's freshly severed head. Never the less, from David's tousled hair, half-hidden beneath his laurel-topped hat, and down to his boots, the David is completely naked.

 'Oh, My God!' Hanna exclaims as she looks all around the sculpture, 'I don't think I have ever seen anything so delicate, so powerful, it feels like ...?'
'It feels like what?' Rita asks.
'Like an everlasting ice cream!' Hanna replies, and then without any warning; she swivells her legs over the barricade, pulls herself up and onto the statue, leans forward, opens her mouth and licks the statue's smooth, cool, face.
'Hanna!' Rita hisses as she gestures for her to come back. David Bell meanwhile just stands open mouthed, whilst Steven does likewise; amazed to see someone whose own beauty and unsettling presence, somehow matches that of the David figure.
As Hanna is ushered away by Rita, a Museum attendant gently wags his forefinger at Hanna, and then he smiles; it was not the first time he had seen similar reactions to the David, and he very much doubted that it would be the last.

Whilst touring some of the other rooms, Hanna becomes particularly enamoured by a painting by Caravaggio, called, The Conversion of Mary Magdalene.

Looking at the painting, David Bell states, 'It's fascinating, the way he uses colour to suggest, mood. I think it was David Hockney, who once described Caravaggio paintings as, the film Noir of art.'

After ending their tour, the four friends have a light lunch in a café, and Hanna was still praising the David statue, when she exclaims, 'I think that the angels in heaven will look like the David!'

Although Steven and Rita laugh, it is noticeable that David merely smiles, rather weakly. Looking at David, Hanna asks, 'What is wrong, David, did I offend you? If so I am sorry.'

'Please don't apologize, besides it was not your enthusiasm for the David that I found … off-putting, not at all. It was the reference to Heaven. I find religion's fanciful fairy stories a bit too much to take.'

'How so? Do you not believe in God?'

'In God, possibly. But I definitely, and defiantly, do not believe in any of the gods that any of the religions have so far managed to cobble together, or their versions of a life after death.'

'How so?'

'Because if there is a conscious, all-powerful, all loving God then such a being, will neither cheat, and most certainly won't be cheated.'

'How so … cheated?' Hanna asks.

'I mean, that any way of life aiming to create a moral paradise, must be founded on honesty, so that it can be honestly built and earned with the honest sweat of our own hands, minds and morality. What it won't be, is some exclusive, after-death holiday resort, which has been cobbled together, by and for desperate people who want to try and cheat death … or indeed god, should there be one.'

Shrugging his shoulders, he continues, 'Death, is not some unwanted gift that can be exchanged at the super-natural superstore, no matter how many so-called, *sacred,* loyalty points you've collected!'

'*My* … you seem so passionate.' Rita comments.

'I am *passionate*, it is because ever since they emerged from their breeding mires of fear and greed, the religions have used their truth-less, sound bites of an after-life, to bleed and numb the very legs of our pursuit of a moral paradise, here on Earth.'

Turning to Hanna and then back to Rita, David states, 'In short, they are a *parasite* upon human morality, and it is why I believe that all religion *sucks* … not *saves*!'

Shrugging his shoulders, he continues, 'However, all is not lost. For there is a stubbornly deep-rooted, survival instinct, which has been found and verified in the noble mind and heart.'

'How so this instinct? Hanna asked.

'It is the instinct of … fair play!'

'Fair play!' Steven repeats with some surprise.

Looking at each of his companions in turn, David Bell qualifies, 'It exists in us, apes, and in many noble species … and perhaps surprisingly to some … it has even been found to be just as deep rooted amongst packs of … wolves.'

Addressing Hanna, he explains, 'The researchers found that when one wolf was given substantially more reward than the others, for achieving the same task, then rather than turning on the wolf, the rest of the pack simply downed tools and refused to take part in the task at all.'

Turning to Steven, David adds, 'Which as it happens, is the most appropriate response to the unfairness of religion. The more we refuse to play their games, the more pointless they become.'

Addressing Hanna, David continues, 'Throughout the history of humanity, it has been shown that when the instincts for fair play and just rewards, are matched against whims of

favouritism, and unjust rewards … in the end, it is fair play that wins out … time and time again. Which is why I firmly believe that in the long run, fair play, will be the noble instinct that religion cannot outrun, outlast or out evolve.'
Although Hanna looks quite taken aback, she argues, 'But there is no need to let it upset you so David. Besides, many say, religious stories are just examples, or how do you say it …'
Turning to Rita, Hanna asked her to interpret, and Rita replies, 'Parables.'
'Parables …' Hanna continues, '… that give examples of a way of life, rather than the stories that must be strictly believed in.'
'Fair enough, but why add all the stuff and nonsense about there being an after-death paradise at all? Let alone all the pretentious posturing about their religion being the supposed, *special confidants,* of some supernatural god's desires and plans?'
'To encourage people to follow a good way of life,' Hanna suggests.'
'That's an interesting phrase.'
'What?'
'*Way of life*!
'How so?' Hanna asks.
Looking at Hanna and Rita, David answers, 'You know, whenever I look at some living being, such as a bird, an animal or even a lone blade of grass. I recognise that it does not have any, right, to extend its life expectancy much beyond the normal span of its own kind. Let alone to create new genetically engineered life forms, or travel to and settle upon distant planets. It does not have those rights, because it simply doesn't have the abilities to achieve such things.'
Indicating to the people all around, he continues, 'Only we human beings have such abilities and potential. However, every living thing *does* have every right to fly, run, or to stand still and grow, so that it may try to improve its chance in life

and that of its kind. It has those rights, because *the way of Life* has provided it with such abilities, and not some religion's so-called sacred parables, about the way of Life. Unless, that is, the leech has gained the knowledge to teach walking, how to run.'

At that moment, Rita reaches out her hand and lays it on David's arm; whether it is intended to be a comfort or a warning, is unclear.

Using his free hand, he picks up his coffee and after taking a sip, he then slowly returns his cup to its saucer, and emphasises, 'So whenever I hear of some preacher, teaching that there is some instant, already-perfect, after-death, *paradise*, which of course, will be exclusively reserved for him and his teacher's pets … *I shudder!* I shudder, because I can't help but liken that preacher to some teacher, who deliberately spits on a child's painting of paradise, because it is not *perfect* enough!'

Laying his hand on Rita's hand, David adds, 'Which sort of makes me question if such a preacher really knows the art of being a real teacher, let alone the art of being an all-knowing and all-loving God.'

At that moment, Rita tilts her head, and asks. 'Then you believe there could be a God?'

Giving Rita a smile, he answers, 'Whenever I ask myself that question, I am reminded of Arthur C Clarke, the science fiction writer's answer, when he was asked about the possibility of there being intelligent life, other than our own, in the universe.'

'And what did he say?'

'Two possibilities exist. Either we are alone in the Universe or we are not - both are equally terrifying.'

Smiling at the quote, Rita withdraws her hand, and David continues, 'It is fear and greed that drives religion. Fear that we are alone in the Universe, fear that there is an endless nothing after death, and greed for more than the vastness of this Life can provide, let alone justify. The fear merely drives

a self-styled form of foolish bravado, but the greed drives a holy-styled form of sacred terror.'
Ignoring a warning look from Steven, David turns to Hanna and continues, 'It is fear and greed that I understand, Hanna … but I refuse to worship!'
 At that point Rita asks, 'But life and the Universe will end someday, can you really condemn people for wishing that there is a life beyond?'
'No of course not. But do not be so dismissive that in reaching out for a *living, breathing, heart beating* moral paradise, then Life itself will reach beyond such interruptions as the death of the Universe, as we presently know it.'
Addressing his three companions, he continues, 'It is estimated that the Universe as we understand it, will die in approximately three to fourteen billion years' time, which is a lot of generations of humanity. Yet, our generation's abilities and understanding of life have accelerated beyond its predecessor's expectations. So can you possibly conceive what our understanding and abilities we will be in another ten thousand, hundred thousand years or a million years' time, let alone a billion.'
Seeing that there is no reply from his companions, David suggests, 'If like me, you cannot, then I suggest that we think on, before we restrain Life's reach to that of some last gasp promise of a readymade eternal paradise, which has to be firmly and sacredly shackled onto Death.'
Sitting back, David Bell concludes, 'For such a grave error is not only dismissive of Life itself, but should he exist, it is an *insolence* to God!'
Turning toward Hanna, David adds, 'And if I remember my childhood bible lessons correctly, then to be insolent to God, is to commit blasphemy, is it not?'
Suddenly, Hanna looks shocked and even blushes profusely, however, whatever she was about to say, she changes her mind and she remains silent.

At that moment, Steven's gives a blatant warning look at David; which tells him to change tack, or there would be immediate trouble, not from any god, but from him.

Waving her hand in a dismissive air, Rita proclaims, 'Enough of religion! It has been around for a long time and can wait. Whilst the latest fashions in The Mall, will not! So, why don't we all go there before they change yet again?'

When Rita's suggestion is met with agreement, and some relief, by her companions, everyone finishes off their drinks and snacks, in comparative good spirits.

Some ten minutes later, the four newly made friends, made their way to the famous The Mall, in Leccio. This was Rita's choice, and she made full use of it. However, after dragging the group in and out of just every top brand shop, she eventually relented, and they stopped for more coffee and snacks.

Whilst the companions ate and drank, and as they looked out towards the ultra-fashionable shops and buildings, Hanna mentioned, with a touch of irony, that although she adored it all, it was so different to the magnificent art and more traditional treasures of Italy, and in particular to the small churches and great cathedrals.'

'Why?' David asks.

'I guess, because they represent the House of God.'

However, David's reaction takes Hanna by surprise when he counters, 'But, we are all the architects of our own moral happiness or doom, Hanna. And we are perfectly capable of trying to build a moral paradise … or even demolishing the partially built one we've already earned, should we so choose to.'

Shrugging his shoulders, he continued, 'So we certainly don't need any religion appropriating our moral Lego-bricks, just so they can use them to build upon their dying hope, that they alone, will be able to secure some sort of exclusive rights of accommodation, in some all-ready-built paradise, for the already-dead and buried.'

Looking at Rita, David quipped, 'Well I certainly wouldn't want any of my children playing around with the dead and buried … besides … playing with Lego is *much* more fun!'

'Do you have any children? Rita asked.

'No, alas. I have no children yet. But if and when I do, then I truly believe, that my *proudest* moments will be when any of my children, commits an act of kindness, *for the sake of kindness itself* … rather than for the sake of gaining a reward, or to avoid being punished … either in this life, or in any so-called afterlife.'

Then, turning toward Hanna, he continues, 'And if your, or any religion does not understand that, Hanna, then somehow, they haven't even begun to understand what it is to be a loving parent, let alone the children of an all-loving God!'

'Really?' Steven quips, 'How almost interesting you are David. But I thought we had our fill of religion.'

Laying her hand on Steven's arm, Hanna said, 'As I seem to be the only defender of religion, perhaps I should have the chance to hear David's views.'

Indicating to the parade of fashion shops, David continues, 'I was going to point out, that the fashion industry and religion are both founded on plagiarising.'

'How so?' Hanna asked whilst looking politely affronted, and then asking, 'What is plagiarising?'

'To steal, or take credit for the other people's success, to rip them off.' Rita explained.

Hanna quickly nodded her understanding, then turning to David, she broke into a grin as she asked, 'Do you mean they rip off ideas or their clothes?'

At that point, all three of her companions laugh, after which Hanna said, 'I'm sorry David, please go on.'

'No apologies needed, it was worth the interruption.' Looking to see that no one seemed to be objecting, he continued, 'Religion was started, by ripping off the beliefs' of ordinary decent people, which are that kindness and decency tend to

lead to a better way of life. In short, the ways of life that any half decent, village council did and do come up with.'
When Hanna showed no objection, he continued, 'Unfortunately, each brand of religion then adapted decency to their own ends, so they could lay claim the sole copyright or ownership of decency itself. After some time, Christianity continued the tradition, by plagiarizing and adapting the plagiarisms of those previous religions, and most recently, Islam, plagiarized and adapted Christianity's more outdated version, into a more, morally fashionable, version. Anyway, the result is that human morality has been plagued with religion ever since.'
'Plagued and plagiarise are not the same thing,' Rita interjected.
''True! Yet since the religions first began, they have been jointly plaguing humanity by plying us with their grand protection racket.'
'Protection racket, you make them sound like the Cosa Nostra,' Rita answered.
'That is because, as Hanna will be willing to testify, if she refuses to pay their demands, the enforcers, or religious leaders, will outcast her as a moral-piranha, unable to resist the sins of the flesh, and she will be vilified by the religious community. Moreover, she will be threatened with an eternity in Hell. *However,* if she chooses to pay the daily, weekly and lifetime ransoms, then she can be protected from their threats and retributions. Is that not true Hanna?'
When Hanna stayed silent, David turned toward Rita, 'It is noticeable, that regardless of its financial situation or wealth of natural resources, the more a country is ruled by fundamental religious dictates, then the more fundamental abuses are carried out in the name of that religion.'
Addressing Hanna again, he asked, 'Besides, if trying to bribe or ransom life, is a sure guarantee of ending up being short-changed in life, what warranty is there in any bribe or ransom

of your life, after it has ended? Not that may happen for many years to come, of course!'

'Because of the eternal after-life.' Hanna replied.

'The after-life? And do you really hope that short-changing life will buy you even a millisecond, of this so-called eternal after-life, Hanna?'

'But I'm not trying to bribe or ransom life!' Hanna exclaimed in a hurt tone.

Looking with some concern toward Hanna, David asked, 'Then why not stop paying bribes and ransoms?'

When Hanna didn't answer, and Rita looked concern for Hanna, David quickly qualified by stating, 'Of course, the retributions of the current Catholic church are less drastic than their more extreme punishments of old, which are found in any fanatical branch of religion or politics.

'But religion is not political.' Hanna asserted.

'I'm afraid that just because two bedfellows aren't *officially* married, it doesn't mean they aren't cohabitating, Hanna. What is more, even though a religious party claims its party leader is already an all-powerful god, then it doesn't seem to stop them from trying to bully those who they see, as morally weaker than themselves ...'

Before David could continue, Steven quoted, '*Anyone can be big enough to be a bully, but the really telling question is, can you be big enough to stop yourself from becoming one ... because apparently ... size really does matter!*'

At that moment, David looked questioningly at Steven, so Steven informed everyone, 'A mutual friend of ours called Sandra, told me that once.'

'She sounds like a good person, who is Sandra?' Hanna asked.

'Someone who worked for David's Crime Advice service, isn't that right David?'

'Yes, she was, and still is a highly-regarded employee and good friend.'

Feeling slightly uncomfortable, Steven abruptly changed the subject back, by asking, 'Anyway, you were saying about religion, David?

'Yes, well … anyway, just as rival cigarette manufacturers join as one, against any health-related criticism of the tobacco industry, so the rival brands of religion will join as one, against any moral criticism of religion itself, and the so-called sacredness of their joint protection rackets.'

For a moment, it looked as if Hanna was about to reply, but she remained silent.

'If I were you, Hanna,' David suggested, 'I'd stick to following the fashion industry, at least there you can exercise some degree of choice, or you might end up walking around wearing a kebab covering your hea…!'

Immediately realising his slip of the tongue, David Bell waits for his companions (and indeed himself) to stop laughing and thigh slapping, before then he continues, 'Ok … Ok! My mistake. I meant *hijab*, not *kebab*.'

After waiting for a few more moments for his companions to settle down, he continued, 'But, nevertheless, I will suggest that my mistake is a reflection that the hijab itself is a falsehood. A falsehood trying to cover up that all religions want to *silence* any criticism of their dictates about what we are to think, say, when we are to eat and … how we are to dress. However, just like the silence rooms of the Victorians, the more fervently they try to shut out any noise, the more their own intolerance amplifies the slightest of disturbances, into an outrageous harshness, or in the case of religious intolerance, into an outrageous blasphemy.'

Holding his hand up, David continued, 'At best, the hijab and the full body burka are supposed to symbolise that neither female nor male sexuality should dominate the responsibilities to family, marriage or indeed *any* relationship. Which, in principle, is much better than the Western World's over valuation and expectations of sex.'

Opening his palms out, he states, 'Nevertheless, it doesn't explain why, if *any* woman wants to display her commitment to responsible sexual relationships, she can't wear a simple, specifically coloured ribbon, wristband or whatever.'
'Sky blue one, with pink and green stripes!' Hanna enthusiastically stated.
Nodding his head toward Hanna, David continued, 'But, some Islamic leaders insist that women go around with her whole body covered, as if her very gender is morally contagious. Which brings us to reality, that the cover up by the hijab and the burka are far more than some sexual health guideline, gone insane, for they hide an even more outrageous cover-up.'
'Cover-up of what?' Hanna asked.
'That the Islam and Christian religions, both try to cover all women beneath a shroud of misplaced blame. Just like many repeated patterns of misplaced blame, places the emphasis on the victim of abuse having to constantly protect themselves against the abuser, rather than the abuser having to stop the abuse. As to why this pattern appears so frequently in religious practices, is a matter of judgement. Nevertheless, by restricting women's dress, expressions of thought, and their social, financial, and educational opportunities, their *loss* of equality, responsibility and justice in life, is *religiously* guaranteed.'
Turning to Rita, David explains, 'All of which, *surprise, surprise, surprise,* has never been of the slightest of help to any healthy sexual relationship, or indeed any relationship … apart from the worst types, of course.'
When Hanna let out a sigh of released tensions, David is unsure if the sigh meant that she agreed with him or not; so, after a short pause to draw in breath, he gestured to five nuns, crossing the piazza, as he states. 'Not that walking around in a nun's habit, hijab, or prayer cap, is any reliable sign of taking moral responsibility anyway. Which brings us to the most corrupting cover up of all!'

'What do you mean,' Hanna asked.

'Those nuns, may be in the *habit* of doing charitable works all their lives, yet beneath their habits, they religiously support a regime that conspires, with like regimes, to *rule* … by using fear, greed, sexual, physical and emotional abuse, protection racketeering by issuing threats, violence, and never-ending torture, plus, a host of falsehoods and wrongdoings, which any branch of the Cosa Nostra, would welcome with open arms!'

Addressing his companions, David Bell concluded, 'In short, it is of little consequence that a person is dressed in a nun's habit, a hijab, a dog collar or a prayer cap, *underneath*, they are still … *gangsters* ... dressed up, in sheppard's clothing.'

At that point, Hanna gave David a serious look of disapproving shock, and Steven turned to Hanna and said, 'My apologies, it seems that the pigeons are not the only ones who swoop on the unsuspecting.' He then turned to Rita and said, 'Excuse my friend's bad table manners.'

Rita then turned and smiled at David, then she turned to Hanna and said, 'So, as I was telling you my darling, the latest …' however, Hanna quickly recovered and told her companions, 'I think that now David has swooped, we should at least let him have his fill, that way he can continue our tour of morality, on a full stomach.'

Bowing to Hanna, he replied, 'I will only say one more thing, before my unintended bad manners, leave me banished to the purgatory of not having your and Rita's company.'

'And that is?'

'As far as playing their cards right, the religions believe they always have a cold deck, which always gives them an unbeatable hand.'

'How so? Hanna asked.

'Well … if there is a heaven and obeying your particular religion's rules can get you in, then you can go and joyfully prance around with all the other obedient lambs. You may even meet up with your previous Earthly religious adviser, so

you can thank him personally, and then you can both wag
your fluffy tails at each other and …'
Quickly lifting her chin, Hanna suggested, 'I think you are
being, how you say …' turning to Rita, Hanna spoke in
Italian and Rita replied, 'Sarcastic!'
'Are you being Sarcastic, David?'
'A little,' David admitted with an apologetic smile, yet his
face grew more serious as he stated, 'Nevertheless, if there is
no afterlife, let alone a paradise after death, then the religions
can play their final *joker* card with impunity. Because your
hand, and you Hanna, alas, will already be dead … and dead
things can't feel cheated, or even express disappointment …
let alone anger.'
When Hanna made no reply, David continued, 'And whilst
you may be dead and gone, your religion will continue to play
on and on … until … those who are living, can at last toss the
pack of lies, aside, by accepting the everlasting justice, of an
everlasting, nothing-death.'
'The justice of a … *nothing-death*?' Rita asked.
'Well, for a start, if death really is a never-ending
nothingness, then you really do having *nothing* to fear from
being dead … absolutely nothing at all!'
Pausing for a moment, David looked around, and gestured
into the piazza again, and then to a small group of tourists.
'As for the natural justness of such a nothing-death? Then if
that man, who is wearing the bright yellow T-shirt, should
suddenly be struck down and killed by being hit by a falling
meteorite, his death would be sad, *incredibly* unlucky, and
under the laws of natural physics, totally justified. *If* … on the
other hand, the meteorite missed him, and he escaped death,
merely, because he happened to be wearing a *blue* T-shirt,
instead of the yellow one, then it would be a total perversion
of the laws of natural justice.'
Seeing that there was a curiosity but no argument, he
continued, 'Since the very beginning of life itself, and no
matter how terrible sad or terribly unlucky, any death may

have been, the laws of natural justice have *never … ever …* sentenced any living thing to death, without dispensing an *equal* justice to every living thing that has previously died … regardless what colour T-shirt they were wearing, or what fashion of religion they were following, or not. So, the justice of an everlasting, nothing-death, is the ultimate, justice, because it applies to the living and the dead, both equally and everlastingly.'

Turning to Rita and Hanna, David continues, 'In death, there's nothing … to fear, desire or serve. Nothing to hear, feel or observe. No horizon, depth nor any height. No glory, shame, wrong nor right. No minus, plus, nor the slightest division. Only in Life are these things here for you to refuse or choose, yet only in death, is there no turning back.'

Pausing just long enough to take another sip of her coffee, Hanna points her coffee cup toward the piazza, and then she gives David a ruthful smile.

'*To be honest* ... David. If that man has the disrespect to wear *that* coloured T-shirt, with that coloured jacket, then he *deserves* to be hit by a *hundred meteorites!*'

After waiting for Steven's and Rita's spontaneous laughter and applause to die down, and grinning broadly at Hanna, David saluted his own coffee cup towards her, and replied, "*Spoken like a true-blooded, Italian!*'

Suddenly Rita got up to leave, saying, '*Ten minutes!* I'll be back in ten minutes!' She then disappeared, and 23 minutes later, she reappeared, with a smile on her face and a Gucci shopping bag in her hand.

'What have you bought?' Hanna asked, whilst almost jumping out if her seat with delight and curiosity.

Sitting down next to Hanna, Rita handed her the bag and said, 'It's for you.'

Looking as if she doesn't know whether to feel delighted or astonished, Hanna plumps for both, and she withdraws a box, which is wrapped with the Gucci logo wrapping paper. Next, after making sure there are no coffee or food stains to mark anything, she puts the box down on the table. She then takes a swift drink of her own coffee; takes the box up again, lays it down on the table again, takes a swift drink of Stephen's cognac, and then proceeds to slowly unwrap her gift. After untying the ribbon and easing the wrapping back, Hanna then opens the box.

'Oh! Rita, it is so … *beautiful!*'

Holding the dark green, silk scarf up to show everyone, Hanna places the scarf around her neck. Then, looking at Steven, and with her eyes shining, she asks, 'Isn't it beautiful?'

'Yes, it is, it's very beautiful, and so are you!'

'The colour matches the green silk in the Caravaggio painting, The Conversion of Mary Magdalene,' Rita explains, and then turning back to Hanna she adds, 'I bought it to remind you of this day and our trip.'

Leaning forward, whilst being careful not to drag her scarf in the coffee, Hanna kisses Rita on both cheeks; at which point, Rita smiles and says, 'A kiss is fine my darling ... but, no licks thank you!'

Smiling at David and Steven, and then turning to her best friend, Hanna answers, 'I shall wear it to remind me that our friendship, will never go out of fashion.'

When the four of them left the café, Steven felt surprised as Rita linked her arm into his arm.

'You like Hanna, don't you?'

'Yes! I like her a lot!'

'Good!' and with that, Rita disengaged her arm and returned to Hanna and David.

Chapter 11 -The Cleric

That evening, as Rita had already pre-booked an appointment for the following day at nail salon, and Hanna wanted to explore the charity shops; instead of spending the next day visiting more of the tourist sights, the four friends decided that they would go their separate ways and meet at a restaurant in the city's central piazza, for an evening meal. However, in the early morning, and before the women had risen, Steven and David had spent time on their respective training – and after reviewing a 3D google map of the church - they then started going over the requirements of a placarding of a church; situated on the outskirts of a town, just over 15 or so kilometres away.

By the mid-morning, both men had arrived in a small town. As they park their car, the heat from the sun is baking the car, both men inside, and the surrounding landscape.

Immediately after pulling the handbrake on, David firstly dons, and then quickly removes a ski hat and jacket; which he intended to wear to help disguise his appearance.

Dressed in a newly bought designer T-shirt, white shorts and a pair of trainers, there is not much more that Steven could remove, without offending the Italian sense of propriety for town wear. Never the less, he does push his newly bought designer sunglasses back far enough onto his forehead, so that he could get an unobstructed final check; that all that they needed to placard the church is there and to hand, in his newly bought, designer shoulder case.

By now, in order to prepare for the unexpected, the front of the slogan-bearing placard, is hidden beneath a sheet of easy peel, white opaque film; which has a printed map of Italy, with the logos' of famous places of interest, and the main routes of travel between them, clearly marked. This way of temporally hiding the incriminating, Curch of Free-Heroes poster from casual view, was David's creation, and he is rather pleased with it, as is Steven.

Having checked that all is as it should be, the two men began the seemingly meandering stroll; that not only avoided any obvious CCTV but also headed towards the potential church. Five or so minutes later, they enter the part of their journey that takes them through a maze of disused brewery buildings, situated on top of a hill that overlooks the small town. Passing through the door-less back doorway of a disused, one-time family home, Steven casually ducks his head to avoid a large, low hanging spider's web spanning the top quarter of the doorway. However, as he steps through the doorway and raises his head again, the sunlight temporarily dazzles him.

Instinctively Steven turns his head away and blinks several times, then he opens his eyes more fully - to behold bright sunlight, sparkling off the dome of a mosque. The spectacle of the mosque, situated about halfway down the hill that the men are already on, holds Steven's attention for about the length of four heartbeats. Grinning, he turns to David and announces, 'Do you see that, David, I think that maybe Allah is trying to send us a message?'

'*What*?' David impatiently demands; frantically trying to brush the remains of the cobweb from his face and hair!

'I said,' Steven replies, whilst flicking a spider husk from the top of David's left shoulder, and then pointing towards the mosque's glittering dome, 'I think that Allah is trying to send us a message.'

'Never mind what Allah is doing, we have business elsewhere,' David states as he gets a comb from his pocket, and combs through his hair.

'Really! But I thought our business is with all religions, of all sorts. Why leave the Muslims out, you're not being prejudiced are you?'

David Bell looks at his companion, thinks about trying to ignore him, then decides to answer him, 'If, as Karl Marx

once famously said, *Religion is the opium of the masses ...* then in my view, *Islam, is the crack-cocaine!*'
'Go on, this sounds interesting, why crack cocaine.'
'Because Islam, *injects* a highly intrusive, and addictive prescription of *rituals and demands*, straight into the minds and muscle memories of its users. Particularly, its demands of ritually praying five times a day, learning the Quran by heart, fasting from dawn to dusk through the month of Ramadan, and the ritualistic wearing of specific clothing.'
'I believe *crack* is snorted rather than injected.' Stephen proffered.
Removing his jacket and brushing it with his hand, David continues, 'As it happens, it can be, and is quite often, diluted with water and injected. But leaving that subject aside, my point is, that similar demanding religious ritualization's had been practiced by monks, nuns and the like for centuries before. But Islamic demands, brought the effect of such ritualistic, *snorting*, out from the seclusion of the monasteries, and straight into the everyday habits, homes and lives of everyday folk. And it is *that,* so-called achievement, which makes Islam more addictive and dangerous than Christianity. Particularly a Christianity that has been diluted by the ever-increasing flow of open education and reasoned argument.'
 Brushing remains of the spider's web from his jacket, David continues, 'In general, the Islamic religion is mainly a re-hash of the Christian religion, and those of the many that went before. Except, that a self-claimed prophet called Mohamed, updated the Jesus character. Mohamed claimed that Jesus was in fact not the son of God, but, like himself, a prophet of God. Mohamed also conveniently claimed that he was in fact the final, final prophet. Anyway, according to Islam, Allah's, AKA God's words were revealed to Mohamed by the Arch Angel Gabriel, and over the next twenty-three years his words were written down in a book called the Quran.'
'*Twenty-three years!* Steven retorts, before adding, 'That must have been some mighty stutter, the angel had!'

Giving Steven a stony faced, grimace, David continues, 'No, not really. As it happens, the various books of the Bible took about fifteen hundred years to complete. And of course, both the Bible and Quran have been open to many and various interpretations, during and since their beginnings. But in general, the various Islamic scribes had learned from their predecessors, and remixed their form of religion into a more insidious and addictive mix for the masses.'

'Mind you,' Steven continues, 'if I was the final … *final* … reporter of God's words, I think I might stutter on occasions too.'

Giving Steven another stony-faced look, David replies, 'Steven … if you were God's chosen final interpreter, then I should think we'd all be totally dumbstruck!'

Shrugging his shoulders, he continues, 'Nevertheless, beneath their joint banner of religion, Christianity and Islam oppose each other. But the difference between them amounts to a lot more than merely splitting theological hairs.'

'Go on.'

'There is little doubt that if Christianity had been left nailed to its own cross by its own lies, it would have eventually died out, and much of its influences and inbuilt turmoil would have been buried with it, as is being seen in many modern-day countries and societies. But, the Islamic upsurge not only challenged Christianity and the other religions.'

'Who then?'

'It challenged the very demise of the influence of religion itself.

'How come? If it's not that different from Christianity?'

'Because addiction mutates the *personality* of a user, and a user of the addictive Islamic rituals, will see any attack against Islam as a *personal* invasion. So, consequently a user will try to protect his or her supplier.'

'So how do you change their mind, Master Mind?'

'Commitment to religion is not some, ideal, but a, deal done, with one's emotions.'

'Go on.'

'Fundamentally, commitment to any religion is driven by emotions. It is not a physical thing, which is in and by itself, outside of us. Yet it can lead, prod or trip us up from the inside, as surely as any real lighted candle, burning iron, or dead matchstick can.'

At that moment, David smiles, then giving Steven a tilted head look, he qualifies, 'So, just as in the same way as anyone can come to renounce any sort of commitment to … crime … Steven …, a commitment to religion can be revalued, by showing that it costs far more, and pays far less than it promises.'

Steven gives David a look of mixed emotions, nods to the dome of the mosque, and asks, 'So why not target them as well as the Christian lot? I don't suppose it's got anything to do with having some Islamic, crack-head, fanatic trying to chop your head off then?'

As he put his jacket back on, and looking at the dome of the mosque, David states, 'My choice of targets to placard are more a case of practicality. There are simply a lot more Roman Catholic churches than mosques in Italy.'

Steven gives David a look of doubt, and then states, 'I've never been inside a mosque before. They used to use the all-denomination church space in prison for Muslims, Christians, and all sorts. Someone even tried to get a Jedi service going, he even went on hunger strike, but gave up after three days. I met a few Muslims on exercise. One of them had tried to convince an online undercover cop to go around killing Jews. Which was a bit ironic, as the undercover cop happened to be a Jew. Can't say I was over impressed with any of them … all gore more than glory.'

'A bit like your own past.' David offers.

After giving an exaggerated grin, Steven continues, 'Still, I'd like to see inside a real mosque, I hear they can be quite splendid inside. We have plenty of time.'

Somehow, although he did not know exactly why, David Bell feels uneasy about the suggestion, but nevertheless he agrees with it.

Twenty or so minutes later, when they enter the mosque, they behold a light and airy interior. When the two men had passed through the empty reception space, there is only one other person present in the central devotion area. A thin set, thick-bearded man in his mid-thirties, dressed in a business suit and a prayer cap. He is kneeling, facing the alter space and he is keeping his eyes tightly closed; whilst he rocks back and forth in his devotions, he seems oblivious to the presence of either, "Infidel."

Whilst David Bell quietly sits one of the chairs meant for the elderly or infirmed, Steven tours around the airy interior; looking at the designs on the walls, floor and the high domed ceiling. During his tour, he picks up (whilst still wearing his gloves) and peruses various books that lay on the bookshelf. After pocketing a copy of the Quran, and to David's horror, Steven looks at the praying man (who seems to be in his own imaginary world) and then reaching into the designer case, he takes out their poster, and then he removes and stows its front covering. Next, Steven looks over at David, who is already vigorously shaking his head from side to side, and mouthing, '*No, no …no!*'

Steven then quickly walks to what serves as an altar area, places and Blue-tacks the placard onto the wall, primes his phone, takes several photo shots of the whole scene, then returns to David and mouths, 'You can stay if you want, but I'm leaving!'

Checking that the praying man still seems oblivious to Steven's actions, David Bell quickly leaves the praying area, ahead of Steven. However, as soon as David enters the outer reception hall, a man dressed in a white ankle length gown and a white cap, comes out of the nearest office. The Imam is carrying a variety of pamphlets and walking towards the entrance to the praying area. As David passes him, the Imam turns and greets him by saying, in Italian, 'Welcome, can I help you?' David, in return, just stands there, speechless. Presuming that the dumbstruck man standing before him does not speak Italian very well, or not at all, the Imam smiles, and repeats his question, in English.

This time David breaks his silence, 'Err! Yes … No. I …!'

Yet, before David could finish his sentence, Steven, steps up behind the Imam; covers the man's mouth, and jabs a sedative-filled hypo into the man's neck. He then catches and holds the struggling man as he slowly begins to crumple to the floor.

Indicating to the main exit doors, Steven asks David, 'Is it clear?' however, David is now even more dumbstruck.

'Quickly!' Steven orders, 'Before the praying man comes out!'

Coming out of his stupor, David makes his way to the doors, opens them slightly, and peeks out; he then turns back to Steven and gestures that it is all clear, then he whispers, 'What did you put into his neck?'

'A sedative.' Hauling the man up and over his shoulder, and with the shocked David Bell in tow, Steven carries on through the main doors; sees that no one else was in view, he then carries the Imam out and around the side of the building, and into what serves as the backyard of the mosque.

Letting the man down, and standing over him, Steven's face hardens. Glancing over towards the recently arrived David, he states, 'He's got to go.'

'What! What … how do you mean, go?'

'He's seen your face and heard your voice, he now knows you are English; he's a hazard that needs dispensing with before it becomes a catastrophe!'

Although David's face begins to drain of blood, he manages to say, 'Ok, let's not get too hasty here! For a start, he's only seen *my* face. Besides, he's not a threat … unless he reports us to the police!' Thinking fast he adds, 'We can take our poster down, and he'd never know the difference! He will never even realise that it existed. He will think he must have slipped over and imagined or dreamt it all up.'

 Standing almost brazen like before Steven, David suggests, 'Secondly, this is a good place to try the exercise, in the battlefield. Now is the time for you to practice a greater morality than ….'

'We could do as you suggest, 'Steven interrupts, 'but he'd talk. But … there is another way.'

Looking around the area and searching a refuse skip, he quickly found some discarded parcel string, and disused electric wiring. Hauling the Imam over to a tall pole that serves to support floodlit lighting for the rest of the yard, Steven ties the sitting but unconscious Imam to its base. Turning to David, Steven instructs him to, 'Stay here, if anyone comes, say that you heard someone moaning and you came around to investigate!'

Less than a minute later, Steven re-enters the mosque, and finds the praying man still oblivious to all about him. Walking straight to the placard and removing it, he then returns to David, who is feeling almost giddy on the heady mixture of fear and excitement.

'*For goodness sake hurry!*' David whispers.

Without a word, Steven Blu-tacks the placard to the post above the bowed head of the unconscious Imam; next, he takes several still and video zoom shots of the man, the placard, and the rear of the mosque, then turning to David, he says, 'I think Allah's message has finished, it's time to depart!'

Fifteen minutes later, four major Italian news media outlets received a text; telling them to go to the rear of the mosque, where they would find the Imam tied to a metal post, and the latest placard from the Curch of Free Heroes. By the time the first reporting team arrives, a dog is licking the face of the unconscious Imam.

Although most of the main media news channels pixeled out the face of the Imam, they did show still shots of the dog licking the Imam's partly pixeled face. Amongst his comments on the event, one well known social media blogger also speculated, "That bearing in mind the dog's natural purpose in visiting the lamp post, the distraction of licking the Imam's face might well have been a blessing in disguise!" Nevertheless, all in all, the general opinion was that the Curch of Free- Heroes - had pulled of a media sensation.

Meanwhile, back in the nail saloon, and although she was not an extravagant person, Rita took care to pamper herself now and again; and the manicure and pedicure were part of that pampering. Plus, of course, in the nail salon, there was also the added (almost mandatory) pleasure of gossiping.

The hot subject of the day in the nail salon, was the latest scandal about the son of the Italian Minister of Education; who had been having a love affair with the wife of a Russian diplomat. Lolita, Rita's manicurist, mostly thought that the affair was the fault of the diplomat's wife, whilst Rita thought the bulk of responsibility lay with the Minister's son.

By the time that Lolita had started Rita's pedicure, the political ins and outs of the affair had taken second place to the recounting of Lolita's and Rita's experiences of good and bad lovers. The conclusion of the sharing; was that Lolita had more bad lovers than Rita, but Rita wished that she had more lovers than she had. When Lolita asked Rita if she had any great lovers, Rita thought about David Bell for a moment, and then she replied, 'No! But I think I am about to.'

Meanwhile, Hanna's excursion around the charity shops, had been fruitful; in that she had enjoyed a half a dozen good gossips, and one argument (about the shop's dress size labelling policy). What is more, all this entertainment cost no more than the 50% final reduction price for the Egyptian silk, shirt, which she had bought as a present for Steven.

As the two men drove back toward their hotel, David pulled into an otherwise deserted, scenic viewing spot, and told Steven, 'We have to talk!'

Getting out of the car, and ignoring the scenic beauty, both men faced each other, and Steven said, 'Ok, let's talk.'
Taking a non-threatening stance David asserts, 'Now, I know that predicting how things will turn out is never certain, as the shambles with that Cleric just proved, but I have certain views about reality.'
'And what are your views, Oh great oracle?'
'My view is that the ability to deliberately choose to be bad or good, is the tiller by which each person steers towards, or away, from life's moral havens or stormy seas, Steven.'
'This is all getting a bit nautical, my friend, or should I call you shipmate.' Steven quipped.
'I also believe that people's, including my own of course, emotional attachments can seem far more important than any map of logic and reason. Something that is logically correct does not necessarily mean it is emotionally acceptable. In short, no matter how clever or learned you are or think you are … feelings can out-rank thoughts.'
'In that case,' Steven commands, 'I order you to shut up, and let's get back to the hotel and Hanna and Rita.'
Smiling at Steven, David mock salutes him and then carries on, 'So, if total free choice is the tiller, yet your emotions can easily grab control, then there is something else to consider, which although is not a fact of life, it is a very useful guide.'
'And that is?'
'And that is, that although emotions, such as love, anger courage and fear are indispensable, and can make good lookouts, they can often be distracted by monsters of their own making, or indeed by the Sirens of other people's making. Which is why our emotions do not always make the best captains!'
'So, David, if you don't trust your emotions, who is the captain of your ship?'
Smiling at Steven once more, David replied, 'I have found that truth makes the best captain of my ship.'

'But don't you *ever* let your emotions rule you, to take you where they may, man?'
'Of course, I do … and more often than you make think …'
'And what if they mutiny?' Steven asks, of no one in particular.
'Then I must trust that they will not sink the ship, with all hands-on deck … shipmate!'
'And what has this got to do with the mosque?'
'We should have kept on course for the church, and not let a spur of the moment decision rule our heads. I thought your experience as a qualified criminal, and my supposed mentoring, would have taught you … and me, that.'
Smiling at David, Steven nods and salutes, 'Ok, captain I'll take that on board …genuinely. Now can we set sail for home or at least the hotel?'
As the pair travel onward, David Bell also inwardly debated as to how he had let *his* emotions, mutiny against his captaincy of not to going to look at the mosque, in the first place. Furthermore, he also re-pondered, for the umpteenth time, how on Earth he allowed Steven in on the Curch campaign in first place?
Yet, as David is to find out, once one has actually bitten into that *"deliciously tempting cream cake,"* it is not that easy to just, throw it away!
The text on the placard left with the Cleric stated:

The Curch of Free Heroes
The 2nd Quest of a Free Hero.
Responsibility:
 A Free-Hero's quest for responsibility is pursued, firstly, by accepting *total* responsibility for *all* of your past, bad and good choices and actions - so that you in turn, can equally accept that you have the equal ability, freedom and power to choose or change, any of your present choices and actions - no matter what they have been, or who you have been, in the past.

Secondly, it is to accept that any of your daily or lifetime quests may be strengthened; by sharing the burdens (and rewards), with those who can supply any of your quests with any ability that you presently lack.

The 2nd question:
If an all-loving God, truly, believes that such Life qualities as empathy, kindness and an educated free choice; will bring enough multiple rewards, in and by themselves, to save and secure humanity; why would he even want to send us any messages about any after death Paradise or Hell? Or is it the so-called messengers - who lack such a faith in such Life qualities?

www.curchoffreeheroes.info

Chapter 12- Dark roads and wet streams
 Before Steven and David had driven back to their hotel and using their PAYG phones, they saw that the TV coverage and social media were in an uproar. Yet, the clamour was not only because of the Cleric being rendered unconscious, and then used as an advertisement hoarding for the Curch of Free-Heroes' campaign. The loudest uproar was about the

declaration, by Cleric Faeq Mansur, who was responsible for the surrounding district. For the Cleric, had declared a *death fatwa* upon the offenders! In effect, he had called for a religious ruling on their death, by beheading.

'Fucking well marvellous!' David exclaimed as he pulled their hired car to the side of a countryside road so that he could now see as well as hear the breaking news. After hearing and watching for another agonising minute, he continued, 'Before you appeared, I was quite content, living a semi-retired, semi-recluse existence. But after allowing *you* to stay at my home, out of the goodness of my heart, and I might add, and against my better judgement, I am now living in the middle of a bloody war zone!'

After holding his head in his hands, and then facing Steven, David continued, 'Firstly, I am wanted by the whole of the Italian police force. Now, thanks to you, just about every religious fanatic wants to chop my head off, because he believes that he will then take his seat alongside no lesser a personage than Allah! How fucking well … *helpful of you!'*

Speaking to David, as if at first he was genuinely apologising, Steven replied, 'I'm so sorry!' then he added, 'But somehow I must have missed the bit in the news, where it said that the only offender who would be beheaded, might be you. Or perhaps you think that if I converted to being a Muslim, and tell all I know about you, they will only chop off my dick!'

Steven's "apology" had not calmed David's fears, but it did calm his sense of outrage as Steven continued, 'But have no fear, David, my reluctant friend. When I said that no matter what either of us does, it would be protected under the code of anonymity, I meant it! Just as I did, when I said, that I'd see this thing out, until the very end! Or is this your way of trying to back out, now that this thing has got a bit messy. Not to mention, fucking hugely successful! This demand for a death fatwa has given the quests more world-wide publicity than our little stunts at the Roman Catholic churches, could have achieved in a year.'

Looking at Steven, David replied, 'Thanks, a lot for the pep-talk, I could never have got this far into the middle of this bloody minefield, without you. But at least it's good to know that you'll be blown sky high too.'
Getting out of the car and slamming the car door shut, David Bell strode to the bank of a babbling stream, which on some other occasion may have been quite a relaxing experience. As he walked off, he heard Steven close his car door too, and come after him.
As David reached the shallow stream bank, he heard Steven say, 'Of course, although I won't grass you up, I could always *send* you ahead if me, who knows, it might even get me a reward in Paradise. It was not so much the words that Steven said, but the tone of Steven's voice that made David slowly turn to face him.
 For the next five minutes, the two men fought, without a break, until both of them ended up fully soaked, and still wrestling in the knee-high stream. What is more, throughout the struggle, David Bell had the feeling that Steven was containing him, rather than attacking him.
Suddenly Steven suggested, 'Truce?'
'Truce!' David replied, whilst trying to keep his relief from showing.
When they eventually reached the hotel, and their adjoining rooms, and after shaking hands once more; the men went into David's bath suite, cleaned themselves up, attended to their own reachable and each other's unreachable minor cuts and grazes, and then they retired to the balcony, with two black coffees and two large brandies, and phoned and arraigned to meet the women.
When the men met Hanna and Rita, Hanna immediately asked about the marks and bruises on both of them.
'We decided to go hiking in some forest, and soon got lost in a lot of brambles and ditches.' Steven joked.

After some suitable chiding (and admiration) from the women, the subject was closed as the women related their adventures.

When Hanna presented Steven with the shirt, he genuinely thanked her, not only with words … but also with a lingering kiss … so close to her mouth … that it brought a lingering blush to her cheeks.

As Steven quickly returned the shirt into its bag, Hanna stated, 'I simply and absolutely love the shirt, where did you buy it?' The two women then exchanged the details of their trips, until the meal arrived, and then they carried on where they had left off.

After the meal and their "goodnights" to the women, the men retired to David's room. As the sun began to set over on a reasonably calm atmosphere between the two men, David felt far from at ease. Looking out to the darkening horizon he said, 'When I used to try advice a client on the crime advice line, about dealing with their dark feelings or urges, I would sometimes tell them about a certain type of darkness.'

Looking at the attentive Steven, David then turned back to the darkening sky, then proffered, 'The darkness, can be found deep in the countryside, in the depths of a wood, or even on a country lane at night, under a cloud thickened sky. To most city dwellers who happen upon this sudden, darkness's, it comes as a surprise! It is a dark far blacker than when one merely closes one's eyes in the safety of one's bedroom, surround with the familiar. For on a country lane, there is a choice to make. The choice of walking further into the pitch black, in the hope that you will eventually find a welcoming light or stay where one is … in the dark.'

Turning again to Steven, who was now lit more by the room's lighting than that of the setting sun, David continued, 'I would then advise the client, that in such times of darkness, it might well be a good idea, to use the light from their mobile phone, to shed some light on the road ahead,'

'If they have a phone.' Steven quipped.

'True!' David replied, 'But then, making sure that you have a phone with you, on a dark journey can be pretty useful. Just as it is, to be able to phone the advice line, in dark times.'
'What's your point? 'Steven asked.
'Travelling besides you, on this adventure, has become like walking along that dark country road, and the further we go the darker everything has become, including you, my friend!'
'So, what do you want me to do ... hold your fucking hand?' Steven retorted, 'You're a big boy now, and my guess is that it's the road that we are on, that makes everything appear darker, including me.'
For a few seconds, Steven looked into the mid-distance, then he ventured, 'But if you don't want to continue before we have reached our agreed destination, whether it turns out to be a good or bad end, then don't. As for me ... I'm going on, with or without you, my erstwhile friend!'
'It would help if I could at least see how we can possibly get to the end?' David asked.
'By seeing it all the way to the end. The one thing for sure is that now the stakes have been raised, we both need to raise our courage.' Then laying his hand gently on David's shoulder, Steven said, 'We will need to watch the road ahead, as well as each other's back …' then smiling, he added, '… not to mention, watching out for each other's head!'
Looking at his former sworn enemy, David Bell nodded, and for a moment he waited for the last rays of the sun to disappear behind the distant mountains until there was a darkness behind and in front, then he made a toast with his coffee cup and said, 'To the road ahead!'

Chapter 13 -Proof of authority

The following morning the four companions crossed the famous Ponte Vecchio as they made their way to David's choice, the Museo Galileo. For a while, the group meandered between the exhibits, pausing at some and bypassing others. Eventually, they arrived at David's favourite exhibit room, which held an extraordinary collection of celestial globes.

Looking at the various globes Steven commented, 'They're impressive, but they're not exactly earth-shattering are they Einstein?'

'As it happens,' David answered, 'it was Einstein who called Galileo, the father of modern science, and to my mind, and many minds much greater, his work is pivotal in the spread of truth and indeed justice!'

Giving David an askew look, Hanna asked, 'What has the globes to do with justice?'

'I think the globes are absolutely, fantastic, so let's move on,' Steven said, whilst trying to divert the conversation.

Ignoring Steven's ploy, David continued, 'In past times, only royalty, politics and religion have been seen as the main rightful authorities of morality. However, when, Galileo's famous work, called The Dialogue, proved that the rest of the universe did not revolve around the Earth, as the church proclaimed it did, the church accused him of being, vehemently suspect of heresy, and the Dialogue was placed on the Index of Forbidden Books. He was then placed under house arrest for the rest of his life.'

'How so?' Hanna asked.

'Because the religions' greater fear and anger, was not just that the Dialogue went against the then, *gospel version*, of the physical universe, but because it also meant that truth, did not necessarily revolve around the *gospel* truth, which in turn was the basis of religion's so-called divine authority over all people.'

Gesturing to the displays, and briefly glancing and smiling at
two American tourists (who thought that they had the good
fortune to have stumbled upon an official guided tour of the
museum), David continued, 'Whereas religion demands blind
faith towards their authority, Science has evolved the concept
of demanding verifiable proof before claiming that any idea
as a scientific authority.'

Turning once again to the tourist, David explained, 'But,
since Galileo's Dialogue, verifiably *proved* that religion's
version of the universe revolving around the Earth was
completely untrue, people began to place verifiable proof
before blind obedience to religious claims.'

Returning to his companions he concluded, 'And the more
and more religion failed to come up with any such proofs
about its claims, the more religion seemed to be living in its
own, made up, self-serving world.'

'But I have heard on many scientific claims have also turned
out to untrue too!' Hanna exclaimed.

'Yes, you blaspheming heathen!' Steven also exclaimed, in a
theatrically, offended manner, whilst putting his arm
defensively around Hanna's shoulders.

At this point, the two tourists began to doubt about being part
of an official guided tour, but as David Bell again turned to
them and smiled, and even continued by briefly but directly
addressing them, their reluctance seemed to diminish.

'That is true,' he continued, 'yet science, unlike religion, has
never claimed its interpretations of life are infallible. Which is
why it has dedicated itself to exploring its own possible
ignorance about life. And that at least helps to guarantee one
thing.'

'And that is?' Rita asked.

'That only the most vigorously tested of scientific claims will
earn the authority of being reliable enough to live one's life
by.'

Addressing the tourist and his friends, David continued, 'In
short, all the religions describe life and death, so as to get you

to obey *their* authority. The Sciences, however, describes life and death, so as to get you to obey Life's authority.'
David looked at Hanna and gave her a muted smile, then he looked to Steven and gesturing to the globes he continued, 'As it happened, the original observations of scientific-astronomy, were turned into religious-astrology.'
'What is the difference?' Hanna asked.
 'Astronomy is the scientific study of the provable movements of the stars, planets, and the universe. It led to navigation by the stars, Newton's discoveries about gravity, Einstein's Theories of Relativity, Quantum physics, and a host of mind-boggling discoveries about life and universe.' Turning to the Americans, he emphasised, 'However, religious, *astrology*, is the totally unproven claim that the movements of the stars and planets, or maybe the arrival of a passing comet, are so-called, sacred, messages from their gods, or goddesses. Rather conveniently, they, the religious leaders, also claimed to be the special confidents and exclusive interpreters of those messages, and of course demands of God as interpreted by the particular religion.'
Addressing the whole company, David enthused, 'What is more, they also claim that if someone in the community, or the community itself, disobeyed the sacred interpretations, then their god would send a punishment, in the form of the destructive flood, storm, or some other tragedy. *However,* if their so-called, sacred interpretations were obeyed, then the god or goddess would send a beneficial event, such as good weather, good crops or good fortune in war, or whatever … thus, setting any unbelievers, against the welfare of the community.'
Addressing Hanna once again, David explains, 'The same sort of scam was played on a personal level too. If some misfortune befell a person or their family, then the religious leader would say that it was because someone in the family, or community, had disobeyed the religion's sacred interpretations or rules.'

Turning to Rita, David qualifies, 'Nevertheless, as science and education began to evolve and spread, people began to realise that their good and bad fortune depended on whether they could interpret, predict and follow the rules of, *nature*, rather than the so-called sacred, rules of religion.'

Pausing for a second or two, David then faced Steven, and qualified, 'Mind you, the same sort of scam is used by the criminal community too.'

'In what way?' Steven asked, with seemingly neutrality.

'Because they both invent self-serving justifications for their own lies which can be used to victimise any unbelievers.'

When Steven made no answer, David turned to Rita, and continues, 'Nevertheless, it doesn't take a genius to realise that it would take a particularly *vast* scam, such as religion, to at least partially cover up the vastness of the ordinary truth.'

'Ordinary truth?' Hanna asked.

'That it is the ordinary, and indeed the priceless, acts of hard work, honesty and caring, which have been committed by generations upon generations of every day, very ordinary people, which has, is, and always be our everlasting saviour from moral disaster.'

Smiling at Hanna, David adds, 'You know, if the religious didn't fear being so ordinary themselves, they would be worshiping it, instead of some extraordinary god figure.'

As he spread his arms, as in a crucifix, David continued, 'The list of religious tall stories stretches from here to here. Nevertheless, if our current and future societies are to evolve further, then we need more than science. We will need a moral evolution. To my mind, it will help if we can create a non-religious way of appreciating, celebrating, and discovering Life. We could even have buildings in which people can reinvigorate their moral and spiritual sense of wonder. In short, we need non-religious churches. Instead of calling them Churches we can …!'

At that point, David halted in mid-sentence, as Steven raised his head, in a manner that was a definite warning.

Suddenly, the American man turned to his wife and pointed to his watch, and his wife looked aghast; quickly leaning forward to David Bell, she said, 'I hope you didn't mind us sneaking in on your guided tour,' she then started to get some money out of her purse, as she continued, 'I feel so guilty, is there any way we can donate something to your good self or the museum …'

Addressing the couple, David quickly held up his hand and replied, 'Please, don't feel guilty in the slightest. Besides, guilt is something you must pay off, whilst gratitude is something to be spent. So please feel free to take whatever you have gained, with you.'

Putting her purse back into her handbag the woman said, 'You're very kind sir, and very knowledgeable.' With that said and done, the couple nodded to all four companions, and departed.

As the couple walked away from the exhibit, the woman tourist took her husband's arm and said, 'My, these Italian tours are so informative, and so *passionate!*'

Ten minutes after they left the Science Academy, the four friends walked as they idly chatted, and Steven could not help but notice that Rita seemed to be a lot more attentive and warmer towards David. In fact, as he watched them, she was leaning her head on his shoulder.

'Tired?' Steven casually asked Rita.

'I think you English would say, I am knackered ... yes?'

Suddenly Hanna stopped walking, 'But you mustn't be,' then turning to Steven, she explained, 'we haven't been to your favourite place yet – and we are planning to go to Turin tomorrow – not that there aren't many great places there to visit.'

For a moment, Steven, seemed to be considering something, then after looking at David, he replied, 'By a strange coincidence … *we were planning to go to Turin too*!

Giving both men, a knowing look, Hanna and Rita linked arms with the men, and Hanna stated, *'It is settled then!'*

Then, as Steven briefly smiled ... or was it a smirk ... at David
Bell, he added, 'But eventually, I would like to see the
Pope … at the Vatican!'
Stopping in her tracks, Hanna enthusiastically informed
everyone, 'But that is easy! We can easily visit the Vatican.
There is a train to Rome every hour from Turin. The Vatican
is a glorious place. But if you wish to see the Pope, then you
must go to the 'Peoples day' It is at midday, though we must
be there by at least nine in the morning. I will find out when
the next blessing is, if you want me to – and we can all go …
together!'
As he re-linked arms with Hanna and gave her a kiss to
acknowledge her offer, Steven could almost feel David Bell's
eyes burning holes into the side of his skull.

Chapter 14- Steven's unexpected surprise

After the four companions arrived at hotel dining room for breakfast; before going to the railway station to catch the train to Turin, Hanna put forward, 'It is such a beautiful morning, I choose we breakfast in the park opposite.' A short while later, just before the group started to enter the park, Hanna saw a street beggar and she immediately began to rummage inside her handbag and brought out her purse.

'Really Hanna,' Steven suggested, 'you do no long term good by giving him or his type money. Most of them are either alcoholics or drug users, or both. You may as well go up to the nearest group of drug pushers and give your hard-earned money to them.'

In response, David quipped, 'There but for the grace of goodness go you or I.'

Rita meanwhile, said nothing; as she knew only too well from previous experience, that it was quite pointless to try to stop Hanna giving a beggar money.

Whilst Hanna paused to take in what Steven had said, the beggar used a fashion magazine to brush away the bits of rubbish from around his begging hat. Nevertheless, before Hanna decided to part with the coins in her hand, she turned and quietly suggested to Steven, 'But if no one helps him, he might go and rob or steal from someone!'

'Then save your money and give it to some charity that helps people get off drugs! But don't give it to someone, who, according, to your latest reasoning, is a thief or robber!'

Looking from the beggar to Steven, Hanna paused, and then she put her money back in her purse, 'I will give it to the collection box at the next church that we visit!' On that point, Steven and David exchanged a look of irony, and they all walked on; whilst the beggar gave the middle finger to Steven's retreating back.

Soon, the companions arrived at the park's café, and they chatted as they breakfasted; then as they watched the people feeding the various wildfowl, Rita pointed to a goose. The goose in question, a brown-headed goose, from Canada, had marched, rather than waddled, up to several tourists at the water's edge. Having reached its target, the goose pecked at one of the men's trouser leg; and after giving it two firm tugs, stepped back, looked up at the man and then waited with an expectant air … but to no avail. Within a minute, the goose moved to a different group; this time tugging at a woman's shoe strap, and then to the amusement of the woman and her friends the goose received its due payment of pasta.

Having finished their breakfast, the four friends made their way to the park's main gate, yet as they did, the last thing that Steven, wouldn't have prepared for, happened - even though he had felt it coming since the first time he had seen Hanna at the restaurant. He felt, as is if he were falling in … *love*.

For a moment, Steven thought this love thing might be a case of serendipity. Apart from the Sandra and Crimetest disaster; he felt that he had always been lucky in his past, at least as far as his criminal exploits went … so why not so in his 'normal' exploits too. For being in love was normal, in terms of normal human behaviour.

Although many people would rejoice in such an unforeseen surprise as Love, falling into their world, it worried Steven. It was an unknown, and Steven did not like unknowns, they were full of unpredictable outcomes in the outer world, and his inner one. In addition, for someone like Steven; who liked to feel in control of both worlds, he worried and even feared that such a powerful emotion as love, could turn him into an emotional moron?

However, he also considered, that David Bell's prediction; that by giving up crime, it made more room for things - such as love – to appear, might be true.

He knew the symptoms: thinking continuously about one person, his body responses rising when he is in her company, or about to be so - these were all classic symptoms of someone *infected* with Love.

Although he was normally a secretive man, at least as far as sharing his inner emotions with other people were concerned; in this situation, he began to think about sharing his dilemma. He could, of course, ask David; but he would go on about therapy, and then he (Steven) would get annoyed. Alternatively, he could of course, admit his feelings to Hanna herself, but that course of action would still be full of unpredictable outcomes.

Just then, and without any consciously deliberate decision, Steven found that he had slipped his arm through Rita's arm, who in turn looked up at him and smiled, questioningly. Slowing his pace slightly, so that David and Hanna moved out of earshot, Steven ventured a question, 'Why did you say, Good, when I told you that I liked Hanna, very much?' Immediately Rita became alerted, and Steven could feel her 'antennae' begin to sweep for all possibilities that might be heading her way. In response, Steven smiled warmly, and said, 'It's just that I value your opinion, not only as Hanna's friend but because … quite frankly I respect your opinion, you have a good head on your shoulders.'

In truth, he meant what he said, and as such, knew that he would have to tread carefully with Rita. Then, he suddenly realised, that he was not entirely concerned for his own future, but he was also nervous for himself and Hanna. He also knew, that if Rita disapproved of his feelings for Hanna, then her influence with Hanna could sway the balance, by some significant measure. Being unusually nervous was not a state he was used to or liked, and it must have shown, for when Rita replied, she touched his arm with affection.

'I shouldn't worry too much about my opinion, Steven. Hanna is a spirit, beyond the influence of most people,' then she added - almost as if it were a warning, 'Even for those who care for her … deeply!'

If Rita was indeed issuing a warning to him, it went home, yet before he could ask further, she asked, 'You do not like the term, spirit?'

Again, Steven felt surprised. It was true he did not normally like such sentimental words as, spirit. However, the reality that somehow the term, spirit, did suit Hanna, took him unawares. Yet this was not all. The fact that Rita had picked up on his discomfort, in the midst of his greater turmoil about her 'warning,' had impressed him even more.

Quickly deciding that he was facing someone who was more than capable of playing, and winning, mind games, he decided to come clean, and bare all, by being honest … at least about his feelings toward Hanna!

Once again, Rita pre-empted him. 'Then I will qualify the term, spirit.' Looking to check, that they were still beyond earshot, Rita continued. 'There is a demon stalking Hanna's persona. At least, in the olden days, it would have been called a demon. Nowadays, it goes under the name of an illness called, Bi-Polar, or a sort of manic depression. She will go through tremendous emotional highs and devastating lows.' When Steven stopped walking, Rita urged him on again. 'When you saw her lick the face of the Caravaggio statue, it was not showing off, she was showing genuine gratitude for the artist and his creation. When she wanted to give that beggar money, she was trying to give him more than a mere subsistence, she was trying to give him … hope.'

Up ahead, Hanna and David turned around and began waiting, but Rita smiled and waved them to go ahead, and all four of them carried on walking as before. 'But sometimes the world,' Rita carried on, 'Sometimes life seems to pour scorn on her attempts to improve it, or even be grateful for it. When this happens, a great … how you say …whirlpool … of sadness pulls her whole being down. She herself once described it as, like being plunged into a waterfall of tears.' Pausing in her stride, Rita looked at Steven and emphasised, 'She also said that such a sadness must have been with Jesus when he trod the earth.' Then walking on again she added, I tell you that, not because I believe in any religion, I don't. But

it is important that you know she gains much support from her belief.'
If Rita meant to move Steven – she did. Then he asked her a question, which in part was also a self-admission, 'Do you love her … too?'
Rita put her other hand on Steven's arm and replied, 'I love her … spirit.'
Just then, Hanna ran back and giving Steven a huge grin she almost shouted, '*David has said it would be great, but I said only if you come too*?'
Returning Hanna's grin, Steven asked, 'Come where?'
'After Turin, we are going to my village, for three days, to see my sister and her newborn son, Philo. He is five weeks old tomorrow. We can shop for presents in Turin, you don't have to buy anything expensive. Then we can catch the train to near my village, and from there my cousin Phillio will pick us up and take us to my family's house.' Grabbing Steven's arms, Hanna explained, 'As our friends, you will be a very welcome too. My brother in law's family owns and runs a restaurant that serves the most delicious aubergine and lamb.'
When Steven readily agreed, Hanna stepped in a little closer, and then kissed twice him on each cheek, and then once on his mouth.
Chapter 15 - Snapshot opinions.
Following the trip to the park, the four companions decided to see an exhibition of photography, at a venue not far from their hotel.
Once inside the four of them split up as they stopped or walked by the various photos. Eventually, the four of them reunited in front of an image. As he looked at the image, David commented, 'It reminds me of Salvador Dali's stunning painting of Christ of St John on the Cross.'
Bearing in mind what Rita had said about Hanna's vulnerability depression, Steven exclaimed, 'Enough of religion!'

'I was speaking in artistic terms rather than any religious ones,' David explained.

However, Steven still gave David a look of warning and walked on, with the others in casual tow. Although no one looked at Hanna, she self-consciously looked at them, and as they stepped aside to let a party of school children through, she said, 'For someone who is not religious, David, you seem to know a lot about it, how so?'

'That's because one of the main duties of the Crimetest's Crime Advice line, toward a caller is to uncover the lies underneath their wish to commit a crime. So, I'm pretty much used to looking for lies, and it happens Religion has a lot of them.'

As the companions moved into a wide exhibition room, Hanna asked, 'Do you think that religion is a crime?'

No, of course not, no more than being gullible is a crime. However, I think religion is a great wrongdoing against humanity.'

'How So?'

'It promises to be a saviour of human morality. Yet, no matter what side of the divide they are on, virtually all the studies based on reasonable proof, come up with the same conclusion.'

'Which is?' Hanna asked, without accusation.

'That religion is no better at preventing crime or wrongdoing than any other, non-religious, form of social influence or control, such as Democracy, Dictatorship or Communism. Even the act of prayer is no more effective at achieving what the prayee wants, than any other form of positive motivation … or even plain ol' random chance.'

'Then if religion does no better than the others why do you want to ban it?' Hanna asked.

'*I don't!*' David replied in a shocked manner, 'I'm just trying to uncover its lies. After that, it is up to individual people or the various religions to decide what they want to do. Besides, as I have often suggested before … a life without total freedom of choice, even a wrong choice, would be no more than a hell … without sin.'

For a moment, Hanna thought about what had been said, then David asked, 'Would you have being non-religious, banned?'

'No, of course not!' Hanna replied in an equally shocked manner.

Noticing that Steven had just given him yet another warning glance, David continued, 'Please don't get me wrong Hanna, I do not blame people for falling for the lies, I just want to uncover the lies.'

Pointing to some wall mounted photo exhibits, David continued, 'The religious view on the self, self-expression, and self-development is that, viewing yourself, or enjoying a momentary *selfie* of yourself enjoying life, a personal moment, or even friendship, is merely an act of pompous, selfish vanity … unless … of course, religion is in the picture also!'

At that point, Steven immediately took out his phone then took a selfie of Hanna and himself. Continuing as if he hadn't noticed Steven, David stated, 'In short, according, to the religious view, any form of self-expression or self-development, which does not include religion in the picture, should be viewed as the undeveloped, *negative* self, compared to the fully developed religious self.'

Holding his hand up, to momentary interrupt David, and then took a selfie of himself and Rita.

At that point, David Bell emphasised, 'Even though the need for any religion is psychosomatic, anyway!'

'Psychosomatic?' Hanna asked.

'It is when a person is so anxious about being vulnerable to an illness, they feel ill anyway, and sometimes even they feel the symptoms of the illness that they are so worried about, without actually catching it. In terms of catching the *religious illness,* a person is led by a specific religion to believe that she or he, and indeed humanity, is more morally ill, than they

or humanity really are. And so, that person then goes and seeks the so-called cures offered by the religion.'
'And what would your diagnosis and cure be?' Rita asked.
'My personal diagnosis is based on human history.'
'How so?' Hanna asked.
'Human beings throughout history have and will continue, to behave as best as they know how … regardless of the abundance or lack of material wealth and health. Even in the midst of wars, the vast majority of civilians *and* combatants will try and behave as humanely as the demands of war allow.'
'And your cure?' Rita asked.
'That we need to stop taking religious cures to cure the illness of religion. There are many other non-religious and worthy ways to offer education and personal good support throughout life, including such things as, moral support and advice, a sense of belonging, and a personal and shared responsibility.'
 Holding up his hand to again momentary interrupt, Steven then took a photo of David, who carried on, 'It's just a matter of looking both ways, instead of only one way, before crossing the road. And it's a lot safer than trying to cross a road by using the trials and errors of blind faith, that's for sure.'
Looking up suddenly, Steven said, 'They should use that as an advert, on those road safety posters.'
'What?'
'They could have a crashed car and dead driver, in the road, with the slogan … *you can change your mind but not your body – don't drink and drive!*'
Looking at David's surprised reaction to the interruption, Steven said, 'What? You were talking about crossing the road.'
'It's brilliant!' Hanna said, 'You should write to the road safety people and tell them!'
Lifting her head Rita suggested, 'If it's not too much, you could have an arrow on the poster, pointing to the body of a

child, further back up the road, and some writing saying, *Or anyone else's body either.*'

 'That good.' Steven acknowledged.

'Maybe you should write, my Italian is not anywhere that good?'

'We can do it together.'

'Yes, as soon as we get back.'

At that moment David and the rest of the group became mesmerised by a photo of a woman in a wide-brimmed straw hat, which created a dappled effect across her face.

When they began to walk away, Steven showed his selfie images to Hanna and Rita, and finally to David; who casually appraised the images and then commented, 'The ones with Hanna and Rita look great … it's just a shame that you're in the picture also!'

Taking his phone back and flicking through the images, Steven commented, 'I don't think I spoil the pictures at all!'

Stepping forward and then kissing Steven on the cheek, Hanna confirmed, 'Nor do I, my darling, nor do I.'

When the four companions left the photographic exhibition, David and Steven walked apart from the woman for a while, during which Steven confided to David about Hanna's vulnerability to depression, and that he would much prefer that he laid off the religious bit.

David Bell immediately agreed that he would.

Chapter 16- Pixies, thunderstorms, and families

On the train to Turin, the companions met a twenty-four-strong group of "pixies" and "elves," who were dressed in traditional pixie and elves outfits; and carrying, to a man and woman, bottles and cans of alcohol. The pixie and elves were on their way to an international hockey match between the Italian league hockey champions, whose name demanded a chorus of cheers whenever mentioned, and a team from Rumania, whose name drew a dirge of jeers.

Although the group was boisterous, they were in good spirits and well behaved, and apart from one partially drunk pixie; who kept trying to insist that Hanna and her friends share some of his pixie magic enhanced larger, the pixie's company were entertaining. By the time, the train pulls into Turin's main station, it is a dismally dark afternoon. Hordes, of low-slung rain clouds are harrying, deluging, and drenching the city in torrential rain. After waiting for over half an hour beneath the station's forecourt canopy, the four companions eventually catch a taxi.

By now, with the onset of the storm clouds, the city's street lighting had come on automatically; giving the houses and streets an eerie half-twilight, half-daylight hue. As they travel along, the companions stare out, with an almost hypnotic fascination, at the passing street scenes of crowded cafés, doorways and bus shelters. Above the streets, the pleated rows of tiled roofs; seem to shimmy, beneath their sliding skirts of rain, as their pearled-hems of fluttering raindrops, breakaway and sail off with windswept abandon, before they disappear onto the glistening wet pavements below. As the companion's taxi speeds along; gushing rainwater is swept along seemingly gushing streets; until the wide mouths of the street drains, gurgle the waters down.

Suddenly, two bedraggled and panicking sewer rats begin to abandon their once safe underground thoroughfares. '*Look there are rats!*' Rita points and exclaims, as the taxi speeds past.

'The heavy rain drives them out!' Hanna shouts. Then, as her voice battles with the relentless drumbeating of the rain upon taxi roof, she adds, whilst making a sign of the crucifix, *'Once the rain has disappeared, they will go back to their homes.'*
On the half-deserted streets, people who would normally walk, sprint against swathes of gust-blown rain; whilst others, duck under, weave around, and expectantly collide with the torrents of cascading rainwaters, which have long overwhelmed the roof gutters, above. Sweeping the litter along with them, the rain-rivers cleanse the pavements and cobblestoned roads; until the littered waters swirl across the expansive piazzas. As the taxi drives across one such piazza; a few people, just saunter, swagger, or simply stand still and surrender to the downpour. When one dripping wet, elderly, man stands still; opens his arms and starts singing the chorus of "Va Pensiero" (the chorus of the Hebrew slaves), several more equally saturated, enthusiast, join in (or way out) of tune.
Eventually, as the rain begins to lessen, and the taxi climbs above the city centre; Steven opens the passenger window, and the sudden, yet unmistakable smell of freshly rained upon earth fills the taxi's interior. Then, as the road runs above and parallel to the city for some five minutes' drive; and as the storm clouds begin their raked retreat from the victorious, dazzling-blue, sunlit sky above; the four companions, behold the panorama of the bejewelled, city of Turin, as it shines, sparkles and shimmers beneath their mesmerised and awed filled eyes.

Chapter 17 - Mary Mother of Jesus and the Quran

The following day, Steven came to David with a plan, 'I know we need to think about the whole campaign some more, but one thing for sure is, there is one more placarding that we can do together, because it's too good a one to resist!'

Pulling out his non-registered phone, Steven Google mapped an area about 15 kilometres away from where they sat. In the middle of the map, stood church.

'What's so good about it? 'David asked.

'Nothing in particular, except that it has good exit roads and public transport. It's just off the main route. Hanna and Rita want to go and see the Turin Shroud. If we tell them that we'd rather do something else instead, we can take a train to the town where the church is, look at it to see how the land lies. If all is well, we can leave the placard, and be back before their hearts start to yearn for our company again. Plus, I've scrutinised recent images of the interior and can see no sign of any CCTV cameras. But it's not what is already there that makes it so good, it's what we are going to leave there!'

With that said, and despite David's pleading and insisting, Steven would say no more; apart from that it would be a symbolic gesture of defiance, rather than anything that could physically harm anyone.

After Hanna and Rita had accepted to go their own way; enacting the placarding plans became straightforward, and two and a half hours later, the men had arrived at the village, and were reconnoitring the church; which David and Steven agreed was ideal for leaving the placard.

However, when they returned to the church, fifteen minutes later, they are surprised to find that it is being patronised by a large group of Chinese tourists; necessitating a hurried turn around by the two men, to avoid ending up appearing in any photos or phone videos. Nevertheless, after returning less than a half an hour later, the pair of them walk into a deserted church.

Now all the pair had to do is leave the placard and Steven's surprise on the statue of Mary Mother of Jesus; nestling the baby Jesus in her arms. Without hesitation, both men calmly perform their respective duties; David attaching the placard around Mary's neck, and Steven leaving an open book upon the infant Jesus.

'What's the book?' David asks, as Steven steps back and takes the video shots of the scene.

'It's a copy of the Quran.'

'*The Quran!*' David Bell repeated, 'So you mean, that you left it there, so it looks as if Mary, the mother of Jesus Christ, is now reading the Quran?'

'Yes. I took a copy from the mosque when we were there.' Steven replies. In truth, David quite likes the idea and so without any great regrets, both he and Steven left the church. The placard that they had left, stated:

The Curch of Free Heroes
The 3rd Quest: Empathy:
Empathy opens out to greater knowledge and freedoms, than
charity or competition. A Free-Hero's pursuit of empathy is
one of a genuine, emotional insight, alongside a practical
insight of another person or group of people; without having
to follow (or trip up) in their footsteps.
Emotional empathy: is the act of imagining one's self feeling
a victim's emotional sufferings; although very valuable, if
overused, it can cause feelings of emotional distress,
helplessness, victim blaming and ultimately an avoidance of
empathising with a victim.
Practical empathy: is the recognising the hands-on, practical,
perspectives of another's situation; yet without feeling as
much emotional discomfort as in emotional empathy. A
combined use of both types of empathy, increases the
opportunities to find realistic and acceptable ways for
everyone involved, to tread a more able and free path.

The 3rd Question:

As the pursuit of true justice is always a three-legged race –
somehow best run side by side instead of face to face - what
is gained from falling for racial, gender, ethnic, or any other
form of divisive prejudice?

The www.thecurchoffreeheores.info

Chapter 18 - Hanna's village

Back in Turin, and after a meal, the group casually explored the city, without having any arguments about religion at all. However, it was obvious that Hanna was so excited about visiting her family, the four of them decided to cut their tour of Milan short, and head for Hanna's village the very next day.

When Steven and David first saw Hanna's village from a distance, they were delighted. The 900-year plus old village; made up of about 800 or so houses, both surrounded and crowned a majestic edifice of rock. Indeed, some of the older buildings seemed to have been carved out from the rock itself. Nearly all the buildings had whitewashed walls and orange-clad tiled roofs.

As they arrived at the village centre, both men could see, with feelings of mild trepidation, that nearly every house, shop, and building, bore some religious emblem or token on their doors and walls. As they passed what seemed to be the main church, David gave Steven a fleeting glance, which all but said, 'This whole place is *so* out of bounds!'

However, such warning looks were to prove superfluous, as he was to find out as soon as the pair of them were alone, when Steven stated, 'We can forget any thought of pulling off any sort of stunt or campaign *anywhere* around here!'

'Do you hear me arguing, in the slightest?' David asked.

Hanna's family house is old and large, without being grand. The two guests are given a large bedroom to share, with two separate beds. The bedroom furniture, bears the signs of many generations of use, as does the wash basin, table, and chairs. The room has a small balcony that overlooks a spacious, private, inner square.

If either man still had any lingering ideas about trying any stunts in or anywhere near the village, they were corralled into a far-flung, moral ghetto of unforgivable meanness; by the warm welcome of Hanna's family. The children of the immediate family, whose age range seemed to differ by one year for each child, were highly excited about the visitor's presence. Whenever Steven or David were out of their room; which appeared to be out of bounds to all the children, they either had at least one child either hanging from their hand, arm or seated on their knees.

As in many parts of Italy, family mealtimes in Hanna's village regularly saw most of the family, and its clan like extensions, gathered in one place at one time. Quite often between fifteen and thirty people of assorted ages were seated for the evening meal, which (weather allowing – as on most evenings), was eaten in the central garden square.

The main course of the meal was brought straight from the family restaurant, some two streets away. However, the preparation for the arrival of the meal prompted a circus of loosely organised chaos; with half of those present shouting orders to others, who then immediately retorted with equally boisterous replies or arguments. Adults shooed children and young adults out of the way, then commandeered them a minute later to lay, fetch or carry some of the many side dish and condiments. Most of the clamour was typical, good-hearted but dramatically theatrical, Italian, banter!

'Where is the vinegar?'

'It's to your right!'

'What is it doing there - it should be in front of me!'

'Well if you turn to your right it will be in front of you, you idiot!'

'Bravo! How brave you are, if you were in front of me right now, instead of lazing over there, then by the grace of Saint Lucius, I'd show you how brave you are!'

'If I were standing in front of you right now, then I'd need Saint Lucius to hold me up and prevent me from collapsing from hysterical laughter!'

With everyone (barring inevitable latecomers) seated, the head of the family, Don Gusto Milanesi, said a prayer of thanksgiving. After the prayer, a perpetual state of loosely organised verbal-chaos held court during the consumption of the meal itself. Like the meal's preparation, most of the verbal battling; consisting of salvos of information, mockery and retorts, came from one, two, three or even four sides of the dining area, and it ranged across just about every subject possible – apart that is from religion.

As the only non-speaker of fluent Italian, Steven was able to enjoy the spectacle for its own worth. Even though David understood the Italian language to a fair extent, he was at times overwhelmed with the sea of words. However, what was abundantly clear to both guests, that in spite of the apparent discord around them; if any outsider became a threat to any member of the family - then the grip of clan loyalty would surround that intruder, with the finality of a shuddering noose.

Once the English guest had time to settle in at the table, and start their meals, politeness and natural curiosity about the visitors, made sure that neither David or Steven were left closed mouthed for too long. Steven gave a brief history of his life (leaving out any illegal bits), and he was listened to with polite interest; particularly after Hanna's father loudly admonished two bickering teenagers, who were sitting half way down the table.

However, there was genuine interest (and some uncertainty) when David Bell (after being prompted by Rita) began to tell of and explain about Crimetest. By the end of his story, most people seemed to think it was a good story, particularly when one elderly woman concluded, 'If you want to catch a fox, then you may have to pluck a few chickens.'

In answer to the old woman, David saluted her by raising his glass of wine and saying, 'I do not think any criminal would be able to resist against your great wisdom.' Mirroring David Bell's salutation, everyone saluted and applauded the old woman. Yet no, sooner than the salutations had died down, then one of the previously rebuked teenagers asked Don

Gusto, to tell about the time when the Mafioso, had come to the village.

'We had two outsiders, one time,' Hanna's father, began to relate to Steven and David. 'They claimed to be members of the Costa nostra. They were joined by two brothers from our village, who are not the brightest in our midst. For about six months they managed to frighten some local shopkeepers into paying them protection money, if you please!'

At that moment, Don Gusto interrupted his story telling, to again loudly admonish and then give a final warning to the same two bickering teenagers, after which they fell silent. Don Gusto then continued, 'Then they tried the same trick with our baker, but when he resisted, they foolishly roughed him up, not much, but enough … *but* … they forgot that he was already under the protection of his … wife!' At that point, several grownups made various gestures of serious impending trouble.

'When she found out the truth, she marched her husband to our village priest, Father Padovesi. He called the mayor and then the whole village to the church. Father Padovesi gave everyone there a sermon, on the sins of worshipping … *false idols*!' At that point several people at the table made the sign of the crucifix and then carried on listening to Don Gusto who continued.

'That same evening the mayor and the men of the village, including myself, marched the outsiders to the church, and then into the graveyard. Our Mayor told them, 'If you or your kind ever come back to our beautiful village again … then you will stay in here …*forever*!' At which point, many of those around the table nodded their heads in agreement, and Don Gusto continued once again, 'The outsiders understood only too well, and they never returned. As for the stupid brothers, they were easily led in the beginning, so it was not too difficult for Father Padovesi and their families to lead them back into good ways.'

The whole meal lasted for a little over two hours, and by the time it was over, Hanna asked the two men if they would like to go to freshen up before she and Rita showed them some more of the village. As soon as they were alone in their room, Steven said, 'There you see, a good priest can rally his people against evil.'
David looked at Steven, and then answered, 'But they still ended up paying protection, to the church.'
Steven then looked at David and replied, 'If I were you, I wouldn't mention that to them, unless you want to share the same fate as those two from the Mafia.'
'I won't, but I wonder what the priest would do if I told him that he was a front man for the grandest protection racket of all time.'
A short while later, Steven, Hanna, David and Rita walked through the village. As they walked, Hanna told of the village's history, which also meant the history of her own family. The family and village had long aligned itself to Giovanni Visconti, who died in 1354. Visconti was an elected Roman Catholic cardinal of Milan, but Pope John the12th, refused to recognize his position, so, the Cardinal who was also was a military leader, fought against Florence, and used force to capture and hold other cities.
When Hanna brought the group to the church, they found a crypt, to which she had the key. In the crypt were generations of her family's forebears, including a one who sailed with Christo Columbus.
After locking up the crypt, Hanna seemed to invite all three of her guests to visit the room of records, situated at the rear of the crypt - but Rita made a point of declining the offer, and almost dragged David off towards village centre once more.
As soon as Rita and David had almost impolitely departed, Hanna walked up to Steven and said, 'Would you like to come to the room of records with me,' then holding up an old, iron mortise lock key, she informed him, 'It has very

interesting and rare records, but it is rarely visited ... and I have the only key!'

Whether the ancestors of Hanna would have approved of what she and Steven did, on the dust covered oak table, in the room of records, remains unrecorded in any book or on any parchment, and neither is it recorded here. Suffice to say, it had not been the first time such an act had been completed there, nor, what with two more days and nights to go before the visitor's departure - would it be the last.

When the time eventually arrived for the four companions/lovers to leave Hanna's village, no one was more saddened to do so than, Steven. His time there had been almost a "Saul on the road to Damascus," time. However, Steven's conversion bore no religious overtones; instead, his heartbeat with ... Love.

Although Steven's thoughts and feelings turned almost exclusively towards love, families, and even having babies; David Bell was still of a mind to continue with the campaign. When he came across Steven, looking wistfully at his beloved Hanna sitting alongside Rita on a nearby bench, which was several decibels away out of hearing range, David decided to test the situation.

'I don't suppose there is any chance that you might wrestle your gaze away from your newly beloved, and turn your attention to the matter of our campaign, is there?'

Putting a half-lock on his intention to return to Hanna's beauty, Steven answered, 'Like you, of course, are totally immune to the lovely Rita's charms.' Receiving no answer, he chided, 'Your immunity, must come from knowing all about love and the psychological foibles of sexual and emotional attraction.'

Looking at Steven, David replied, 'Although I will always love, Claire, I'll admit that I find Rita very attractive. But we, that is you and I, can't leave our business half finished.'

'Just because *we* don't finish it, it doesn't mean others won't take it up.'

'Yet I thought you were the one who said, if we leave it half cocked, then no one will take it seriously.'
'I said they'd give us short shrift, sure, and I still believe that, but things are different now. Before I only had my freedom to lose, now I have a lot more.'
Looking at his ex-adversary, his homicidally psychopathic ex-adversary, for another second or two, David Bell pondered about exactly what to say next, then he suggested, 'I can carry on, on my own, I guess. You have taught me quite a lot in a short time. I guess what I'm saying is that I don't need you now! I can go on alone.'

Chapter 19 - The ABC of faith

After leaving Hanna's village and family a long way behind them, the four lovers decided that they would stop at a lakeside restaurant. Whilst waiting for their main meal to arrive; and to Steven's annoyance, the conversation again turned to religion. Once again, bearing in mind what Rita had said about Hanna's vulnerability to depression, Steven was worried; that if David Bell questioned Hanna's religious faith too rigorously, then it might trigger a depressive reaction in her.

However, he had also noticed, that whereas Hanna's tone was once confrontational towards any questioning of religion, it was now more inquisitive. Moreover, as on this occasion Hanna herself had initiated the discussion about morals, Steven was handicapped in trying to change it to a safer topic, so he did his best to stay neutral.

After eating a couple of the olives and sundries from a dish on the table, and placing the olive stones on the table, David Bell answers a question from Hanna about Life.

'Life has taught me what I hope are two very valuable lessons,' proffered.

'And what are they, David?' Hanna asks.

'That it is impossible to *not* make mistakes in life.'

'And the second?'

'That sometimes the most valuable lessons learned from a mistake, are taught after you deliberately choose not to repeat the mistake.'

Gesturing to the river, David continues, 'On the south-east coast of England there is a place called Fairlight, which has a coastguard house with a large radar that scans the sea. I like to go there sometimes. It's sort of symbolically reassuring to believe that someone is constantly looking out for our safety upon the seas.'

Turing to Hanna, he emphasises, 'But if any so-called guardians of our moral horizons, produce false horizons and deceptive life-charts, then the costs of such a deception can be Titanic.'

'How so?'

'Ever since the ebb and flow of Life began in the primeval seas, all living creatures have feared being sucked down by a whirlpool of their own current, ignorance's. It is of course, a very natural and human fear, which sadly the religions trawl through, with their leech-pooh-lures, of a life beyond death, and their wriggling greed for far more, than the sheer immensity of Life can support … or ever afford to justify. For until something has been truly earned, it remains unaffordable.'

Shrugging his shoulders, David adds, 'Unfortunately, the religions have not learned, that their rituals of praying for people's salvation, does not make preying upon their fears and greed, any more affordable.'

With that, he pops an olive into his mouth, and then places the stone onto the table, in front of him.

Although Hanna is looking decidedly interested in David's answer; to his surprise, she suddenly asks, 'If you had to pick one religion, which one would you choose?'

Looking and checking that neither Steven nor Rita objected to him answering, David replies, 'The English version of Quakerism, which is also called the Society of Friends. But only if I had to choose. For like all the others, the Christians, Muslims, Hindus, and just about any other religion you could name without having to Googling it first, choosing just one, would be like trying to vote for your favourite loan shark.'

With that said, he picks up an olive, and after popping it into his mouth, he placed the olive's stone onto the edge of the table, and continues, 'And by that, I mean, they will all try to rip you off, until you have neither a leg to stand on, nor an arm to pull yourself up with.' He then flicks the three olive stones off the table edge, and into the river below.

Although he was addressing his three friends, David realises that had taken on his persona of a conference speaker. So, in order to adjust back to an equal level, and pausing to allow the waiter to lay the coffees, he then plays "mother" to his friends, by offering to pour the coffee, milk, and sugar.

'I think you maybe a closet waiter, David,' Rita teases, 'for you always like to serve tea and coffee. I'm sure that if we let you, you'd cut up our meals, so they are easier for us to swallow.'

Holding up the cream and sugar in each hand, David grins as he replies, 'You are right, as usual, Rita. If I were not who I am, I could happily earn a living as a waiter.'

Giving David a sideward glance, Steven half asks, half jibes, 'Then perhaps we should start calling you Mother from now on?'

However, before David replies, Rita retorts, 'But that is such an English view, Steven. In Italy, we consider the calling to be a waiter as a masculine trait.'

Then as quick as a flash, David looks at Steven and quips, 'Perhaps then, you should address me as … father,' then grinning even more broadly he adds, or even … our father.'

At that point, all three of his friends burst into a round of mock laughter and salutations.

Pausing to sip her coffee, Hanna half asks half challenges, 'So what would you do, if you were washed up on some desert island, and found the natives had started to worship you as a God ... David? What would your divine guidance be?'

Once again, before David can make his reply, he is interrupted, this time by Steven, who turns to Hanna and suggests, 'Spare him his blushes Hanna, at least give him the chance of being a mere messenger, from their God?'

David Bell smiles, and replies, 'Well I certainly wouldn't proclaim that faith in me alone, is something to be praised.'

'That away to go David,' Steven interjects, 'Dash their hopes gently.'

'I am just pointing out the dangers of using religion, as a serious vessel for morality.'

Steven then leans back slightly, however, Hanna leans forward and asks, 'How so?'

'Because, it can only stay afloat by promising their faithful, a fairy-tale landing in a Never-never land.'

'Never-never, land?' Rita queries.

''Never, ever ... never! Has any religion provided any *solid,* verifiable, proof, that their promised afterlife land, exists. Even though it is *that* promise, above all else, which acts as their institutional, lifebelt.'

'So how come they have managed to survive, people aren't stupid?' Steven challenges.

'The problem with religion,' David answers, 'can be hinted at by the phrase, *I think therefore I am.*'

'Go on.'

'*I think therefore I am.* Therefore, a person's chosen religion, tends to be reflection of the chooser's own persona. If the person's mind is loving, then so will his or her reflections of that religion, be loving. If a person's mind is malevolent, then so will his or her reflections of that religion, be malevolent.'

Looking at Rita, David continues, 'This dual persona of the *already* half converted, is one of the reasons why religious blind faith is so influential, because it's *not* blind at all. The follower already sees their own wishes in their chosen religion anyway. The so-called, blind faith of a religion, is not blind at all, it already preaching to the half converted in the first place.'

Shrugging his shoulders, David continues, 'Unfortunately, religion's problem escalates, when a malevolent person reflects that their own meanness, etc, reflects God's personality, rather than merely their own damaged one. In short, it works like a self-fulfilling prophecy, except, that the malevolence of the prophecy takes on a holy, persona.'

Turning back to Hanna, David states, 'Religion has managed to stay afloat because, although faith is their cruellest lifeline, it is also their most effective lifeline!'

'How so, cruel?' Hanna asks.

'Because faith in the unproven, is *cruelly dependent,* on people attaching it to themselves,' David replies with obvious anger.

In a bid to calm himself, he pops another two olives into his mouth and after chewing them, he calmly places the olive stones onto the table, and continues, 'Religion is a belief system reliant on faith. Faith is the act of replacing verifiable proof, with emotionally attached beliefs, or feelings. Just like astrology, faith healing, and all the other charlatans, all religious leaders insist on *absolute faith* in the unproven … as being the true proof of being *worthy* of salvation.'

'That is true but having faith in goodness is good.' Hanna replies, without showing any sign of a challenge.

'Of course, it is, but standing up for something good, and bowing down to something good, are not the same things. Besides, Hanna, what if there were no God or an afterlife, but just these four score years or so, would you still fight for things such as justice, truth, and empathy?'

This time Hanna's tone and face expresses defiance when she answers, *'Yes! Of course!'*

'Then I must conclude, my dearest Hanna, that your faith in such things, is far stronger than your religion demands that you believe.'

Shrugging his shoulders, David emphasises, 'You don't need to be attached to any religious puppeteer Hanna. You just need to cut their strings, lift your head, and stride toward the things that *you* would and do freely desire anyway, regardless of whether there is a God or not.'

When Hanna does not answer, David suggests, 'Because religion's most verifiable proof of being the sacred interpreters of their God's words, is that no one has been able to prove that they're *not*, they are open questions about their faith in the unproven.'

'What questions?' Rita asks.

'I call it the ABC of verifiable proof.'

'ABC?' Hanna asks.

'It goes like this. Imagine that you have been *falsely* …
accused of a crime. Now, question A is, would you want to be
tried by jury A, who will rely upon verifiable proofs of your
guilt, or innocence. Question B is, or would you choose to be
tried by jury B, who will judge whether your guilty or
innocent, by relying upon totally, *unproven* claims?'
'I guess I would want the first one,' Hanna replies.
'There you go. When it comes to truth and justice, you prefer
verifiable proof over blind faith,'
'But what is question, C?' Rita asks.
'Question C is, if you are indeed *guilty* of the crime and want
to try and pervert the course of truth and justice, which jury
would you choose … A or B?'
When neither Rita nor Hanna answers, David concludes, 'The
danger in religiously worshipping the unprovable, is that it
can motivate blasphemy of the provable.'
He then flicks the two olive stones off the table and into the
river, and pronounces, 'It is as easy as … *A … B … and C.*'
At that point, Rita hands David a side plate, then indicating to
the dish of remaining olives she asks, 'Are you going to make
every point in the same fashion my darling? Because if so,
could you be a *hero,* and save a Jesuit, a Taoist and maybe a
Mormon for the rest of us? At least, until the main course has
arrived?'
As all of four companions grin; for a fleeting moment, both
men independently wonder about Rita's emphasis on the
word "hero" but then both dismiss it as mere coincidence.
Refusing the offered side plate; and pushing the dish of olives
into the centre of the table, then looking around, David says,
'Do you know, I'm famished, where is our food?'
Reaching for an olive, and smiling, Rita answers, 'Don't be
so *impatient* David … have a little *faith* … my dear!'

Chapter 20 - The Milan and Tehran synods

Three blocks due east from the main Roman Catholic cathedral of Milan, the private offices of the Proctor of Milan sits resplendent, with its mixture of 17th-century furniture, and modern-day office necessities. Squeezed behind the Proctor's office; there is the "Outreach" room, where the hum of computer consoles; imperceptibly reverberates the faintly incensed-tinged air, which has sauntered along the portrait-lined corridors and seeped into the whole fabric of the building. As a sign of the politics of the incumbent residency of the Proctor's post; the once renowned portraits of the infamous Medici family have been removed from the public's gaze.

Leaving a window ajar to disperse the smell of recently applied furniture polish, Cardinal Tivo turns to address the assembled company; who include two more cardinals, three bishops, and the Pope's personal secretary.

'As you may well be already aware,' Cardinal Tivo announces, 'it is my sad duty to inform you, that those responsible for the attack on our churches, and the assault on a Muslim Cleric, have now added another atrocity to their list of crimes.'

Looking around the company, the Cardinal emphasises, 'There has been a *fresh* attack on a church, and they left an open book of the Quran in the arms of the statue of the Mary, the Holy Mother of Jesus.'

As soon as the silent chorus of shaking heads and raised arms subsides, the Cardinal continues, 'From the information gleaned from their website, named The Curch of Free Heroes, their campaign is an attack on all the major religions. Unfortunately, since the attack on the Cleric, and the public declaration for a call for a death fatwa against the guilty ones, the guilty have merely attained even greater worldwide publicity.'

'The Muslims should have done as we did and kept things in low key.' Bishop Paroni sighed.

Nodding his agreement, Cardinal Tivo qualifies, 'Admittedly, the issuing of a call for the death fatwa, has undoubtedly given impetus to this group of blasphemers. However, by having some personal relationships with the Muslim section of the Committee for Interfaith Cooperation, I have been able to discuss such matters, alongside our mutual concerns, with his Excellency Sheik Shamim Said.'

'Trying to steer a straight course after the boat has been holed?' Monsignor Galvin interjected.

After 34 years serving the church, Monsignor Galvin did not believe in God or an afterlife. As far as he was concerned, anybody who believes or at least wishes for either, is weak-minded. Nevertheless, if the promise of an afterlife made the weak minded, pursue a reasonably good life before they died, then so much the better. For despite his known doubts about the afterlife, the Monsignor did believe in the church, or more succinctly, in the power of the church to propel and steer a true course of salvation for the thing he loved the most, which is Life and humanity, with all of its faults.

He likened the two arms of the church; a belief in a God and an afterlife, to the oars of a boat; a boat trying to cross a lake; a storm-prone lake that spanned the lifetime of any and every man, woman or child, born into this world. To lose either oar, would mean having to develop the skills of a lone gondolier, to both steer and propel a true moral course. Such skills of navigation were no easy task to learn or put into practice, as the Monsignor had discovered as a young man seeking to learn the craft of a gondolier. Admittedly his chosen church had sprung a few worrying leaks along the way, and there were other religions of course, but what matter the name on the prow, as long as the boat got you to the other side.

Monsignor Galvin had been a lover of the water since he was a young man and he had joined a rowing club. During that time, he had learned much about the water, such as how to read the various signs on the water's surface. Yet sometimes, there were no signs, such as when an oarsman would "Catch a crab," an underwater current or eddy, which could snatch an oar clean from a rower's grasp and even from the boat. However, to lose both oars, meant being at the mercy of the unthinking winds of misfortune, and the turbulent eddies of human emotions; for then disaster could proceed at a very swift pace.

Coming back from his memories, the Monsignor sees that Cardinal Tivo is addressing him, 'Not at all, Monsignor Galvin. I have spoken very recently with the Muslim committee, and I can assure all here, that these offenders will not go uncaptured or unpunished.'

'Do you mean that you condoned this fatwa outrage!' then turning to the Papal Secretary, the Monsignor demanded, 'Does his Holiness the Pope know about this?

The Papal Secretary says nothing in reply but turns his face to the other assembled hierarchy. 'We, of course, cannot be seen to condone violence. Yet I am pleased to report that we are using all available non-violent assistance, in our search for this blasphemous criminal group. Only this morning I had an hour talk with the Commissioner of Detectives, in this very room. I have also been in communication with our own private agents of enquiry, as well as the other avenues of enquiry that we have. I refer of course to our billion and more worldwide followers. Through our World Wide Web for Catholics online, we have already sent out communiqués, requesting any information concerning this abomination towards our church.'

'It's a shame that we were not so forthright in securing information about the abominations of those in our own priesthood a while ago, let alone to the problem of the so-called, third world.'

Although Monsignor Galvin's sometimes-sharp comments and attitudes often grate with official opinion and policy, they generally command a wide tolerance from his peers; not only for the sake of the appearance of inclusiveness but also as an occasional reality check.

Giving the Monsignors a curt smile, Cardinal Tivo advices, 'Let us try and keep to the matter in hand. Through the generosity of a few favoured individuals, the police have announced a fifty-thousand-dollar reward for the capture and prosecution of the offenders. There is also a worldwide hunt for the perpetrators of these crimes, by the world's media, and our own billion strong faithful. With faith, perseverance and with the essential help of Our Lord, these wrongdoers will be captured … or scared off.'

THE MUSLIM SYNOD

A ten-minute, lover's stroll, from the offices of the Proctor of Milan, the Muslim equivalent of the Italian Synod, reaches the same conclusions as for the Roman Catholic one. In the matters of placarding of the church or the mosque, let alone the assault on the Cleric, there is not enough evidence to come up with any specifically named suspect. Accordingly, the committee decides to wait and see what develops from further investigations. However, that is not the only issue on their agenda for that afternoon; for there is the issue of the proposed death fatwa, upon whoever committed the assault on the Cleric. For an answer to that question, the Grand Mufti had been consulted.

Speaking directly to Faeq Mansur, the Cleric who had called for the death fatwa, the leader of the meeting pronounced, 'Whatever your personal feelings are on this matter, you had no authority to publicly call for such a drastic action.'

'Drastic action!' Faeq Mansur retorts, 'I call such action merciful! In the old days, this blasphemous act would have demanded death by far more merciful ways than beheading!' Ignoring the outburst, the leader carries on, 'We have had a directive from Mecca, which specifically rules, that your actions went beyond your responsibility to our guidelines, and those of Allah, may his name be praised. The result is that your call for a death fatwa has been rejected.'

As soon as he heard the rejection, the rebuked Faeq Mansur storms out of the room, and whatever the council's leader was about to say to him, he no longer said.

Chapter 21 - Steven and scorched wings.

After their riverside lunch, the group window-shopped (with both couples walking arm in arm) through the old town. As they climbed a steep hill, they happened upon, and entered a 16th century Church, to listen to an orchestral rehearsal of Vivaldi Four Seasons. Although the conductor interrupted the music on several occasions, his interruptions were usually quite humours. What is more, if one listened attentively enough, one could hear the difference between pre-and post-instructions. To his surprise, Steven finds that it is not only the music that is moving - but also, the orchestra's pursuit of collective harmony, moves him too.

At one point, Hanna could not help herself from bursting into spontaneous and loud applause, which was immediately supported by her companions, and answered by several orchestra members, as they played notes of 'Thank you' with their respective instruments.

After the rehearsal, the group returned to their hotel to rest before the evening's entertainment and evening meal. The women went to their room and the men to theirs.

Nevertheless, by the time a quarter of an hour of just laying around had passed; Steven has become restless and bemoans, 'It feels as if I've been sitting around for years!' Turning to David Bell, he adds, 'Besides, as much as I like the company, I could do with some space.' With that said, he gets off the bed and heads toward the door, adding, 'Don't worry, I'm not eager to be returned to prison, I'll behave myself.'

'Glad to hear it!' David replies to Steven's back, as it exits through the closing door.

In fact, Steven does not intend to do any wrong whatsoever, as he heads toward the old town once again. As it happened, his intentions are quite the opposite. Previously, whilst the group had been window-shopping, a pearl bracelet caught Hanna's attention so much, that she pointed it out to her companions. Noticing the reasonable price of the real pearl bracelet, Steven decided that he would sneak back later, and buy it for Hanna. Thus, it was, that with enough cash in his pocket, and good intentions in his heart, Steven now set off to buy the necklace.

However, the plans of men, mice, and oysters do not always go according to plan. In the narrow and maze of streets of the old town, Steven has ended up getting so lost, that he could not even see any shops around, let alone the jewellery shop. He tries asking an old man for directions, but the language barrier is too much for either man to overcome. As he soldiers on up the hill to try to gain a better view of his whereabouts, Steven looks into the open doorway of a small church and spots a priest.

'Buongiorno, 'Steven greets the priest, 'Do you speak English?'

'Buongiorno!' the priest returns, 'And yes, I do speak English, and Spanish and even a little German.'

Stepping inside the church threshold, Steven asks, 'I am afraid I am a bit lost, I was looking for the old town, where the shops are, can you help?'

'Of course,' the priest replies with enthusiasm, 'I am Father Alberto. You are not far from your way, and you are not the first to stray.' Father Alberto; a man in his mid-forties, smiles, and then puts on a sad face, 'It is unfortunate that the hill climb is so steep, that we get few tourists visiting our humble place of worship. So, if you would care to look around whilst you are here, then please, you are welcome.'

The fact that the priest had not given any directions yet and seemed to be waiting for Steven to accept the offer of a tour first, annoys Steven somewhat. However, after a short but heavy silence, the priest gives Steven the directions to the Old town shops.

'Thank you for your help.' Steven replies.

'Don't mention it.' Father Alberto acknowledges, 'It cost nothing to help a traveller who is lost.' The priest then pauses, gestures to the collecting plate just behind him, and suggests,

'But if you would like to show your gratitude by donating to our much-needed collection ... then I am sure the Lord will bless your journey, both in this life, and the life that is yet to come!'
It wasn't that the priest was asking for money, which so annoys Steven. The reasonable price of the pearl necklace would dwarf any reasonable donation. He is annoyed at what he sees, as an affront to common courtesy. If he had asked a street beggar for directions and had received a request for money; Steven would have laughed and might have given the beggar some money for his cheek. Yet somehow, the priest's request seems to be taking him (Steven) for granted, which was something that Steven detests!
'*Excuse me?*' A stony-faced Steven demands.
Looking at this tourist, Father Alberto begins to blink, as if he is unsure of the situation. Like Steven, he too feels under pressure, not so much from Steven, though in the priest's opinion the man is being rather abrupt. The real pressure came from the church. For the last year or more, he had been getting strong hints that his humble place was too humble; or at least he was acting too humbly to increase the monthly revenues from his parishioners. Along with these hints, came the suggestion that if things (i.e. he) did not improve; he would find himself and his church being reduced to a part-time occupancy.
By his eighth blink, the priest has made up his mind, 'I said if you would care to donate …'
In his efforts to calm himself, Steven suddenly recalls a poem he had read many years ago, so he asks, 'Do you like poetry?'
Surprised at the sudden shift in direction, Father Alberto replies, 'Yes, I like it very much.'
Looking around at the church, Steven then recites the poem:
'*I was chatting to God the other day... whilst I was sipping some hot tea in my local café. When he happened to mention in an offhand way, that he was thinking of packing it in. He said that he might retire to Bournemouth, upon the sea, and*

maybe dabble in some shallow sin. Nothing too risky ... just a dabble ... nothing more, just a gentle paddle 'tween the deep and the shore. Just a casual stroll, maybe once or twice a day, after all, he didn't want to get carried away. I was thinking, he said, you could take over my job. There's plenty of over-time, so you'd earn a few bob. Think about it, God said, and he wished me a nice day. Then he left, leaving the bill for his tea and angel cake ... for me to pay!'

 When Steven had finished, the priest said, 'That is a very thought-provoking poem. Do you know the author?'

'No.'

At that point, Father Alberto considers adding a rider to his implied compliment about the poem. Looking at the man in front of him, and wondering about the man's temperament, he considers his intended rider carefully.

'Then … I would think,' Father Alberto suggests, 'that the author's message is that, no matter who we are … we all have to pay the price of our original sin!'

Grabbing the priest by his dog collar and vest front, Steven knees him in the groin and then pushes him onto his knees. Towering over the priest, Steven then asks, 'How about I donate to charity, by sending you to your maker right now!'

To Steven's surprise, the Priest answers, 'I may walk in the valley of death, but I fear no evil!'

Somehow, to Steven, the priest's words have the ring of finality. Yet Steven is not used to backing down, 'Ok, you win, you've convinced me that you are stupid enough to be a dead martyr to a dead cause.' Then looking around he sees that the entrance to the church is still clear. He then steps behind the priest, twists him around, so they were now both facing the entrance; cocks his arm around the priest's neck. Steven then he pulls out his phone, activates the photo app, and asks, 'But what about your flock, your parishioners Mr. Reverend, or are they just lambs to be slaughtered on your slab. Would you be willing to sacrifice their lives too?'

Speaking through his half-strangled throat, Alberto half pleads, half accuses, 'For God's sake, what are you doing, you are in the house of the Lord?'

Tightening his arm around the priest's neck, Steven emphasises, '*I mean*, that if you don't renounce your faith, *before* your next sacrificial lamb trots in here, I will shoot the sucker or suckers, before they make it past the first row of benches!'

Although Father Alberto cannot see any gun, he feels that this mad man, could well have pulled out a gun, he also feels very shocked and frightened.

Nevertheless, as Steven is a man who likes to keep his word, at least unto himself, he had already internally qualified his meaning of the word "shoot,' to merely mean to 'shoot' a photo of anybody that walked in.

However, Father Alberto was not to know of Steven's qualification, so when he answers Steven's threat, with, 'Their souls are in the hands of the Lord, as is my own ... and yours!' Steven's anger suddenly begins to reach a level of spontaneous combustion, which would not have felt out of place within the preverbal fires of Hell itself.

Yet, to his own utter amazement, and in a bid to cool his hot temper, Steven takes several deep breaths and then almost without thinking; he tries to perform a "surprise" distraction exercise.

Glancing around, he sees several rows of candles sitting in a black, wrought iron stand. People paid money to light the candles and then prayed for what or whomever, they chose. Buying the use of such a candle supposedly increased the chances of God, or one of his Angels, answering the prayer. However, the "surprise" that happens upon Steven, is that he notices the *presence* of the half a dozen or so, dead moths, which are strewn around the base of the candle stand. Clearly, the "sacred" light of the candle flames had attracted the moths, and then scorched their wings beyond use, and then died.

Returning his attention to the priest, and gesturing toward the moth carcasses, Steven states, 'You see those moths, they are just like your fucking parishioners. You offer them a light in the darkness that burns their fucking wings off.'
Struggling to speak, Father Alberto proclaims, 'Yet they will still be raised up into Heaven, by our Good Lord!'
Squeezing his arm even tighter around the priest's neck, Steven's eyes close, almost as if they were acting on their own accord. Waves of darkness swamp his inner vision, until he sees an unbidden flash of light illuminating a partial memory, partial dream. Before him stands a past victim, Rita Knightly, the local beauty queen he had murdered during the time of his Body Part Murders.
Except, this time she and he are not alone, for Rita, is taking part in a pageant of Steven's past Body Part Murder victims. As Rita gleefully steps forward, and then in the hushed silence of the auditorium, she begins to flaunt her fatal injuries - until a voice, which Steven knows only too well - breaks the silence. He immediately recognises the voice of Sandra Lott, the Crimetest Advisor who had been paramount in his downfall and imprisonment. As each contestant moves centre stage, whilst gesturing to his or her wounds and mutilations, Sandra; dressed in evening wear (and an unseen audience) enthusiastically applauded the contestant. Finally, after all the contestants had lined up together, and had either bowed or curtsied, Sandra steps boldly forward and announces, 'Unfortunately, folks, there is no winner, because you're all … *fucking, losers*!'
With Sandra's announcement, all the victims burst into tears, and (whilst taking care not to squeeze any wounds or mutilations too firmly) they begin hugging each other. However, at that moment, Sandra raises and then slowly opens a large, golden envelope; then she draws out a golden card, reads it, and announces, '*But* … it is my privilege, and a great pleasure, to announce, that the biggest loser of all, is …
… … *Steven … Nobody!*'

Seemingly unable to tear away from his taunting fantasy, Steven feels as if he his lungs are about to collapse, then suddenly the inner scenes change into a clear, real memory of his school days. On this day at school, he is in the school playground and he is surrounded by a group of his peers, who are shouting, *'Steven Nobody!' 'Steven Nobody!' 'Steven Nobody!'*

Just as suddenly, Steven's waking vision returns, and he finds that he is looking at the burnt carcasses of the moths. Without giving any conscious command, his body reacts by jolting him backward, and he sees that the face of the priest is turning a purple shade of red; and that the priest himself is about to lose consciousness. All of which is enough to convince Steven to deliberately, thrust the priest away, and take a huge breath in.

Next, Steven raises his arm high into the air, as the priest immediately tries to shield himself. Then, looking up into the camera lens of his phone, Steven takes a selfie of himself, standing over the priest. Keeping his arm raised and feeling as if he is some warrior-angel, raising a sword of justice, Steven glowers down at the priest, and proclaims, *'You are the nobody! You and all your kind!'*

With that proclamation, Steven releases the priest and rapidly heads for and out the main doors. As Steven storms out of the church, he has the simultaneous feelings; of a much-confused groom who has just been dumped at the altar - and a very much relieved, parent of the self-same groom!

By the time, Steven had returned to the hotel, there is a message on his phone, it is from the man dealing with obtaining the false documents, which Steven needs to make his new life in another land, more permanent and secure.

The message states, "Come anytime."

Chapter 22 - Getting one's affairs in order
When Steven returned to the shared hotel suite, he did not tell David Bell, of the church incident. However, he did inform him, 'I need to go and meet with someone!'
'Someone?'
'Someone who can arrange my next move, to a new country.'
'When will you be back?'
'In about five hours'
'Ok! Have you told Hanna, or do you want me to improvise another excuse, out of thin air?'
Steven gave David a look of mock surprise and replied, 'No, don't worry, I won't be relying on your amazing powers of concoction, I will tell her myself. By the way, I mentioned to Hanna that I might well be going to live in another country!'
'Really, where?'
This time, Steven gave his friend a look of mock threat, 'Do you really want the burden of knowing my eventual destination?'
'No, of course not, but I must admit to being curious.'
'Unfortunately, so will a lot of other people be, including the police.'
'Of course,' David agreed, holding up his hands, 'So, how did Hanna react to your news? Did you tell her where you were going, or when?'
'I told her the continent, but not the country,' Steven paused to collect his words, 'She was sad, very sad that I was leaving, but she was very enthusiastic about the continent where I intend to go. She even said, and I quote. It's such a wonderland of opportunities. Then she added, and even emphasised, that she had always wanted to go there herself!'
David merely raised his eyebrows.
'What's that look supposed to mean?'
'Nothing, it's just that we both know that Hanna is a born enthusiast, it doesn't mean that she is not genuine, but it doesn't mean that she is ... necessary truly committed by her enthusiasm!'

'I also …' Steven adds, '… mentioned, that I would not want what I had just told her, to be known, even to Rita or yourself, because there were people who would like to know where I was going to be. People who would not have my best interests at heart!'

'And she said …?'

'That I could trust her to have my interest at the centre of her heart!'

'In that case,' David suggested, as he looked at his wristwatch, we have time to do a couple of exercises. You've missed a few in the last scheduled session, so the more you get under your belt now the better for you, and Hanna, in the future!'

Steven smiled, sighed, and then raised his hands in surrender. Just under three hours later, Steven shook hands with a burly man, wearing a bespoke tailored suit; which flattered the man's frame as much as it complimented his tailor. After exchanging cash and documents, Steven asked, 'Can you get the same set of papers and documents for someone else, a woman?' When the man replied that he could, Steven handed him a photo of Hanna, 'Let us say within a week?'

The burly man nodded, 'Yes, of course, I can get the papers, but things can't be rushed if you want good papers.'

'Ok! Go ahead with it, make her country of origin Italy, and her first name Hanna, but the rest I'll leave to you.' After shaking hands once more, the pair went their separate ways. By the time, he was back with the group he was in a bright mood. By now any news about the exploits of Curch of Free Heroes was appearing amongst the top five news stories. The last outing, in which a copy of the Quran was placed on the statue of the Virgin Mary and infant Jesus, inspired rumoured accusations; that it was, in fact, a Muslim inspired attack. The rumours began to multiply and heightened the outrage and enthusiasm of the commentators on the various social networks. There were even in-depth debates by various political and religious spokespeople.

To Steven's relief, there was no media news at all about his assault on the priest. Two hours after Steven had stormed out of the church, a report landed on the desktop of Cardinal Volta. The report contained the summarized version of the assault. The report was in-line with an edict sent to all parish priests; that all suspicions actions, particularly by any English-speaking man or men, were to be reported directly, and firstly, to the office of the Cardinal - before any further action was to be taken.

After reading the report out to the assembled company, the Cardinal looked out of the window, pondered, then turned back to give his opinion, 'There is no definite proof that this assault is their work. The priest, Alberto, does report that the altercation did include references to religious matters. If we accuse them of being involved, and it turns out to be the work of some drunken tourist, we will appear to be zealous. So, my personal recommendation is that we will wait, and in the meantime, I will personally speak to Father Alberto about this matter.'

Chapter 23 – The confessional

Although Steven was relieved, that there had been no media coverage of his assault on the priest, something worried him. What it was, he could not tell, and that worried him even more.

As he looked his friends, sitting with him at a cafe, he felt a sense of foreboding, which in turn was distracted by Rita's question to David.

'Then what is good and what is bad, David?'

Holding up both hands David replied, 'I don't know, but I do have a fundamental guide to morality.'

'What is it? Steven asked.

'That the best thing to slip in-between an unstoppable force and an immovable object … is a question mark. And that one prompts me to say another one, which is, the more you try to squash the people who your prejudices place beneath you, then the lower the platform of your wisdom will rise.'

'Very good. And how do you deal with your prejudices David?' Rita challenged.

'I try to deal with my instinctual prejudices …'

'How so instinctual prejudices?' Hanna asked.

'Things like racial, tribal, social divisions. I put myself in their places.

Ah! You mean good ol' empathy.' Steven said, without any apparent sarcasm.

'Yes. Good ol' empathy. Let's say, that I as a white man, who was trying to do the best for himself and his family, whilst also doing his best not to cause any harm to others, was accused by someone, of being a no-good layabout and thief, merely because of the colour of my skin is white. I ask myself, how would I feel about that?'

'And?'

'I would feel outraged of course. So, next, I would take that outrage and apply it to my prejudice, my instinctual racial prejudice.'

Is racial prejudice instinctual or learned?' Hanna asked.

It's both, which means that there is no need to feel guilty about feeling it … unless you practice it.'

For a moment, the four companions were silent, then Hanna asked, 'Are you my friend or my enemy David?'

David, thought for few seconds and answered, 'I hope the truth of my actions will help you decide on that.'

Suddenly Hanna looked at Steven, smiled and asked, 'Are you my friend or my enemy Steven?'

Surprised at the question, Steve's heart rate increased, yet any intention that he should also leave her behind when he eventually left Italy, diminished into the ridiculous, 'I will hope *my* actions will prove that to you.'

Leaning over, Hanna kissed him, and the matter seemed to be over with; then turning to David, Hanna said, 'You are right, about prejudices. They lead to so much suffering. The church is full of prejudices, but I would not like that they would suffer for their … mistakes, but that they would learn from them.'

As Hanna said the words, Steven recognised what was troubling him. It was not that he felt bad about the priest – it was that he knew Hanna would think him bad, for attacking the priest.

As the others chatted, Steven thought about discussing the whole mess, with David Bell, but he would only get into a flap, and then probably go and do something goody, goody, stupid.

Whether it was her instinct as his lover, or that of a naturally empathetic person, Hanna immediately picked up on Steven's mood.

'You seem unhappy, is there something wrong?'

Normally he could convincingly hide the truth from anyone, but with Hanna, Steven just smiled, shook his head, and said, 'It's something that I have to work out on my own,'

Returning Steven's smile, Hanna held his hand and said, 'I know it might sound silly, but whenever I needed to share a something, that I wish to be ... private, even from my friends

or family, I go to confession. I know you do not believe in the church, but the act of sharing my worries has always helped me in times of need, so if you want to share anything with me, you can anytime.'
At first, Steven dismissed such an idea, but then, the idea of talking to a priest, suddenly appealed to his sense of outrageousness. He also reasoned that the idea might have some advantages. At least that way he could have a confidential sounding board, so long as he didn't disclose too much.
After their drinks and snacks, the four friends left the café, and after saying that he felt that he wanted some time alone, to clear his thoughts, Steven kissed Hanna, told her that he'd be back soon - and then he went off to find another priest.
Even before he had reached any church, Steven decided not to verbally object to any references about God and the like; for they could hardly be avoided by a priest in a confessional. However, he would simply translate the word, God, into "Me or I," that way he could re-apply any religious tone, into his own situation.
He didn't obtain a confessional slot until the second church; the first had a queue of seven sinners wanting to be saved. Fortunately, the second church had only one sinner before himself, and before three minutes had passed, he was seated in a small cubical, with a pierced grill between himself and his Italian, English speaking priest. After a short preamble, in which Steven falsely identified himself as a long-lapsed Catholic, he launched into his confession, 'I have committed several sins ... since … of late,' Steven admitted, as he tried, unsuccessfully, to stifle a sudden urge to giggle, then after finally getting a better control of his emotions, Steven apologised.
'There does no need to apologise,' the priest replied, 'the prospect of releasing the burden of mortal sin, can be both a relief and joyous thing to do for the heart and soul.'

Taking several deep breaths, Steven started out with his
confession. 'I have … betrayed, some dear friend, by
committing a sin that they would not want me to commit, and
I have not told them.'
It took the priest only a moment, but the reply was confident.
'To betray a friend's trust, and not tell them is regrettable, as
one should be honest with one's friends. But by asking for the
greater forgiveness of our Lord, then it is given.'
Taking a deep breath and remembering his intention to apply
the priest's words to his own personal situation - and that he
would not turn violent - Steven interpreted the priest's
counselling as; he should forgive himself for not telling
Hanna about attacking the priest. Nevertheless, as Hanna had
said, he should, learn from his … mistakes.
Steven then moved onto his next dilemma for the priest to
consider, which was, ''I have also placed my friends in
danger. I am faced with the prospect of giving up my love for
a woman, for the sake of her safety, and that of my friends.'
'Is this woman a believer in our Lord, and the teachings of the
Holy Church?'
'She sent me here,' Steven replied.
After pausing to consider Steven's answer, the priest replied,
'Then you will have a good and worthy friend, and you
should stay with her, for God will guide and protect you
both.'
Steven interpreted this; as that he should do all he could
to stay with Hanna, whilst believing that he himself had the
ability to guide and protect them both.
Steven then made his last confession, 'I may have to give up
many things that I value, to commit to a cause that may save
many from the devises of a powerful corruptor!'
The priest again thought about the question, and then
answered, 'If your commitment is truly worthy of any cause,
it is that which ends in the service of our Lord. For that is the
beginning of a journey that ends amongst the wonders of
paradise, and for which, the abandonment of your friends, or

your commitment to any other cause, would be but the casting off, of one's shoes, so that one could walk upon the water!' Steven's conclusion to that answer was; That regardless of Bell's, Rita's or even Hanna's commitment or involvement, he will attempt to see the placarding through to its end at the Vatican, and that whatever her answer may be, he should ask Hanna to go across the water, and emigrate with him.
With his confessional, over, Steven thanked the priest. As he left the confessional box, he thought about leaving some money in the collection box but decided not to. He then left the church a much happier man – just as Hanna had predicted.

Chapter 24 - Steven's sermon
When Steven left from his confessional meeting with the
priest, he spent his time wandering around, for a while. He
was quite happy to spend time on the move and in his own
company; it was as much or even more about the journey as
the destination. On this occasion, he spent a fair amount of
time thinking about what would happen when he met with his
friends, again.

 He wanted to do something to impress Hanna, as she had so
often impressed him. However, as he wandered, he tried to
come up with an answer, yet by the time he had turned back
to meet with his friends, he still had not found anything to
impress Hanna with. However, the death of an English ex-pat
was soon to intervene.

Shortly after the four companions met up again, they were
passing by a small local church, in which it was obvious that
a funeral was taking place. From various signs on the flowers
and wreaths, it was equally obvious that the deceased called
"Billy" was an Englishman. As was common at funerals, a
flower seller had set up his portable stall nearby. Seeing the
stall, Hanna impulsively bought a bunch of mixed blooms,
and then insisted that she wanted to pay respect to, 'Poor
Billy and his family.'

Steven immediately agreed with Hanna, and taking her arm,
he accompanied her inside the church, followed by a more
reluctant Rita and David Bell. The congregation was about
thirty to forty in number, and after dutifully laying the flowers
amongst the other tributes; Hanna stood at the back of the
church, and respectfully listened to the eulogy for the
deceased, which was being given in English by one of his
friends.

After the woman had finished and had stepped down from the
lower of the two pulpits, the priest took his place on the upper
pulpit. He was about to bring the service to a conclusion,
when he noticed and acknowledged a raised hand at the rear
of the church. After Steven, had acknowledged the

acknowledgment by the priest, he strode forward indicating that he wanted to climb the steps of the lower pulpit, and so the priest invited him up.

As Steven briefly surveyed the mourners, some of them looked back at him as if they were trying to place his face. Meanwhile, at the back of the church, Steven's three companions stood with their mouths open at various stages of openness.

Nevertheless, it came as no surprise to his three friends, that once he began to speak, Steven's natural commanding presence immediately captured, and then began to hold the attention of the congregation. As his deep, calm voice resonated around the interior of the church, everyone looked up to him; apart from David Bell; who appeared to be praying, as he lowered his head even further and further.

'I knew Billy,' Steven misinformed everyone, 'only for a brief time. But as I recall our friendship, I am reminded of a saying. And it is with Billy in mind that I will quote it for you, for it will always remind me of him, and of the person he was.' Steven then looked towards the coffin, then back to the congregation, and then he quoted from the Terrence Malick film, "The Thin Red Line."

'If I never meet you in this life … *let me feel the lack!*'

As the words resounded around the church, the woman who had previously given her own eulogy, sobbed out loud; whilst her friends on either side, placed comforting arms around her shuddering shoulders. Looking into the mid-distance, Steven paused as if recalling some event, then returning to the present, he stated, 'The Billy that I knew, was a staunch supporter of anything that expressed a love of people, and a love life. Billy, tenaciously fought against the bullies and takers in life.' At that point, some of the mourners looked as if they were trying to place this description of Billy, with the Billy that they had known. Carrying on regardless, Steven stated, 'And it is with that in mind, I am going to ask you to do … donate … something.'

Briefly holding his hand up, Steven continued, 'Not now. Not even tomorrow, unless you wish it of course. But within the time of one year from today.'

Looking over the assembled mourners, Steven asserted, 'Within the next year, *you* will come across some wrong in the world. Some off-putting smell, that is becoming a foul stench. Some act by others or even yourself that will cause you to feel … a lack … in your personal life, or in the world about you.'

Leaning forward, Steven continued, 'When you feel that … lack, I want you to donate some time, some effort and even some pleasure, into ridding your world of that foul odour. Not by spraying it with some sweet-smelling excuse not to act, but by using hard words, hard work, and hard facts.'

Briefly pausing once again, Steven then concluded, 'I am sure that Billy would ask this of you, and perhaps one more thing too, and that is. If you choose *not* to donate to this bequest, as is your personal freedom to do so, then let the world feel the lack.'

As Steven stepped back down again, there was a silence, until the priest thanked Steven for his words, and continued with the funeral ceremonies. Steven and his three companions did not stay for the end of the service, choosing instead to quietly leave the church. As they strolled down the road, Hanna stopped directly in front of Steven, and firmly kissed him on his mouth, and then she held onto his hand, as they both walked on together.

Chapter 25 - Fresh cream and strawberry flan.

Faced with having more to lose than he had ever faced before, Steven began to have some second thoughts about the risk he was taking, by being out and about in public whilst helping Bell with his campaign. Consequently, his pre-planning and preparation for the next placarding the next curch were even more meticulous. However, when it came to his natural inclination to be top dog, his one-up-man-ship tussles with David Bell did not waver.

As the pair, dressed in their second hand bought clothing, are about to exit the car for another placarding, David instructs, 'Ok! This time, we just place the placard on the statue, take the photo shots and leave! If anyone disturbs us, we walk away, and we do not touch them or even speak to them … right!'

'What if it's Jesus?'

'What?'

'What if Jesus happens to walk in, rallying the troops and all that?'

David gives Steven a look of scorn then answers, 'Then you ask him for proof of identity. You know, holes through his hands and feet, or perhaps miracle or two, or failing those, a recent credit card statement with his address on it!'

'Right!' Steven replies, and then adds, 'What about if his disciples show up?'

Again, David gives him a look, 'Use your own judgement, but under no circumstances, must you assault or kidnap them!'

'Right!'

Having laid the ground rules, the pair put on their sunglasses, and then their hats, which they pull forward to hide their faces as much as possible, then they move off in the direction of the chosen church. The church is not out of the ordinary and stands at the far end of the outskirts the small town.

All is going to plan, with Steven standing guard at the main entrance, and filming David's actions from the rear view.

After David hangs the placard over the head of the Mary Mother of Jesus statue; and whilst he is taking the video shots of the placard and statue, he suddenly turns slightly, as he senses an unexpected presence behind him.
'Pop this over her head.' Steven suggests, whilst proffering a dinner-plate sized, strawberry and fresh cream flan.
'No! Where did you get that?'
'It was on a table, just inside the door, with some other food. They must be having some sort of celebration or thanksgiving service or other. It will liven the photo up a bit.'
'No!'
'Why not?'
'Because,' David replies, looking nervously towards the now unguarded main entrance, 'we are trying to educate them, not deliberately insult them.'
'Oh! Like they don't insult us every day by churning out their bullshit?'
'I don't care. I am not doing it!'
'Coward!'
For about five seconds, David neither looks towards the door nor anywhere else, except into Steven's challenging eyes.
Then he shrugs his shoulders; takes the flan from Steven's hands, looks up at the statue, and in one smooth movement he shoves the flan - straight into Steven's face.
'Coward?' David asks, 'So, how many people do you know who would shove a cream cake into the face of a known serial killer?'
Immediately offering Steven a white cotton handkerchief, David says, 'Ok! I'm sorry, I should not have done that. I would have been more sensible to put it in my own face.'
Then looking towards the main and side doors, he adds, 'The entrance has been unguarded for too long, we should really leave.'
Dismissing the offer of the handkerchief, Steven uses the front of his shirt to wipe the residue of the flan from his face.

David, in the meantime, wipes most of the back-splatter from the flan, off his own face, shirt front, trouser legs and shoes. Having cleaned most of the flan from his face, Steven nods his agreement, and then using his gloved hands to pick up the plate and remains of the flan from the ornately tiled floor - he wipes the remainder of flan onto the head of the statue. Then picking up his sunglasses and hat, he finally heads toward the door, followed by David.

As David and Steven begin heading out of the small square in which the church stands, and after he has finished wiping the cream from his ear, David drops his handkerchief into a builder's skip. If Steven had seen him do that - he would have told him to pick it out and take it with him.

Once in the car and away from the immediate area, the two men talk, with David opening the exchange.

'Ok! Once again, just so there is no doubt, I apologise about the flan. I was in the wrong. I apologise.'

To David's surprise, Steven smiles and answers, 'To be honest with you, David, if you had done anything like that, back in the days, I would have killed you.'

'And now?'

'And now, I admire your guts and inventiveness. It was a good move … and it shows that your training is progressing. My guess is, that two weeks ago, you would have been far too nervous to even think of that, let alone do it.'

David Bell had to agree, and not only to keep the peace. 'You are right. And I also guess that it may also be that your training is starting to kick in. I mean training to be a … less harmful sort of psychopath.'

Steven smiles, nods, and then says, 'I get your point. And as it happens, I think that my new-found desire to play practical jokes, particularly on so-called successful establishment figures, is a very worthy replacement therapy for wanting to kill them. In fact, I don't even want to kill anybody. Not successful ones, nor annoying ones, I don't even want to kill *you* anymore!'

Looking at David's face, Steven grins and quickly adds, 'Don't worry, I was just kidding about the last one … I still want to kill you!'
'Thanks' a lot!' David replies, but as he starts the car and drives along, he is thinking, "It will be like a drug addiction. To get a higher fix next time, he will have to make each prank even more outrageous than the last. It will be catastrophic!'
As they drive along Steven's smile returns and breaks into a grin as he proffers, 'Of course, as an alternative, I could combine the two of them, and take up playing *fatal* pranks, on successful people. Hey! Maybe that was what you were trying to tell me with the flan business. That I really can have my cake and eat it!'
The placard they left behind stated:
The Curch of Free Heroes
The 4th Quest: Equality:
The pursuit of equality by a Free-Hero; is achieved by balancing equal ability with equal opportunity; rather than trying to equalise ability.

The 4th Question:

As life is an unattainable, yet increasingly rewarding pursuit toward achieving a moral-paradise upon Earth (or any other planets that we may yet settle upon), why settle for any promise of an exclusive, "We are much holier than thou," ready-made, after-death paradise?

www.curchoffreeheroes.info

Chapter 26 – A time of sadness and the giggles

After the four friends headed and reached, Venice. Venice is one, if not the most splendid of Italy's jewels; embedded upon silt, mud, wooden pylons - and astounding feats of engineering.

During the next three days, the four friends managed to explore a mere fraction of the mesmerising maze of canals, bridges, streets, alleyways, piazzas and intriguing buildings, which made the myriad of Venice.

They did however, manage to visit the covered Rialto Bridge, with its shops on each side; which merely hinted at the history spanning between Venice's great trading empire and the rest of the world. They also managed to visit The Bridge of Sighs; whose enclosed corridors once reputedly echoed with *sighs* of prisoners, as they were transferred between the old and new prisons of the Doge's Palace.

On their second day, as the heat of midday sun baked the stunning, Piazza San Marco, the four friends sipped cooling drinks at a bar, and looked out toward the Basilica and Doge's Palace; whose grand buildings symbolised the religious and civil powers of olden day Venice. Indeed, at its height, the Doge's Palace became the shining zenith of democracy and civilization, encircling the world.

The morning of the third day saw the friends take a canal trip, via a gondola, under some of the many bridges, and past many of the intriguing houses fronts. However, in the afternoon they took a motor launch to the "Isle of the dead." Poveglia, is one of four (out of five) remaining octagonal forts, which the Venetian government built to control the entrances to the lagoons. The island became a quarantine checkpoint for all ships, goods, and people travelling to or from Venice. However, when a plague was discovered on two ships; the plague quickly spread to Venice. The island was sealed off and used to imprison plague victims; prompting the many and macabre tales of grotesquely infected Venetians dying in agony - before returning to haunt the island.

In 1922, the island became home to a mental hospital where a doctor, allegedly, experimented on patients, by using crude lobotomies. He later threw himself from the hospital tower after claiming he had been driven mad by the ghosts.

As with all places of such imprisoned sickness and insanity, Poveglia (and Auschwitz and the like) had a muting effect upon those who visit there; in vastly more safer times.

Rita, summed up her feelings by saying, 'Such horrible deaths to protect the living.'

David pondered on saying some anti-religious statement, but quickly decided better of it.

Steven was briefly (and somewhat regretfully!) taken back to his choices and actions in the Highgate catacomb.

It was, however, Hanna who perhaps best summed up their collective feelings by saying, 'I am glad that I am with good friends in such a place.'

After the afternoon's sobering trip, the four friends seemed to make an extra effort with their respective relationships.

First thing, on the next morning, Steven told his three friends that it would be better, and less embarrassing, for all concerned if he spent the morning alone. He further (and falsely) explained that he occasionally suffered from, Irritable Bowel Syndrome; a recurring stomach upset, which when triggered, necessitated him being within easy reach of a lavatory, at all times. He further assured them, that as the bouts only lasted for three or four hours, and he was positive that he would be able to meet up with them that afternoon or early evening at the latest.

So, after receiving much sympathy, from Hanna in particular, the friends agreed that as soon as he felt more comfortable, he would phone David, and all of them would o meet up later.

Later that afternoon, the four friends were re-united.

However, as soon as Steven was alone with David, he briefly told him, that after recovering very quickly, he had gone to a church, situated in a town, north-west of Venice, to see if it was possibly worth placarding. What is more, he thought that it is worth placarding, however, this time the timing of the raid was to be different.

Later that evening, when the two men are sitting in David Bell's hotel suite, Steven explained the plan more fully, 'Since we have attracted so much news coverage, we can't be sure that a watch on the churches, and any CCTV coverage, isn't being constantly monitored, either by the police or the Italian equivalent of Neighbourhood Watch.'

'So, what are you suggesting?'

'We need to gain access at night, when the church will be locked and empty.'

Hearing this, David Bell looked apprehensive, but Steven pressed on, 'When I was at the church, I saw that there is a CCTV system operating inside, and it covers the outside front, but not the sides or rear.'

'Really, why not?'

'Because the building's outside architecture has too many deep alcoves at the sides and rear for cameras to cover. However, if we go in at night when no one else is there, we can wear hoods or even masks to hide our faces.'

'But, how do we get in, surely that will mean committing burglary and that is definitely a crime?'

'If we steal anything, yes, but we will be leaving something not taking something.' This answer seems to placate David, at least for the moment.

'As for getting in, I've already left a toilet transom window slightly ajar. The full window itself is secured by an inner window latch, which needs a window key to open it. The transom is fairly high up, but from the outside, all it will need is a leg up, and one of us can easily climb through. Of course, if someone has closed the transom in the meantime, then we'll have to abandon the plan. Breaking the window, even quietly, could alert somebody. But if the transom is still ajar, one of us can open it fully and climb through, get into the church, placard the statue of Jesus, video it, then climb out through the transom again. And we'll be well away before

you could say the Lord's Prayer. After that, we wait until we are well clear of the town, then upload everything to our website and the media outlets.'
Holding one hand in the air, Steven pauses then suggests, 'Now I certainly don't mind going in, but as part of your training, I suggest that it is you who goes in.'
Looking at David, Steven paused, then emphasised, 'I've still got the hire car I used to get there and back, parked around the corner. If we left now, we could be back well before dawn.'
At 2am, and despite his worries about committing a crime of burglary, David is getting a leg up from Steven; and climbing through the previously opened transom window.
Eight seconds later, there is a loud clattering and thumping; then ten seconds after that, Steven looks up to see the worried face of David, poking through the open transom window, and urgently whispering, 'The loo door is locked from the outside, I can't get out!'
'Force it open!' Steven insists.
'I can't, it opens inwards. I haven't got anything to force it!'
Without further ado, David starts to climb back out; as he manages to get his shoulders out, he also manages to step on the toilet flushing handle; thereby sending the toilet into a noisy flush mode. Becoming even more desperate, he twists his body so that he can grab hold of the short stub of the overflow outlet pipe, which is sticking out of the outer wall. Grabbing the pipe, he manages to pull himself halfway out - until his grip on the pipe slips; leaving the upper half of his body to jackknife from the knees - so that he is now hanging upside down, out of the transom window.
 Looking at David Bell; hanging upside down, waving his arms about in the night air, like a hysterical bat - immediately sends Steven into fits of hysterical laughter - whilst David just glares at him … just like a demented bat.
Five minutes later, and after both men had almost composed themselves, they are walking down the narrow back streets

and alleyways of the town. In consideration for David's feelings, Steven keeps a few paces behind; whilst making every effort to subdue yet another fit of the giggles.
Turning around and seeing Steven trying to stifle another fit, David Bell demands, 'I suppose that is what you call being a true … *professional*?'
Predictably, this sends Steven off into so much hysterical laughter, that David just gives up, and leaves him to his own amusement.
Just before 5am, the pair of failed burglars go to their respective beds, to catch up on some much needed, sleep.

Chapter 27 - The calling card

The morning following their failed attempt at placarding, David Bell is feeling a bit under the weather. Nevertheless, Steven is eager to gain a success. Having trawled through the various websites, it was Steven who came up with a Church that was only 10 kilometres from where they were staying. However, when Steven showed David the Google map 360-degree, version of the surrounding streets, exterior, and interior of the church, it plainly showed that there were surveillance cameras in operation. So, after watching the video shots for less than a minute, David pointed out, 'But there *are* cameras inside, look you can see, and even you agreed that everyone will be on high alert!'

Steven, on the other hand, was not so easily put off, 'I know about the cameras. But they won't make any difference, for I, my comrade in adversity, have a plan!'

Pin-pointing the view of the church interior, Steven explained, 'All the cameras we can see are overhead, the take shots from above head height, which means that someone can go in, dressed in a hood of some type, without their face being shown.'

'But they will still be able to see what you're doing, and if they see you hanging a placard anywhere, they will have the police there within minutes.'

'Then … we'll just have to work in mysterious ways.' Steven replied, as he got up and made ready to go out.

'What do you mean in *mysterious ways*, there will be no mystery about being caught.'

Turning around and holding his palm forward, Steven ordered, 'Get behind me, Oh Faithless One, for I am going … shopping!'

Just over an hour later, when Steven got back from his shopping, he refused to tell David what he had bought, let alone why. All he would reveal was, 'We, or rather I can be at the church by mid-day. Hanna and Rita have already said they want to sunbathe on the beach. I've checked the weather forecast and it's going to be hot all day. I'll tell them that coming from England so recently, I'm still not used to the Italian sun, so, instead I will go off and look at a couple of exhibitions of modern art. Hanna has already said it's not her favourite art, so I doubt if she will want to miss out on the beach. I'll take the hire car to the town where the church is and leave our calling card. We won't need a full-size poster, but we will need a pithy quote, something that can be written on a calling card. I'll be back well before the three of you have bronzed your sun-soaked torsos. Then we can all have a splendid meal in some splendid restaurant!'

'What are you going to do, leave a card instead of a placard, that's not very … impressive … besides what about all the CCTV cameras?'

'Oh! Them. They're not a problem, in fact, they will be of great service to us. Of course, the cameras will capture me as soon as I walk in, but I'll be well disguised, and I will be gone long before any camera operator can call any police. And before you ask again, I promise that it will be impressive, and there will be no kidnapping or any violence!'

The same afternoon, as Steven had promised, and after phoning David to find their exact position, he arrived at the beach. Whether the obvious joy, particularly from Hanna, at his arrival was even more ecstatic because of the ice-creams that he was carrying, was difficult to tell, yet even David greeted him without any obvious hint of concern.

As soon as the group settled down to soak up what was left of the afternoon sun, which was still hot enough to rapidly melt the ice-creams, Steven stripped down to his boxer shorts style trunks, and then he sat down in between Rita and Hanna.

'My God!' Rita exclaimed, holding her hand to her face, 'You are as white as marble!'

Steven looked down at his body, looked up at the grinning faces of his friends, and quipped, 'Well I have spent the last few years in ...' pausing just long enough to see David's expression flood with worry, Steven concluded, '... England.'

Whether by intuition, humour or coincidence, Rita quipped, 'I thought you were going to say prison,' before adding with a smile, 'You look so terribly pale, even for an English man.' Before either Steven or David could react, Hanna sat up, lunged forwards and passionately kissed Steven on his mouth; when she came up for air, she caressed his chest with her hand and said, 'I think you look like a marble statue of a Roman God!'

Taking Hanna's hand, Steven kissed it twice, smiled ruefully, and warned, 'Didn't you know it can be dangerous to go around kissing Roman Gods? I might turn you into an animal of some sort!'

Hanna kissed him on the mouth again, and then replied just as ruefully, 'I think you already have!' With that said, all four friends settled down to enjoy the Italian sunshine.

By the time the group had reached the restaurant, and ordered their wine and meals, David Bell's curiosity, about the church had tipped into anxiety. Since his return, Steven had not said a word about his absence; though in truth, as they had been in the company of both or at least one of the women, it would have been nigh on impossible to have given even a summary of the events. But now, as Hanna and Rita had gone to the restaurant loo, David wanted to know.

'Ok! They will be in there for ages, you know how long women take in the loo, and they'll be queuing up for at least another five minutes!'

Looking over at Hanna and Rita, who were indeed queuing and chatting with several other women, Steven plucked his shirt away from his chest; apparently the Italian sun had left its trademark on his newly pink chest and legs, then he replied, 'Are you worthy of asking such a request of a Roman God?'

'I'm impatient enough to throw this wine over a Roman God if he doesn't tell me what happened at the church!'

'Ok! Ok!' Steven relented, as he raised his arms in surrender (whilst remembering the strawberry flan incident). Bringing

out his mobile phone, Steven opened several apps' and then
settled on a news channel. David could hear the announcer
reporting on a scandal in the Portuguese banking sector.
Lowering the volume so that it would not be overheard or
annoy the neighbouring dinners, Steven handed the phone to
the cautiously relieved David.
Less than a minute later, David saw the news broadcast about
the church. He saw the interior of the church, as recorded by
one of the CCTV cameras. The scene showed about forty or
so worshipers, most of whom were about to, or were already
kneeling for prayers. Although there were no sound
recordings, in the background the priest could be seen reciting
from a book.
Then gradually, the people at the front of the congregation,
started to look up and around them; and then some of them
started to wave their hands or hymn sheets in front of their
faces, as if they were hot or were shooing away flies. Next,
the people in the rear section followed suit. Then, David
could see that the priest had stopped talking, and that some
people were loudly complaining. Next, he could see that
many of the congregation were getting up and heading
towards the main exit, some of the people were even starting
to panic!
But now it was David's turn to panic, as thoughts rushed
through his mind, ''Had Steven hidden a beehive in the
church? Or even worse, had he planted some sort of
firebomb?'
Looking up at Steven, David asks, 'What did you do?'
Looking around to see that the Hanna and Rita were still not
returning, then glancing at the large, muted, TV screen on the
restaurant's wall, which was also showing a muted but
subtitled news broadcast, Steven leaned forward, and
whispered, '*Stink bombs*!'
'Stink bombs?'
'Stink bombs.' Steven repeated, 'I put four of them under
random kneeling cushions one row from the front. As soon as

anyone knelt on one of the cushion, it would crush the stink bomb and release a … God almighty … stink!'
Keeping his voice down, but no longer whispering, Steven continued, 'There were several people there when I first went in, but I was disguised well enough. Each time I left a stink bomb under a kneeling pad, I went over and lit a prayer candle, then returned to a different pad. I took the chance that no one would go and kneel on them before the priest called them to prayer - and it paid off!'
With that, Steven lent back and took a sip of his mineral water, then lent forwards again. Then still, keeping his voice low, he continued, 'I also phone videoed myself placing the first two stink bombs, to prove it was us, or rather, the Curch of Free-Heroes who left them.'
Pausing to see if the women were still not returning, Steven then gestured to a wall mounted TV screen, which was still showing scenes from the church. David could also see the screen was showing the security CCTV recorded scenes of the havoc inside the church.
Looking at the wall TV, and the rolling Italian language subtitles, David found that he was watching a reporter standing outside of the church. The reporter was relaying that, "This outrage had been executed by the infamous anti-God group, the Curch of Free Heroes."
'We are not anti-God … we are anti-religion,' David whispered, as he watched the TV view zoom in as it showed a close-up of the stained underside of one of the contaminated kneeling cushions. The camera shot then panned out, and zoomed in, to reveal a hand holding a small business style calling card; whilst the reporter's solemn muted voice reported, "This is the calling card that the perpetrators left under each booby-trapped cushion."
The camera shot then zoomed in further to show the five-star logo, and the printed website address of the Curch of Free-Heroes. The camera shot then showed the card being turned over to reveal the message on the back, which simply stated:

'Something smells rotten in the state of religion!'
Handing David an unused calling card, Steven told him, 'It's
not one of our prepared quotes ... but it's pretty good, and it's
apt for the situation. As soon as you get the chance you can
upload image of this calling card, and the Fifth Quest onto the
website. And you can emphasise the fact that we are anti-
religious, and not anti-God as such. Unless that is, you want
to give me the password for the web site's supervising
access?'
At that moment, David looked across the restaurant and
casually pocketed the card as he saw that Rita was returning.
Looking at Steven, he replied, 'Saved by the returning Rita, I
think.'

Chapter 28 - Discovered

In the dwindling, but humid remains of the day's heat, and as
the four friends walk back to their hotel; David removes his
jacket, folds it over his arm, and fans his face with a brochure
advertising a local theatre venue. Just then Rita, who is
walking several paces behind with Hanna, calls out.

'Wait Darling, you've dropped this!'

Turning around, David, to his horror, sees that she is holding,
and now reading the calling card that Steven had passed to
him in the restaurant; and he had slipped into the top pocket
of his jacket when he had seen Rita returning from the lady's
loo.

Still holding the card, Rita looks at David; who already feels
his face blushing. Then she looks back to the card; turns it
over and reads the quote - which only an hour before had
been solemnly read out by the TV reporter on the restaurant's
muted and subtitled TV screen - and which had been seen and
commented on, by Hanna and Rita.

Looking at David, Rita asks, *'Something smells rotten in the
state of religion,* David?'

When David holds out his hand to receive the card, Rita
instead hands it to Hanna; who in turn reads both sides, opens
her mouth as if to speak, but says nothing; looks at Rita, then
at David and Steven, and then hands the card back to Rita,
who takes the card, holds it lightly between her forefinger and
thumb and states to David and Steven, 'I think we need to talk
about this!'

'Yes … of course we …' David starts to reply, whilst
feverishly hoping that Steven would come up with some sort
of innocent explanation.

'Oh! Of course, for sure!' Rita interrupts, 'for sure, and of
course we all need to talk … but when I said …we … I meant
Hanna and I.'

Glancing back to Steven, who seems calm but says nothing,
David replies, 'Of course.'

Fifteen minutes later, Rita and Hanna return from their walk and talk, and then they sit down in front of David and Steven, who are already sitting at one of the outside tables of a coffee shop. The brief conversation between the waiting men had been tense and had ended with Steven insisting that 'We will wait and see what they say. But I suggest that you let me do the initial talking for us.'
As soon as Rita and Hanna sit down, Rita leans forward and addressing David, she asks, 'How did you come by the Curch of Free Heroes' calling card, only hours after the TV news has said that one had been left in the church, where a load of stinky bombs had been put under the kneeling mats?'
When David turns to Steven, all eyes turn to him. Before answering, Steven, looks at Hanna for some moments, without answering; until he decides that the best policy is honesty.
'It started out as a gesture against religion, something that might make them at least think about their responsibilities. Then, unfortunatcly, things went beyond our intentions, at the Mosque, and the responsibility is with us, to either give up and turn tail, in the face of religious power, or stand our ground.'
Looking to Hanna, Rita says nothing but looks at David, and after smiling at Rita; Hanna then looks back to Steven, as she explains, 'I have been a Catholic since I can remember. But since meeting the two of you, I have doubts, *serious* doubts!'
Addressing David, Hanna adds, 'Don't worry David, you have not been the main cause. My private doubts have been rising for some years now. I used to see the church as the guardians of good, but now I too, see them as imposters of goodness, running, as you say, their protection rackets. Like, as you say, a pack of gangsters, in shepherds' clothing.'
Then, turning to face a surprised Steven, Hanna continues, 'But above all, I too see the greedy insolence, of their promises of a paradise after death.' Looking straight ahead,

Hanna concludes, 'It is here in this life that we must, at least try to build Paradise!'

Nevertheless, turning back to Steven, who now looks more shocked than surprised, Hanna almost pleads, 'But this Free Heroes affair is *very* dangerous … and *that* is my main worry.' Taking hold of Steven's hands, she pleads, 'I would be *crushed* if anything happened to you.' Then looking at all three of her companions, she adds, 'But I will be loyal to you all.'

After thinking for about a moment, David warns, 'Your loyalty to the church will try to pull you back.'

Hanna's reply surprises not only the two men, but its intensity even takes Rita aback, 'I do not mistrust my sense of loyalty, David. I mistrust the church … *for abusing it.*'

In the silence of the following moment, a waiter comes to the table to see if the women wanted to order anything, and when Rita and Hanna politely indicate they wanted nothing, he politely thanks them and goes about his duties elsewhere.

After a short pause, David says, 'I am sorry to you both!' Then looking straight at Hanna, he qualifies, 'Not for my views on religion, but for placing both of you in this position.' Turning directly to Rita, he asks, 'But what about you Rita, you haven't said anything about your views yet?' Smiling broadly and placing her hand on David's arm, Rita answers, 'My affections for you, my darling, have little to do with my wish to help your cause. I became a recruit in waiting, long before you even thought of placing your first recruitment poster.'

Rita then addresses both men. 'And *now,* we can discuss how we can help. For a start, Hanna and I can help in the field and off. We presume you started with ten posters in all. Which leaves five, to deal with, presuming of course, you are going to post the fifth one on the web site?'

'We haven't had the chance yet.' David replies.

'We know, we checked before we came back to you.' Hanna states.

'We can be lookouts.' Hanna put forward. 'You may be right David, and I think for a while it is best that I do not go into the churches.' In answer to David's cocked head and raised eyebrows, Hanna continues, 'It is unwise for an ex-lover to go straight into her ex-lover's arms at their first reunion. I will be a soldier behind the front line, until I get my ... place ... better.'

Lifting her head, Rita continues, 'Women favour resolving differences by using co-operation instead of conflict. This is natural feminine quality, which the church and politics twist and turns against us. But these same qualities can be our joint strengths as well as our vulnerable points. We can use them to pull together, as your famous English boating song says. We can pull together our strengths, such as our love of sharing, including sharing our feelings and hopes.'

 'And we love to gossip!' Hanna announces with glee, and then adds, 'We can use that online, to spread the word about the aims of Free Heroes.'

Having finished their rally, the two women sat back and look at the two men, who in turn look at each other, with bemused astonishment, before Steven says, 'And so it happens!'

For the next few minutes, Steven and David are like two spectators watching a friendly game of tennis. Rita opens the play by stating, rather than suggesting, 'We can help spread and coordinate any growing interest of the social media outlets.'

'We can also put a woman's point of looking at the whole thing,' Hanna adds.

Rita then adds, with heightened passion, 'Women have been pushed down, silenced or at best have been patronised by every religion that I have ever heard of. We have been using sex to gain love, for millennia, just as men have been using love to gain sex. It's served as the mainstay bartering system between the two of them for millennia. It is *also* why the religions are so authoritarian about sex.'

'Why?' Steven askes.

'Because they want to be known as the mainstay suppliers of love. The trouble is, that religion has and is run by people who have been using love, to gain power and authority, as well as sex, for millennia.'

At that point, David Bell umpires, 'Do you know the majority of modern day converts to religion are female?'

'Yes,' Rita answers with a smile, 'I Googled it some time ago,' but as her smile disappears she continues, 'all the better motive to speak with those women.'

Then leaning forward Rita looks at David and Steven and serves what would be her winning ace, 'To slightly misquote your famous William Shakespeare.

'It is time to let loose the ... bitches of war!'

As a way of accepting and cementing their new alliance, David tells his fellow campaigners, the Supervisor's password; so that any of them could upload content directly onto the website. The only exception was that no one, but he, could authorise the uploading of a Quest of the Free-Heroes, for that access, he would keep a separate password to himself.

 Looking to Hanna, Rita, and Steven, David holds up his hands, and says, 'Ok! So, if we are as one, then we must all be aiming for the same goals.'

''How so?' Hanna asks enthusiastically.

'Well, the first thing we need to take on board, that the pursuit of justice always a three-legged race that is much easier won, when it's run side by side, instead of face to face.'

'Ok! I can get that, but how do we use that?' Rita asks.

'Well, we need to combine, the best of humanistic ways and needs, alongside the best of religious ways and needs, which although we hope will eventually become non-religious, they must be rewarding by in and by themselves.'

'Such as?'

'To begin with, we need to provide a Humanistic figurehead.'

'How so?'

'Take the spiritual logos, of Christ on the cross, the Muslim crescent moon or the multi deities of Hinduism, which act as figureheads for their followers. We need to provide a universal, humanistic figurehead, to symbolise our overall aims.'

'How so?'

'As with the multi deities of Hinduism, we can also have a series of symbolic figureheads of the pursuits of the humanities, such as justice, peace, education, the sciences, and so on, but I think …'

'And Love, we must have a figurehead of love!' Hanna enthusiastically demands.

'And Love. So, what would the humanistic figurehead of Love be, Hanna?'

Whilst Hanna ponders, Rita suggests 'A combined heart and brain.'

'Or a combined a vagina and penis?' Hanna suggests with a mischievous grin.

'Tricky choice!' Steven comments, with a smile.

'Perhaps,' David continues, 'for the main logo, it might be appropriate to keep the five, four-point stars, or bird shapes, in the pattern of a phalanx. It's what I've been using on the placards so far.'

'How so is a phalanx?' Hanna asks.

'It's the shape that geese fly in,' Steven explains, using his hands to demonstrate. Turning to David, he asks, 'Why appropriate?'

'Because it can represent the famous poem about stealing the goose.'

At that point, Steven looks at Hanna and quotes, '*The law locks up the man or woman, who steals the goose off from the common, but leaves the greater villain loose, who steals the common from off the goose.*'

After a quickly laying her hand on Steven's arm Hanna replies, 'Yes I know this poem. I like this poem very much,' then turning to David she asks, 'Why so that poem?'

'Because the religions continually try and indeed succeeed, in stealing our common-sense-goodess, so they can claim it as their property.'
When Hanna and Rita nod their approval, David carries on, 'Next, we need to provide rituals. Spiritual based rituals have so far have been almost, exclusively the domain of religion. Yet most people like having regular rituals. Confucius realised, that regular, positive rituals provide that needed emotional traction, to pull positive concepts, such as loyalty, respect, and love, along, so that they can become a regular practice for us. It is the ritual that transforms or pulls the body, mind, and heart along, not just the so-called godhead to which they are focused upon.'
'So how do *we* provide that?' Steven asked.
'In short, we have to provide a personalised, ritualualistic way of motivating a person to give a regular daily or weekly commitment in time and effort to their chosen humanistic pursuit.
'Such as?'
'Like the the various saints you see in stained glass windows, we have to provide a set of humanistic, figureheads, or Secular Spirits, so people can personailse what they choose to commit themselvs to. It could be a symbol of education, law and order, human relationships, a branch of the sciences, or whatever he or she believes will simultaneously better them self, and humankind. Over a week, year, or lifetime, such commitment can be a profound support to a sense of self-worth and community belonging.'
 'Next, we need our own Bible or Quran.'
'A Bible?'
'Yes. We need, the Book of Free-Heroes. An on-line book of proven moral guidelines, not just parables, but verifiable, true stories about real people who have in some small or large way, sanctified the principles of Human goodness.'
Suddenly, Hanna announces, *'I'm sorry, but I need the loo!'*
However, as she got up and went to leave, she turns to David,

she asks, 'In your first placard, it says that a Curch is a place for the Secular Spirit. How so Secular Spirit?'

'Have you heard of the Magna Carta, Hanna?'

'Yes, we were taught it at school. It came from England, it said that even if he is a king or a beggar, no man is above the law of the land.'

'That's right, and it has been used as the moral foundation for trying to build fair and just societies around the world ever since. However, did you also know that within ten days of the Magna Carter being ratified, the Pope in Rome issued what is known as the Papal Bull. A Papal ruling, in which he declared the Magna Carta to be null and void … for all time?'

'No, I don't think so, if we were then I can't remember. But why would the Pope do such a thing?'

'Because, the Magna Carter made, or at least attempted to make, *all* people *equal,* under the law of the land. But religious leaders, monarchies, dictators and their organizations, shy away from seeing themselves as the moral equals of the very people who they are supposed to be serving.'

Shrugging his shoulders, David concludes, 'The Magna Carter contains the *secular spirit* of pursuing a fair and just way of life, Hanna.'

For a moment, Hanna grows thoughtful, and then she states, 'Maybe, I didn't forget that they didn't tell us about banning it, maybe they didn't want to tell us.' With that, she disappears into the bathroom.

Within two days of the two becoming four, Hanna's and Rita's anonymous social network sharing, and "gossiping" began to have a self-propelling effect upon the overall interest of the Curch of Free Heroes' website – rather than just the headline exploits of the placarding. Then suddenly the principles of the Quests began to go viral.

Although the spread had started on websites predominantly aimed for women, it soon became apparent that it was not exclusively so. Social posts, activating debates, heated arguments, outright accusations of blasphemy, and moral education abounded. The flavours of people's comments ranged from candy sweetness, to sour grape bitterness, and even outrights threats to life.

Reading out one the favourable posts, Hanna quoted, *"Just because you have been cruelly crucified for being the son of God, doesn't mean that you are the son of God!"*

'I like that one,' Steven commented.

Scrolling down further, Hanna said, 'There's one from someone called DMKYO. *Religion gives the cowardly mind a false bravery, so that it can condone what the courageous mind refuses to do to the cowardly.*'

'That's very good and very true too,' Rita said, 'Anymore?'

'Here's one, named, Way to go.'

Leaning forward, Rita said, 'Go on.'

'All religious prophets and leaders insist that their God needs interpreters, because people are too stupid to understand him, too corruptible to obey him, and too suspicious to trust him. Way to go with praising your God's genius for creation, religion.'

'Way to go!' Steven echoed.

'Here's one. It's called, a slight of religion ....'

'Go on,' Steven encouraged.

'Magic and religion are not the same things. Magic is about the illusion of power created through slights of hand and mind. Religion is about the illusion of power created through slights of mind and morals.

Here's another one, Hanna continued, *'To some people, Paradise is about having a full stomach, empty hands, and a grateful mind. To others, Paradise is a about million miles away. To the religious, Paradise is just around the corner from death.'*

Looking up at her companions, Hanna added, there are requests for people to have sit-ins protests too.'

'Really.' David, commented.

Looking down the posts Hanna exclaimed, *'There's lots more!* Here's another one.'

'Go on,' Rita enthused, 'Read it out!'

'Religion, who needs it, apart from the religious?'

'Simple and to the point,' David Bell commented; then briefly gazing into the distance, he proffered, 'They are all great, the posts, I mean. But I must admit, I also like the classic one from Epicurus, the third century BC thinker, who is reputed to have asked.

Is God willing to prevent evil, but not able? Then he is not omnipotent. Is he able, but not willing? Then he is malevolent. Is he both able and willing? Then whence cometh evil? Is he neither able nor willing? Then why call him God?'

Giving everyone a satisfied smile, Rita said, 'Mmmmm! I like that one a lot.'

Turning to Hanna, Rita asked, 'Are there anymore from, Way to go?'

Scrolling down the posts, Hanna answered, 'There are so many, and I need to rest my feet, I'll go into our rooms and see.' Placing his arm around Hanna, Steven said, 'I'll come with you.'

However, just over twenty minutes later, David and Rita are lazing on their bed; when there is a rapid triple-knock on the door and then Hanna burst in, followed by Steven. Holding up her tablet, Hanna announces, 'Somebody has started a crowd funding project to buy *Curches!'*

'What?' David asks.

Quickly handing her tablet over to him, Hanna explains to Rita, 'They want to buy up property, and buildings and even disused churches, and turn them into *Curches.* They even give the same description of a Curch as we do, you know, a haven. There are two lawyers, and there are others. They have already started the fund with a hundred and eighty thousand dollars, and it has already climbed over to nearly three hundred thousand!'

Within two minutes the four companions are huddled around Hanna's tablet; whilst David Bell reads out the information and gives his reactions, 'It looks a genuine group sure enough. They intend to run the Curch pretty much as the guidelines that we set up on the Free Heroes website.'

Looking at the other three, Steven suggests, 'It's going to get very interesting if they start a real Curch, in a real building, especially if it is in an ex-church they've bought up.'

'I guess we'll have to wait and see, but a real Curch!' Rita exclaims with a wide grin, and then adds, 'But you're right, it will be *very* interesting to see how other people will react.'

'I shall give some of my money to it!' Hanna announces with conviction, 'I don't have lots, but I shall give some.'

Leaning over and kissing Hanna, Steven suggests, 'If we want to, we can all send some together.'

Turning to Steven and Hanna, David warns, 'You're right of course, you're both right, but we must make sure we send it anonymously. It would be a shame if our generosity led to our capture and imprisonment.'

As soon as the words "capture and imprisonment," was mentioned, Hanna's smile quickly fades. However, it is Rita who expresses her view, 'Way to go with a spoiler alert, my darling, especially with one that we already knew might happen.'

Looking at his friends and holding up his hands, David says, 'Sorry! I was trying to be cautious, not pessimistic.'

'Pessimistic? What is this?' Hanna asks.

'*Boringly dull!*' Steven quips, without the slightest hint of any humour.

'But we haven't done anything really *bad*.' Hanna replies, then adds, 'Although I did not like it when the statue of Mary was left with the cake on her.'

'You're right, and that was a mistake that won't be repeated.' David states to no one in particular, and then rising from the bed; he walks to the window, looks out to the distant horizon, turns back around, and facing the others and says, 'But it won't be our view of things, that will be taken into account if we are caught. There is also the matter of the Muslim Cleric. Even though the two of you had nothing to do with that, you might be blamed too. There are people out there who would go to extreme lengths if they knew you were involved with us.'

'But we both knew about placarding the Cleric before we decided to join the campaign, and we also knew about extremist,' Rita asserts, as Hanna nods her head in total agreement and says, 'We talked about it a great much before we told you about wanting to become … Free Heroes!'

As soon as the words "Free Heroes" is spoken, both David and Steven hang their heads, and then raise them again in a mixture of concern and admiration.

Looking to David, Hanna asks, 'Wasn't it you, who once told me, David, that the most precious thing any human being has, is the freedom to deliberately choose to do bad or good. Is it not possible to choose both, at the same time?'

After a moment of thought, David answers, 'Yes, I suppose it is.'

'Then I choose to try and be a Free Hero, even if bad things happen to me.'

Looking at each other, two men exchange looks of thoughtfulness, until Steven says, 'I think that if we don't agree with these two, my friend, then it will be us who should be left behind … for the pigeons to *swoop* up.'

Two hours later, the four companions drive through the outskirts of a small village, and the mood in the car is pensive. As they pass by an animal rescue center, it is feeding time, and the air is full, with the baying of the hounds.

When David Bell posted, the 5th Quest, it stated:

The Curch of Free Heroes
The 5th Quest: Honesty
A Free-Hero's Quest for freedom through honesty; is progressed by accepting that honesty with oneself, and with others, is a friend and not something to be overly feared. However, just as a friend's grip may hurt as it prevents you from falling, or a medical sticky plaster may hurt when it is removed; honesty can also hurt - after dishonesty has already caused the harm and damage in the first place.

Nevertheless, honesty can also prevent falls (from grace) and damage (to friendships) from happening in the first place.

The 5th Question:
If it is impossible to prove that a claim is true, how honest is it to promise that it is ultimate truth?

www.thecurchoffreeheroes.info

Chapter 29 - The 2nd Synods

When Cardinal Tivo, the leader of the Roman Catholic Synod, addressed the fellow members, he spoke with an air of authority that had come from a lifetime of studying human nature, and he spoke in an optimistic tone.

'An astute detective, working the attack in which a strawberry flan was used to desecrate the statue of Mary the Mother of Jesus, spotted a white cotton handkerchief near the scene of the crime. He noticed what appeared to be dried strawberry and dried cream on the handkerchief. Putting two and two together, he sent the handkerchief for a forensic analysis. It came back with a positive human DNA reading. A further search has revealed a match.'

Pausing to look at the assembled company, the Cardinal continued, 'The man is called David Bell. He is an English man and has a criminal record for heroin distribution. His DNA was matched from the criminal records data base, in England.'

'A drugs trafficker!' Cardinal Lupo exclaimed.

Holding up his hand, Cardinal Tivo, continued, 'In fact things are not quite as they may seem. It appears from a summary of events, that there were no indications that he was a common drugs dealer, and in all probability, he was not motivated by personal financial gain.'

'*What*?' Cardinal Lupo asked, with some incredibility.

'His motives were to try and bring down a drug baron who was responsible for the death of his daughter. He was also apparently trying to promote the concept of legalising heroin, in an effort to change the procedures on the war on drugs.'

Leaning forward, Cardinal Tivo emphasized, 'He was sent to prison, but since his release from prison, he has built a high reputation in the world of crime prevention. He is the founder of an organisation called Crimetest.'

Throwing his hands in the air, Cardinal Lupo interjected, 'Those people! They are the people behind the attempt to start a … phone in … for criminals, if you please!'

'True.'
'And is also the leader of this Curch business?'
'Let us just say that, for the present, that is a possibility.'
'But if he hasn't already fled, then he must still be in Italy. Do we know where he is, can we have him arrested or at least have him questioned?' Bishop Abategiovanni asked with some urgency.
'As yet, his whereabouts are unknown. However, even if he is discovered, arresting him may not be the wisest course of action to undertake.'
Taking a moment to bring some hard copies of David Bell's file, up onto the long table, the Cardinal gave them to be passed amongst those present, then he addressed the conclave.
'On the advice of our legal department, such a step would be presumptuous. Just because someone was near or even at the church around the time of the crime, does not mean that he committed the crime. He could easily say, that when he saw the desecrated statue, he tried to wipe the desecration away, but fearing that he might be discovered and then blamed as the perpetrator, he departed, dropping the handkerchief.'
Looking at the disappointment, and the defiance, around the room, the Cardinal then warned, 'This man has many powerful allies from his work in crime prevention. Those allies are made up powerful individuals and institutional supporters. To arrest him, would not only lead to that support possibly turning on us, but also, it would give further unwanted influential publicity to this, Curch of Heroes cause!'
'Free Heroes,' Monsignor Galvin corrected.
'Pardon?'
'Free Heroes. They call themselves the Curch of Free Heroes,'
Bowing to the Monsignor, Cardinal Tivo replied, 'Your knowledge is, as always, welcome Monsignor Galvin. However, as was in the assault on the Muslim Cleric, it is unlikely that these outrages are the actions of one person

alone. It is open to mistakes by other members of this, Curch of … Free … Heroes. As a result, of that possibility, then they may be not so free, for much longer. Therefore, I agree with the senior investigating officers in this case, that when Mr Bell is located, a twenty-four hour a day watch will be placed on him, and any of his associates that he is with. Other than that, we wait, keep things confidential for the time being, and hope for any further developments.'

Holding up one hand, Bishop Abategiovanni asked, 'On the matter of confidentiality. Will it not seem … inconsiderate, if we do not let our Muslim counterparts know of this development? After all, one of their brethren has been seriously assaulted'

For a moment Cardinal Tivo, bowed his head as he pondered the matter; however, before he answered, Monsignor Galvin looked at the bishop and almost accused, 'And what possible action could the Muslims take, that we, or the police and courts, could … or would not … take?'

'I was merely asking for clarification.' Bishop Abategiovanni replied.

At that moment, Cardinal Tivo gave his opinion, 'For the moment we will keep everything as it stands.'

The 2nd Muslim synod

Three hours later, the Muslim equivalent of the Roman Catholic Synod, had also gained the same incriminating information about David Bell. They had also reached the same conclusions as the Roman Catholic synod had reached; that there was not enough hard evidence to prove that David Bell was directly involved in the vandalism of the churches. Nevertheless, in the matter of the assault of the Cleric, there was more promising leads, in no other than the Cleric himself.

 Addressing the committee, the leader pronounced, 'He has been shown a passport photograph of Mr. Bell, and although he cannot definitely say it is the same man who was present during the assault, he has said that it may be.'

'Doesn't he know?' Cleric Saad Akbar, whose call for a death fatwa had been previously rejected, asked with obvious disbelief, 'How many blasphemers assault him each week?'
'He has suffered a serious assault, with a very strong sedative that can confuse the short-term and medium-term memory of anyone, Cleric Akbar. The man he spoke to wore sunglasses and was in front of the wall lighting, which made it difficult to make out his features clearly. Do you seriously think that he would not positively identify this Bell as one of the assailants if he could?'
'Can't we hypnotize him? Witness have been hypnotized and remembered things that even astound themselves.'
'Such things have already been considered by others than yourself, Cleric Akbar. However, without further evidence, such an identification would not stand up in a court of law.'
Turning to the rest of the committee, the leader concluded, 'Accordingly, I am recommending that we wait and see what the police developed from further investigations, and what our dear friend who was assaulted may remember. Allah, permitting, praise be his name.'
When the majority of the committee gave their approval to the recommendation, Cleric Saad Akbar, once again stormed out of the meeting; but this time he was followed by a committee member called Faeq Mansur, who told the committee that he would try to calm the distraught Cleric.
Halfway down the stairs, Saad Akbar was called back by Faeq Mansur, who confided, 'In your understandable outrage, you left your copy of the file on this David Bell. Meet me at the Café Rialto in the piazza, in front of the public library, in one hour. I have some thoughts about how to deal with the outrage!' Then grabbing Akbar by his arm, Mansur added, 'What I tell, must be held in total confidence, Allah be willing! Do you agree?'
Placing his hand on top of Mansur's, Saad Akbar replied, 'May Allah, praise you for possessing more wisdom and

courage than that spineless committee possess between them all!'

At their meeting, Mansur handed over to the file about David Bell, to Saad Akbar. Two hours after he left the meeting at the Café Rialto, Saad Akbar contacted a man called Lateef Kamel, who had long been a part of an extremist branch of the Muslim religion; and who views would have certainly been rejected by most mainline Muslims. After reading through the file, Lateef Kamel asked, 'If I find this man what should I do with him, Allah be willing?'

'The committee has suggested that we leave matters in the hands of police, as and *if* the law allows. They have even ruled that he is no longer under the threat of a death fatwa.' Lateef Kamel made a spitting motion and said, 'They are as weak as women! In my heart, I know that this piece of scum deserves death, and the everlasting turmoil of what will surely follow, Allah be willing. I would behead this blasphemous scum as soon as I found him! Allah be willing.'

Saad Akbar smiled and touched his companion's arm, 'If Allah bids that you receive guidance on where to find this infidel, then you will surely find him.'

'And then?'

'And then ... you must follow what Allah puts into your heart … and hand.' With that agreed, their meeting ended.

As the four companions arrived at a part fishing, part holiday, coastal resort, it was early evening. They booked into a hotel and then went for a meal in a nearby seafood restaurant on the seafront. After the meal, when David Bell went to pay the bill, he brought out his wallet out, and realized that he brought his own personal wallet out with him; instead of the one that he exclusively used for the business of the placarding campaign. Realizing that the other wallet; with a ready amount of high and small denomination cash in it, was back at the hotel, and thinking that the meal had no connection to the business of placarding the churches; David duly paid the

due amount, on his personal debit card, then he put the card back into his wallet and caught up with his friends.
A little over two hours later, and one hundred kilometers away, one of the investigating police officers charged with trying to trace David Bell's current whereabouts, received the information that David Bell's debit card had been used, in Italy, within the last two hours.

Chapter 30 - The 1st followers
The following morning, the friends left their hotel and took a leisurely wander through the town, and then into town's lively marketplace. Surrounding the various market stalls selling a bewildering array of goods, a maze of narrow streets and even narrower thoroughfares ran in all directions. There were also many shops selling just about everything a tourist could desire, from child affordable souvenirs, to foolishly expensive antiques.

As the dominant male, Steven almost unconsciously took on the role of the main protector of his three companions; though as a dominant female, Rita, would have at least disputed his role in leading the group. However, Rita did not possess Steven's long acquired antennae for trouble, which was already unconsciously and automatically sweeping the environment for any anomalies.

The two anomalies that Steven had spotted, had been following him and his three companions, since they had entered the market. Onc man wore a brown hat and casual jacket, both of which he took off, then put back on every few minutes. The other man wore a flat cap and replaced the brown hatted man every five or so minutes.

Casually checking that none of his companions appeared to have noticed either man, Steven told his friends that he wanted to go back to a shop; after which he would phone Rita and find out where to catch up with them. He then dropped back and dawdled inside a souvenir shop, from where he watched the flat hatted man follow the friends across a short bridge, whilst "Mr Brown Hat," also follwed on, whilst talking into a mobile phone.

Although nothing could be proven, yet, Steven strongly sensed that the men acted and "smelled" of police. Three minutes later, he phoned David and asked him and the women to meet at the shop near the entrance to the shopping centre, where Hanna had bought some writing paper, he then switched his phone off.

After a minor rebellion from Rita, the three
companions started to retrace their route - as did the
followers. When the three companions arrived at the shop,
Steven is waiting outside in a taxi. Hustling his companions
in, he told the taxi driver to drive to the railway station. As
Steven looked out of the rear window, he saw Mr Brown Hat;
urgently talking into his mobile, and then raising his arms in
the air in a gesture of exasperation as the taxi disappeared out
of his sight.
However, what Steven did not see, was another man, dressed
a long gown like cloak; come out of the crowd, go straight to
and mount a moped, and then start after the taxi.
In the taxi, Steven chose not to immediately, mention
anything about the detectives; for either David, Hanna or Rita
would probably want to call the whole campaign off - and on
this last point, Steven found to his surprise and excitement,
that he was very reluctant to even consider calling the
campaign off. Instead, he said he would explain everything
once they were out of the taxi and had a chance to talk.

Chapter 31 - The fanatic

As soon as the taxi left them at the railway station, and had driven away, Steven hailed another taxi, and pleaded with his three confused and by now irritated companions, to get in and he would explain what was happening. During the ride, Steven finally told his friends about the police tail, in the souvenir market.

When they arrived at the part of the town that was mainly used for a small but thriving fishing trade, Steven paid the taxi off, and suggested to his companions that they all should find a café where they could talk, without being overheard, and work out what to do next. When everyone agreed they set off along the beach front shops to find a suitable café.

In his past, Steven had been an observant man; for to be otherwise would have probably put him in prison long before he ended up there. But now, he is constantly on the alert, and he is more than alert enough to spot the Arabic looking man; who had dismounted a moped only fifteen seconds after the group had got out of the taxi, and who has been following the group for the last few minutes, and, Steven presumes, probably since the group had left the market.

Although there is no sign of Mr. Brown Hat, or any police, Steven seriously doubts that this latest follower could be another plain clothes detective. The man is wearing a dark, kaftan style robe, and had been ducking in and out of shop doorways, turning around without any apparent normal reason, and would lower his sunglasses whenever he wanted to catch sight of Steven and his friends again. In fact, Steven is surprised that none of his companions had spotted the idiot. As far as he knows, he is the only one with any knowledge that they are once again being followed. However, sooner or later one of his friends would see the obvious amateur, and if that happened, then anything could occur.

Speaking to his three companions in a casual tone, he informs them, 'Don't all turn around at once, but we are being followed again, and this time, I don't think it is by the police.'

After Steven's quick description of the man, David, Rita and Hanna take it in turns to casually look around.

'I see him! Hanna whispers, 'Who is he?'

'I don't know,' Steven replies, 'but I don't think he can hear you from here, so just speak normally.'

Addressing no one in particular Rita asks, 'He's obviously a Muslim, do you think he has anything to do with the attack on the Cleric. Maybe a private detective or somebody?'

'This is getting very scary!' Hanna whispers.

Taking Hanna's arm and giving it a gentle squeeze, Steven replies, 'OK! There's only one way to find out …'

'How?' David asks.

'By asking him.' Steven states, then adds, 'There's a café about a hundred fifty yards ahead, over the road, with the blue tablecloths. I will see you there in a few minutes. In about three seconds I'm going for a wander on my own.'

With that done and said, he gives Hanna a kiss, and peels off from the group before anyone could stop him. As he turns around and walks a few paces, he stops, turns back to Hanna and half shouts, 'I'll meet you back at the hotel.' He then turns again, and walks straight past the man, who seems to be suddenly engrossed in a shop window displaying fishing equipment.

Two minutes later, Steven is watching the man, Lateef Kamel, watching Hanna, Rita and David Bell, as they take their seats at the café. The man is now pretending to study several racks of postcards and trivia standing outside a small grocery type shop.

Bringing out his phone, Steven takes several zoom photo shots of the man, and walks up him. He then blatantly takes a full facial photo of him; presses and swipes the phone screen as if he is scrolling through and bringing up several apps. He then tells the astonished man, *'You can start to follow me now … or your image goes straight to the police!'*

Immediately putting on an innocent expression, Lateef
Kamel, protests. 'I don't know what you are talking about!
Why did you take my photograph?'
As Steven smiles, he is relieved that the man had understood
what had been said, so, raising his phone, he answers, 'Taking
the photo is a neat trick I learned it from a good teacher.' For
a split second, he remembers Sandra Lott's face, then he
instantly returns his full attention to Kamel, adding, 'I also
have video evidence, of you following me and my friends.'
Seeing Hanna rise out of her chair, as if she is about to come
over them, Steven does not give his opponent too much time
to think, 'You, and I, will walk down to beach there, and you
can tell me who you are and why you are following us.' Then
gently waving the phone in the air, he adds, 'It's the beach or
it's the police! And personally, I don't care two fucks which it
is. In fact … *fuck it …!*' Steven then looks around, as if
looking the police.
'*No! Wait!* Kamel, who is now clearly worried, pleads, 'I will
come, I will explain.'
As the two of them head toward the beach, Steven waves
Hanna back, and is relieved that she sits down again.
A few minutes later the two men reach the beach. Steven
gestures to Kamel to go down to a line of beached fishing
boats, then pointing in between two fishing boats, he orders,
'In there!' As soon as they are hidden from view Steven
demands, 'Now, why the fuck, are you following us?'
Taking three short steps back, Kamel swiftly draws out a
revolver, cocks it, aims it at Steven, and snarls, '*You are a
fool!* You should have called the police when you had the
chance, now you will pay for your foolishness!'
As Steven slowly raises his arms to waist height, in apparent
surrender, Kamel tells him, 'If you had not interfered with the
work of a servant of Allah, may his name be praised, you
would have been spared. I meant *you* no harm or the two
women. It is the infidel David Bell, who has defiled the name

of Islam, by assaulting one of his trusted servants! He has a fatwa on his head and soul.'

Moving swiftly, Lateef Kamel reaches inside his coat and brining out a short sword, which even from a few metres away, Steven sees is honed to razor sharpness. Raising the sword to shoulder height, Kamel proudly proclaims, 'This will be the instrument that will send the infidel into the everlasting torment of Hell.'

Keeping a calm exterior that belies his inner fear, Steven calmly asks, 'Who has ordered you to do this? The Muslim leaders have denounced any fatwa. You are just a pawn, a plaything of a … *nobody!*'

Raising his stance to one of pride, Lateef Kamel replies, 'Not all of the grand council are weak as those whose cowardly hearts misinterpret the will of Allah, blessed be his name, into their own cowardly desires.'

Regarding the man before him, Steven notices that the both the gun and the man's hand are trembling. Nevertheless, from his own time as the Body Part Murderer, Steven also knows that a shaking hand does not necessarily mean a lack of resolve, indeed sometimes it means the opposite. However, Steven also had other experiences that could help even out the situation. He is no black belt, but he is efficient enough in the martial art of Aikido, to use an opponent's strengths and momentum against them. So far, the strength and momentum are with his opponent; after all, he has the gun, he has the sword, and in accordance with his faith, he also has Allah on his side.

But it was his opponent's assertion; that David Bell (as the supposed kidnapper of the Cleric), had to be beheaded rather than shot - which becomes the leverage for Steven.

The choice to use the short sword as the instrument of execution, of course, had advantages for the fanatic. Unlike the gun, the sword would be almost silent; it is also the righteous choice of weapon, plus it would leave no ballistic evidence. However as far as Steven is concerned, the advantages of the sword have a single huge potential flaw; for to use the sword - the man would have to come within striking range.

'You idiots make me laugh,' Steven scorns; taking one step forward and then to the side, prompting the man to give a threatening gesture with his gun; which brings Steven to a halt as he continues, 'You have the cheek to attach yourself to the name of God. You're not a follower or servant of God, you and your kind are no more than self-delusional … *pathetics!*'

Before the man could react, Steven emphasizes, '*Then*, to top it all they sent you after the wrong man ... *you fucking idiot!* Bell couldn't kidnap a tub of yogurt without spilling it all over himself! I just used him as a convenient cover. It was me, you deluded fucking pathetic! I kidnapped the Cleric.'

It was not only what had been said, that made Kamel pause, but it was more in the way it had been spoken; the look of ridicule, and the sheer passion behind the sneer.

'Then why should you admit it?' Kamel asked.

Because if you try and attack me,' Steven replies as he holds up his camera phone, 'I'll send your photo all over the world-wide web. Suddenly, the ridicule and sneer disappears from Steven's face, but the authority remains as he pronounces, 'Besides, I, *unlike* you, try to protect the innocent rather than slaughter them, even if I must risk my life for their innocence. And I certainly wouldn't condemn someone to death, for *my* actions, I am no *coward!*'

As intended by Steven, the situation is a bit of a no-brainer for the fanatic; who immediately swaps his grip on the gun over, with the sword, so that he has a firmer grip on the sword, then, with an almost benevolent smile, Kamel says, 'It is clear to any worthy servant of Islam, that you have been sent to me by Allah, blessed be his glorious name. And blessed be his glorious will … that fooled you into trying to blackmail me with your silly camera trick. And made your anger trick you into admitting your guilt. It is you who are the *pathetic,* as all non-believers become when they disbelieve in the wisdom of Islam.'

Seeing the momentum of the opportunity, Steven presses it forward, as he emphasises, with a sneer, 'Well at least if I'm going to become a *martyr*, then it will be for something that is *real* … instead of some *fairy story* made up for *childish* little minds … like yours!'

Giving the fanatic a final look of mixed disgust and resigned fate, and with a shrug of his shoulders; Steven takes another photo of the man - then quickly kneels on all fours, and states, 'Anyway, I'm not fucking around any further with the likes of you! You've got ten seconds, after that, I'm walking, whether you fucking like it or not!'

Then whilst holdings the man's gaze, 'But remember, as you strike, your everlasting image will be sent to the people who will revenge *my* death!'

With that, and looking away from the man, and down to the ground, Steven starts singing *"All things Bright and Beautiful."*

Stepping forward, Lateef Kamel is suddenly stopped; by Steven raising one hand up, and informing him, 'The only thing I will apologise for, is assaulting the Cleric … that was not my pre-planned intention … so, with that said … *you can go and fuck yourself!*'

And with that said - Lateef Kamel, the fanatic, steps forward again.

Note: It is a trick of the mind, or more accurately, the memory, which seems to slow, or expand time during a highly dangerous moment; particularly in those moments in which we may glimpse our potential death. It is, of course, not the slowing of time that makes events seem to pass in slow motion, but rather, it is the unfolding of the concentrated memory of such events.

In Steven's moment of potential imminent death, his awareness is concentrated, not on the fear of death - but on the leading hem of the long coat of the would-be assassin.

Watching out the corner of his eye, Steven sees the man slowly take two and a half steps forward; so that he now towers above him. He even allows the man to quickly babble something about, 'Your apology will be judged in accordance with the blessed wisdom of Islam.'
Then, as soon as Steven sees the right-side hem of the fanatic's coat rise, in accordance, with the lifting of his machete bearing right hand - *Steven strikes!*
Thrusting himself across the ground, he slams his weight into the man's weakest points - his knees; forcing the man to tumble backward and instinctively throw his arms to the side - and away from Steven. As the man lands heavily on his back, Steven becomes acutely aware of the slow-motion sounds and sights of the crunching and sliding of the pebbles. As he grinds a handful of pebbles and sand into the man's face, the man instinctively closes his eyes, and Steven uses a hand size stone to strike three vicious blows, to the man's head.
Fortunately, Lateef Kamel would have no conscious memory of the sequence of his death; and therefore, his last moments would have appeared (and disappeared) within a normal time frame, rather than a (seemingly) elongated one.
Nevertheless, back in the world of the living; it was not until after he had made certain that the fanatic was indeed, dead; that Steven's recalls the sound of the revolver being fired. Checking that he himself hasn't been shot or nicked by any bullet, he slowly stands and scans for anyone else who had also heard the shot. For although it would be clear to anyone that he had acted in self-defence - any involvement with the police would be the last thing that Steven wants.
Seeing that, under the circumstances, all is well, he frisks the body, takes out a wallet and ID papers; and manoeuvres the corpse into the foetal position. He then undoes the canvas cover of a near-bye dingy; dumps the dead man, the gun and sword in, and hauls the cover over the corpse. Steven guesses that the scene would probably remain undisturbed until the

boat's owner returned, or the increasing smell of the corpse became noticeable.

Finally, having double-checked that all was still well, he picks up the blood-stained stone, walks down to the shoreline, throws the stone into the sea, and then washes his hands and leaves the scene. As soon as he re-joins his friends at the café he orders a much needed, chilled, whisky and coke.

Chapter 32 - The reckoning

Whilst Steven waits for his drink to arrive, Hanna whispers, 'We heard a bang, it sounded like a gun, are you all right!
David asks, 'Where is the man in the kaftan?'

 After showing an amazed, Hanna, Rita and David the photo shot of the fanatic holding the gun and sword, Steven replies, 'Well … depending on what interpretation of paradise and hell you give credit to, my guess is, he's either getting a truly heavenly blowjob from some ecstatic vestal virgin. Or he's *giving* a truly hellish blowjob to a very smelly, and I suspect, totally impotent, wart invested, underling of Satan.'

Looking at David's expression, Steven could tell that he was not even slightly amused or relieved by this answer; so, he qualifies it by adding, 'It was him or me, and after that it would have been you. I left him in a dingy, under a tarpaulin, in a quiet spot on the harbour beach. But in this hot weather, he will probably be discovered quite soon.'

At that point, the waitress brings Steven's drink to the table of shocked, horrified and worried, customers, and immediately sees that there is something going on; that is so beyond her pay scale that it isn't even worth thinking of worrying about, and so she promptly leaves them to their own devices.

Over the following ten or so minutes, and in between various question and exclamations from his friends, Steven explained what had happened at the beach, and what he thought had been happening since entering the market.

After a minute's silence, a frightened David Bell asks, 'There will be other fanatics and police … and how the hell did they get hold of *my* name?'

Smiling, and showing the group the photo of David Bell, which he had taken from the dead fanatic, Steven answers, 'What with all that was going on at the time, I didn't ask him. But the main thing is that the police and this man's … associates … have your name in the frame. Though apparently not my name. I'm sure he would have taken great pleasure in telling me if they had. I'm not sure, but I don't

think that they have Hanna's or Rita's names either, but they will almost certainly have photos of us all together.'
'They? Who are they?' Hanna asks.
'I got a distinct impression that our late, would be assassin, was to put it crudely, just cannon fodder. He said something along the lines that, not all the Muslim hierarchy were wimps. Which suggest to me, that someone in the hierarchy, who probably has information from the police, gave David's details to him, and the order to kill him.'
'Oh, thanks a lot that is so reassuring!' David exclaims.
'I'm not out to reassure you, I'm just telling you what I know and think.'
Looking at the confused to frightened state of his friends, Steven asks, 'The question is, what we do now?
'Somebody else is certain to have heard that shot.' Rita states.'
'We must call the police!' Hanna exclaims, then looking at the doubt and even discomfort on Steven's face, she adds, 'It is obvious that you are completely innocent!'
Looking at Hanna, Steven states, 'I would still not want to get involved with the police.'
Looking at the even greater doubt and discomfort on Steven's face, Hanna asserts, 'It doesn't matter about the placarding, we will have to take our chances.'
Touching her hand to Hanna's arm, Rita puts forward, 'I don't think that is what Steven meant, is it Steven?'
'No. Not exactly, but what do you mean?'
'For some time now, I have sensed, that if you were not part of the Crimetest's Advice organisation, and you or David have never said that you were or are … then you were a customer at some time. Of course, I could be wrong, Steven?'
Glancing at Hanna and nodding his head toward Rita, Steven answers, 'I admire your perception if not your timing. And you are not completely right or wrong, but I will explain all later, I owe you and Hanna that much at least. However, *before* … any police arrive, I think we should all move to a

safer place. After that, we can all decide what's best for ourselves and each other.'
After arriving back at their hotel, and checking to see that there were no obvious, or even not so obvious sign of the police, or any would be assassins, the four companions are gathered in David Bell's lounge.
When everyone had settled, and with exception of mentioning the Body Part Murders, Steven told Hanna and Rita everything; from his campaign to discredit Crimetest, to his escape from prison and coming to Italy, and even about his ordering a false passport and documents for Hanna.
After his confessions, he ends by saying, 'I know all of what I've told you will come as a complete shock to you, Hanna and Rita. But I want to say, out of respect for all three of you, is since I've known you and with I have learned from David, I feel a changed man … *in so many different ways*.'
For the next few minutes, no one utters a single word.
Eventually, Rita asks, 'What about your man, here in Italy, the one who makes identity papers for you, how safe is he?'
'He'll keep his head well down unless it is pulled up by his hair roots. Would you voluntary confess to being involved in this mess?'
Again no one says a word, including Hanna who continues to stare at the floor.
Suddenly, as David seems to be about to say something, Hanna lifts her head, and looking directly at Steven, she says, 'I think you should know that I have decided, that no matter what happens from now, I will *not* be leaving Italy or going with abroad with you. Italy is my …'
Interrupting Hanna, Steven replies, 'There is no need to explain further. I sort of guessed it anyway. I can't say that I'm not disappointed, but I felt that would be your decision.
After a long moment, of what seems to all to be a heavy silence, Rita looks at each person in turn, then says, 'Well, then, I guess we still have to answer the question, of whether

we want to be hung as sacrificial lamb, or do we want to try and save the whole damned flock?'

'What?' David asks.

'Do we want to carry on with our business with religion, or do we quit?'

'We'll have to quit, of course. This is bloody madness.'

'I guess that is the obvious thing to do David, but the obvious thing isn't always the best thing to do.'

'What? What do you mean, not the best bloody thing to do, what else can we do?'

'We can go through the facts and probabilities and make an informed decision.'

'About what! What facts, what informed decision?'

'Well for a start, wherever and however, this fanatic man got his information about you, it must from a thorough investigation.'

'By who?'

'As I said, my guess is the police.' Steven suggests.

'Somewhere along the line, we slipped up. I've racked my memory but can't come up with anything concrete, but if they had anything concrete, then you and maybe all of us would probably be in a police cell by now.'

'But why would the police tell what they know to some fanatical Jihadist?' Hanna asks.

'They didn't, at least that's my guess.' Rita suggests. 'After all, let's face facts, there aren't that many Muslims in the Italian police. But there are many Roman Catholic police officials, who would pass on any useful information from the police onto the Church. It is entirely possible that someone in the curch hierarchy, then passed on the information, hoping to get their dirty work done by someone else, namely the Islamist. Of course, if anyone found out about that, it would cause a colossal international scandal. But I doubt that the leak came from an idiot, he may have passed it on anonymously.'

Pausing to see if anyone disagreed, Rita continues, 'Nevertheless, whoever ordered the fanatic was privy to some high-level source of information. Which means he or they are in a position of power.'
'Well at least that is something I agree with.' David agrees.
Smiling at David, Rita continues, 'But now that this informer's plans have fallen through, with the demise of our late, would be executioner, he'll be a more cautious about launching another piece of … cannon fodder … particularly if might land on the back of his head. Which means, that sooner rather than later, the main architect of this plan, is also going to become wary about having his grubby little hands in it all and may try to wash his hands of the whole situation.'
With this possibility looking at least likely, Steven, David and Hanna begin to listen more intently, as Rita carries on.
'Of course, we must act quickly if we are to move things on. For all we know the man's body might have already been found. But he might not be found for a week. Nevertheless, if we make sure his body is found, today, the less likelihood of anyone sending a replacement. People in positions of power don't like to give them up lightly. My guess is that he or even they, will keep a low profile for the time being, which means he is unlikely to be sending a replacement killer too soon.'
Once again Steven, is impressed by Rita's abilities to work out the reality of a situation. Then, after holding one hand in the air, he suggests 'If the police get a photo of our late friend, pointing his gun at me, not that they will know who he is pointing the gun at … and they are told where to find his body, along with his gun and killing knife. That sort of find would be all over the news in a heartbeat. We don't have to send anything about who he was trying to kill or why. Nevertheless, it won't take the press too much time to accuse him of being up to no good, a jihadist type of no good.'
Running his hand through his hair, David exclaims, 'This is all getting out of hand. It's a bloody nightmare that's impossible to wake up from!'

'Well, at least it is still possible to wake up from,' Steven asserts, 'which is a lot more hopeful than it would have been if that maniac had found you on your own, instead of me finding him.'

Looking at Steven, David sighs and acknowledges, 'I know, and I suppose I should be thankful. I mean, well … I am grateful to you, Steven. But what are we going to do about it now?'

At that moment, Hanna says 'I think what has been said about the police tracing David's involvement, and even there being a spy in the Roman Catholic church passing the information to the Muslims, is true. I also think that whatever our personal feelings about each other, we must hold onto to what we have won so far, it is our best advantage.'

Lifting his head to look at Hanna, Steven asks, 'How so?'

Smiling at Steven, Hanna answers, 'The placarding of the churches.'

'Go on.' Rita urges.

'Even though this maniac who was sent to kill David, the reason why the main Islam rulers refused to officially issue a death warrant, is the same as why the Roman Catholic Church has refused to let it be widely known that David is a suspect. Neither of them wants to create a martyr. They are both fond of creating one for their own causes, but if David, or any of us are held up as being personally responsible for the Free Heroes campaign, it will create living martyr who is against the interest of religion. A real, living, person, that people can identify with, and rally around, whether it be by holding sit-ins or any other protest.'

Quickly looking distraught, and bowing her head, Hanna exclaims, 'I'm sorry that I encouraged the sit-ins, people could get seriously hurt, or worse, I …!'

'*Stop being so silly Hanna*!'

It was not only the words that Rita had just said, it was the almost angry authority with which she had said them that clearly startled her three friends. Yet she did not falter.

'Stop beating yourself up, you … silly girl.'
'But I have brought danger to all of us, and shame to my family …'
'We all brought, or at least helped to bring this danger upon ourselves. And as for your family, they will treat you as they treated the two brothers who were led astray by the Cosa Nostra. They will forgive you because they love you, as I do too. It is time for you to take some of the love you give to so many other people and start giving to the person who most deserves it … *you*!'
Looking around at the faces of her three friends, Hanna's eyes begin to well with tears; as Rita fishes into her handbag and produces and hands some tissues to her. Rita then advises, 'If those are tears of guilt, then wipe them away. If they are tears of self-love, at last, then cry as much as you want my darling.'
Taking the tissue, Hanna pauses, and then quickly wipes away a tear that had begun to spill down her cheek; she then grins at her friends and says, '*It tickled.*'
Suddenly standing up, Hanna says, 'I'll be back in a minute!' After rushing into the bedroom, and in less than a minute she reappears wearing the turquoise blue scarf that Rita had bought her. Going over to Rita and kissing her on her cheek, she says, 'Thank you … for being my friend.' Hanna then sits down again, smiles at everyone and then briefly frowns and asks, '*But what are we to do*?
The dynamics of the group had changed, Steven was still the alpha male and Rita the alpha female, but it was Rita who had become the pack leader.
 'With each successful placarding, we push a firework further up their backside, and no matter how much bullshit they try to flush it out with, they fail. If we stop placarding, we can hope that they will forget about us, and we can forget about them. It is a choice we have yet to make.'
Then, pausing for a moment, she stresses, 'But before we can make it, there is something …,' looking at Steven, she

continues, '… someone, who can bring the Free Heroes' campaign down, by his self, even though he might not mean to.

Speaking directly to Steven, Rita says, 'Just as you tried to bring The Crimetest's helpline down, by making it appear untrustworthy. I believe that your past, can now make the campaign appear, untrustworthy.'

Looking back at Rita, Steven holds his hands up and replies, 'You are right of course, but what I can do about that, I have no idea. But I do not want to run away from a fight that I at least, helped to start.'

'But no one thinks you are a coward!' Hanna pleads.

'And I am not saying you are one Steven,' Rita confirms as she leans forward and continues, 'and as for an answer to what you can do about your past, there is a way to at least lessen the potential effect on our reputation. If we choose to carry on with the placarding, the police will be on the lookout for David. Obviously, they do not know who you really are, Steven, or you'd be in a police cell right now. But the less you play an upfront part in the placarding, the less you are likely to be caught and unmasked, along with your past, which can bring down our whole … quest!'

Looking to Hanna and then from Steven to David, Rita states rather than suggests, 'I think it is time for Hanna, if she is willing, and myself to start placarding!' Before either man could argue, Rita explains, 'They will not be looking for a woman. Plus, it is not unusual for a woman in mourning to wear a veil in church, not at all. If we are not caught in the act, then one of us could placard a church and disappear, and the police would not have a clue as to what she looked like.'

Leaning forward, Steven advises, rather than states, 'You'd still have to be careful during the placarding, and with getting away from the area, and out of view of any CCTV cameras, before you change out of your disguises and clothes.'

 Pausing to take the information in, Rita answers, 'Yes, you are right. Neither of us are professionals, we will need all the experience and advice from both of you.'
'We also need your support in many ways,' Hanna agrees, 'I don't think we could do this alone, just the two of us, even if we wanted to, not that I do.'
Looking at both men, Rita states, 'Not that I do either.'
Just under one hour later, the photo of the fanatic, and the whereabouts of his body, were downloaded by several main media television stations.

Chapter 33 - Verona

If Rome is the religious capital of Italy, then Verona is its capital of Love. It is the place in which William Shakespeare, placed literature's most famous fictional lovers, Romeo and Juliet; before thrusting them into a maelstrom of love, feuding and tragedy.

However, before Shakespeare's play etched its signature upon the city's heart, Verona had a history worthy of any playwright's imagination. So, when the four companions and lovers of our story spent their first day in the city, they devised a whirlwind tour of the main tourist spots. Originally a Roman forum, Piazza dell ere is ringed with buzzing cafes and some of Verona's most sumptuous buildings; including the elegantly baroque Palazzo Mafia (now a corporate headquarters). Separating Piazza dell ere from Piazza die Signori is the monumental gate known as Arco Della Costa; hung with a whale's ribs that, according to legend, will fall on the first, just, person to walk beneath it; so far, it remains intact, despite visits by popes and kings. On the northern side of Piazza dei Signori stands Verona's Early-Renaissance Loggia del Consiglio, the 15th-century city council (not open to visitors). Through the archway at the far end of the piazza are the open-aired, Arched Scaliger; elaborate Gothic tombs of the Scaligeri family; where murderers are interred next to the relatives they killed.

By 11 am, the four friends respectfully wander through the elaborate ways of the gothic Arched Scaliger, which holds the tombs of the Scaliger clan who, given the time difference and opportunity, would have been equally at home as any of the Bard's villains or indeed his patron.

After stopping for coffee and snacks, they go to the Verona Visitors' Information Centre, and tour the district; whilst their tour guide headset tells them how the city was ruled the modern-day fascist who took and controlled the area from 1938 to 1945, and was the center for the torture and interrogation of the resistance. It was also a transit point for

Italian Jews sent to Nazi concentration camps. The friends also learn about the Verona's historic Jewish Ghetto; with its tall buildings overshadowing the narrow side streets below. When Hanna heard about Rita Rosani, the woman who became the hero leader of the Resistance in Verona, until she was caught and summarily executed at age 24; Hanna cried. After the sobering visit to the museum, the companions walked through the sunlit streets which are now an Enesco World Heritage Site and a cosmopolitan crossroads; especially in summer, when the 2000-year-old arena hosts opera's biggest stars. The opera house was once a 1st century AD Roman arena, which had since managed to survive the ravages of invading armies and earthquakes, to become Verona's legendary open-air opera house, holding up to 30,000 opera goers.

Whilst David booked the four of them into an evening performance of Tosca's "La Traviata," Steven, Hanna, and Rita lunched outside the grand Roman arena.

Basilica di San Zeno Maggiore, built in honour of the city's patron saint, is a brick and stone basilica that is considered by many devotees of architecture, to be a masterpiece. As the four companions walk through the flower-filled cloister into the nave, they marvel at the vast space lined with 12th- to 15th-century frescoes. When Hanna stands before Mantegna's, Majesty of the Virgin altarpiece; painted with such astonishing perspective that you actually believe there are garlands of fresh fruit hanging behind the Madonna's throne – Rita observers that her friend was about to kneel before it - but at the last moment, Hanna seemed to change her mind. Seeing that Rita had seen her doubt, Hanna smiles somewhat nervously, and Rita smiles back, gives her a hug, and the two of them walked out hand in hand.

Across the river from the historic center, the four friends enjoy the Giardino Giusti sculpted gardens (named after the noble family that has tended them since opening them to the public in 1591). At times, as they stroll through the landscaping of mixed manicured and natural settings, they seem to be over-shadowed by the soaring cypress trees, one of which the German poet Goethe immortalized in his travel writings.

Although Verona's worldwide reputation as the city of romance, was made by the growing popularity of William Shakespeare's 15th century, romantic tragedy stage play, Romeo and Juliet a tale of Verona; over the years, the cities fathers have understandably, done all they can to enhance such a reputation. And their most famous enhancement is, without a doubt, the creation of the supposed 'balcony' from the scene in which Romeo romances his beloved Juliet. Never mind that Romeo and Juliet were completely fictional characters, and that the courtyard and balcony somehow seem surprisingly small; romantics from all over the world flock to the 14th-century house, so that they too can add their names to the lovelorn graffiti already adorning the courtyard's causeway. Or place their notes, mainly to Juliet, onto the bronze statue of Juliet. Some who left, or even mailed, notes were surprised to receive letters back; from a dedicated band of volunteers.

It would have, of course, been heartless to try and prevent Hanna from dragging and pushing Steven, up to the balcony; where credit to his sense of propriety, and even to his sense of new-found love, he and Hanna shared a brief, yet passionate kiss – much to the applause of the crowd below.

However, Hanna's and Steven's balcony kiss, was not the only moving highlight that Verona had to offer the four friends. When they beheld the spectacle of La Traviata; an opera, which is arguably the most tragic opera of any Italian standard of tragedy, performed in the candlelit surroundings of the most romantic opera house in the world– all four companions and lovers, gently and quietly wept … in sheer awe.

By the following day after the night's opera, and filled as they were, with the feel-good feelings of Verona, the group had work to do. Over a breakfast, held in Rita's and David's room, each member put forward his or her ideas of suitable placarding sites that she or he had seen. For reasons, best known to Rita and Hanna, David's choice of placarding the Majesty of the Virgin altarpiece was firmly rejected by the women. It was however, David's choice of a lesser known curch that was eventually and unanimously chosen to be the target – and despite the strong objections from the men it was eventually decided that not only, would the placarding be done by Rita – but that she would leave *two* placards at the intended site.

Three hours later Rita, dressed in the traditional Italian widow's attire, of heavy black lace gloves, a scarf and veil; which all but totally obscured her face, and walking with an apparent limp, Rita approaches the altar. As she steps up to the first of the three steps, the earphone clipped to her right ear remains silent; informing her that none of her friends could spot anything untoward. Rita's outward approach to the whole drama is that of seeing the placarding as no more dangerous, or less important, than a completing some much needed, housework. However, ten minutes later, when the four friends hi-five each other, it is Rita's shout of *'Yes!'* that is the loudest.

The message on the first placard that Rita left, proclaimed:

The Curch of Free Heroes
The 6th Quest: Ecology of emotions.
A Free-Heroes quest to achieve freedom, balance and fulfilment through the ecology of his or her emotions; is furthered by freely acknowledging that his or her current feeling (fear, anger, joy, etc.) about any situation, person or group of people, is real. However, even as a good look-out does not always make the best captain of a ship; a Free-Hero does not always allow their current emotion (and its storyline) to determine his or her course of action, but rather, s/he will seek the storylines of his or her other emotions, as well as the bearings of verifiable facts; before setting out on a course of action.

The 6th Question:

Bearing in mind that our emotions, common sense, and history are pathways leading to our beliefs; which religions rely upon blind faith to plot a pathway, and which ones merely use such faith to try to blind us?
www.curchoffreeheroes.info

The message on the second placard that Rita left proclaimed:

The Curch of Free Heroes
The 7th Quest: Reality:
A Free-Hero's commitment to any course of action is more achievable when it is realistic, and not guided by any leech-pooh-promises; from any preacher, spiritual mystic, proclaimed psychic, faith healer or any other person who claims to be a special confidant, guide or a purveyor of any supernatural or un-natural force or being.

The 7th Question:
Bearing in mind that reality cannot be avoided (and that if it could, then it would become even more morally confusing), will paying tributes to any religion; purchase protection from the moral reality of our own wrongful choices or actions – and if it can buy such protection, isn't that a tad morally confusing too?

www.curchoffreeheroes.info

Chapter 34 -Run up the flag.
As the four friends were passing a small village on the outskirts of Rome, Steven asked David to pull in. When Hanna asked him why, he pointed to a church crowning the village.
'That's why!'
'How so?'
'Because it might well give us the opportunity to *flag* up, that we are arriving in Rome. That's how so my love.'
With that said, his three companions looked at the church, and saw a flag hanging from the square bell tower.
 'Do we want to give them warning we are going to Rome?' David asked.
'They already know it, or at least guess it. So, let's make sure everyone knows that we don't mind them knowing. But first we have to find out if that tower is accessible.'
By the following morning, the social media and news media announced that the Campaign for Free-Heroes had struck again. Along with the headlines, there were pictures of the curch tower, flying, not its previous flag; but a stiffened placard of white cardboard, about the size and shape of an oblong coffee table.
When the zoomed-in image of the "flag" became visible, it proclaimed:

The Curch of Free Heroes
The 8th Quest: Orderliness:
Whatever his or her personal circumstances, a Free-Hero will try to live an orderly lifestyle by keeping a practical level of daily; social interaction, physical activity, personal hygiene, politeness, and play.
In addition, to the above, all Free-Heroes are encouraged to use ten to fifteen minutes, during the first-half of their day, for promoting the Ten Quests of a Free Hero – and ten to fifteen minutes, during the second-half of their day, for promoting the Ten DISCARDING's to his or her friends, as well as the local and worldwide communities.
The 8th Question:
If we are all children of (your religion's version) of God, will he feel proud; when any child of his commits an act of kindness, for the sake of gaining an after-life reward, to avoid being punished in Hell, or for the sake of kindness itself?
www.curchoffreeheroes.info

Chapter 35 - Rome

Once the companions reached the city's most exclusive shopping street, Via dei Condotti; the men realised that there was no chance of dissuading Rita and Hanna from window shopping; so they retreated to a nearby bar instead. When the women returned, the men were "rewarded" with a recount of the many things that Rita and Hanna had, almost, bought; and a display of the things they had bought, which were two identical tops, and various articles of makeup.

Eventually, Hanna enthused, 'Now we must go up the steps!' Descending to towards the Piazza di Spagna at its base; the famed 18th century stairway, was immortalised by Audrey Hepburn and Gregory Peck and in the film, Roman Holiday. When they reached the bottom of the Spanish Steps, Hanna turns around to her friends and suddenly announces, '*We must race to the top!*' And with that, she begins racing up the steps before anyone else had moved.

With Rita's shouts of '*Hey! That's cheating!*' ringing her ears, Hanna reaches halfway to the top before Steven begins to overtake, but he is immediately held back by Hanna holding on to his arm and using him to propel herself ahead and to the top.

Standing triumphantly at the top, Hanna welcomes her friends' out of breath arrivals. Steven grins, bows, and gives her a congratulatory kiss on both cheeks. David grins at her. And Rita exclaims, with a grin. 'You're a cheat and you are disqualified and will be sent to cheater hell!'

However, before Hanna could answer, the companions are suddenly captivated by the sound of a solo voice; singing of an aria, coming from inside the Trinità dei Monti church, which stands at the top of the steps. Without anyone taking the lead, they find themselves walking inside, and sitting down on the rear seating. As they sit, they see that the singing is coming from a young chorister, whose lone voice brings shivers to the four companions. When the chorister had finished, he withdrew from sight.

'That was so beautiful, Hanna said, 'It is my new favourite music.' Thrusting her arm into Steven's, she then asks him, 'What is your favourite music?'
'Goodness … that would be like trying to choose your favourite desert island disc.'
'What is this?' Hanna asks.
'It's an old radio program,' David explains, 'in which different weekly guest, are told they are to be shipwrecked on a deserted island. Then he or she must choose eight records, or pieces of music, to take with them. And at the end of the program, they have to choose the one that is the favourite.'
Without any hesitation, Hanna exclaims, 'I choose the aria we've just heard!'
 'I'm not sure,' Steven answers, 'but if I had to choose, for me, there would be something from Hans Zimmer.'
'And your choice?' Rita asks David.
'I choose, the theme-tune from Simon Templar, it's an old radio program.'
Rita, 'I'd have to choose the, There's a Place, song, from the film West Side Story.'
'Ooh!' Hanna croons; as she grabs hold of Rita's hand, 'I love that film and the song, it is so beautiful, so hopeful.'
Placing her hand on top of Hanna's, Rita continues, 'It is both of those things, but the reason I choose it, is that, at the end, alongside its message hope, the composer drops in a chord of warning. I like to believe he is saying that if our dreams and hopes are to come true, then they must go hand in hand, alongside real life.'
Looking at Rita, Hanna states, 'I choose that song too!'
Reluctantly shrugging his shoulders, David umpires, 'I'm afraid you can only choose *one* absolute favourite piece of music, Hanna.'
Glaring at David, Hanna pauses for just a moment, and then she replies, 'Then I *insist,* that I am shipwrecked alongside Rita!'

Laying her hand on Hanna's, Rita asserts, 'That is good, for we will be able to rescue … each other.'
Holding up his hands in surrender, David replies, 'I surrender to the wiser judgements.'
'And what would be your favourite, *moments*, in life, David?' Rita asks.
After thing for a few moments, David answers, I will give you three such times. Being with Claire, my wife, before we … parted. Getting the Crime Advice Line legally accepted. And … any moment in your company, of course.'
Smiling at David, Rita suggests, 'Then perhaps we should not ask you to tell us your number one moment?'
Smiling at Rita, David answers, 'Perhaps not. But it is good that although happiness itself is not everlasting, at least our memories of it can last as long as we do.'
'That is so true!' Hanna agrees, then before she could stop herself, she adds, 'Of course, they say in paradise, happiness is everlasting. Not that I believe them anymore, but it would be nice.'
Looking at Hanna with some curiosity, David offers, 'But, perhaps it will still be possible to provide an everlasting paradise, Hanna.'
'How so?'
'Well, in the future we shall have the abilities to gain during life, what the religions promise, can only be gained after we die.'
'How so?'
'Because, albeit someway off from our lifetimes, people will eventually gain the ability, to have their memories and any chosen personal preferences, transferred into his or her rejuvenated body… almost as if they are a reincarnated person. Through bio and genetic engineering, a reincarnated person could also choose different physical characteristics, intellectual abilities, different gender, etcetera, than they had before. We will even have the choice of everlasting, multiple reincarnations, in short, you choose it … *you be it.*'

'I always wondered what it would be like to live as a man.' Hanna states.

'If you lived in the future, you would be able to find out. Or if you didn't fancy a full person makeover, you might like to take a vacation to your virtual-reality-paradise, instead.'

'And what is a virtual-reality-paradise?' Rita asks.

'A Virtual-Reality-Paradise will be tailored made, in-house virtual paradise. Similar, to the virtual games we play nowadays, but far more advanced. The storyline of someone's virtual-paradise will be based on their unique, chosen personal preferences.'

Thinking for about two seconds, Hanna suggests, 'But, that could quickly turn into a virtual Hell!'

'Very true! However, it could also be a sort of learning curve, a playable version of what the religions call purgatory, or a learning limbo, in which people will hopefully learn from their mistakes, but without inflicting the aftermaths of the mistakes, on to real life, innocent bystanders.'

'But I don't want a life that is ruled by machines ... even if it does make me happy!' Hanna states.

'And you are right to be concerned, Hanna. For, science alone will not magically give us a get out of jail card. AI or indeed any science should not let us abdicate, or outsource our responsibilities to one another, or indeed to Life.'

At that point, Steven asks, 'That's all very nice, but what happens to us poor shmucks in the meantime, who don't get to your everlasting life and virtual paradises?'

'The same as happened to all those shmucks who made it possible for you, me and the rest of us, to get where we are today, they die. Why? Would you prefer that our primordial ancestral, shmucks had given up, and slithered back into the primordial sludge?'

When Steven just shrugs his shoulders, David turns to Hanna and continues, 'Our morality and happiness will depend on our own fingers, thumbs, smiles and frowns for its continuation, Hanna ... and not on any so-called super-god or

super-artificial intelligence … for to hand responsibility to either would be a tragic betrayal against our primordial ancestors, as well as all who have managed to follow in their footsteps.'
When Hanna remains silent, Rita asks David, 'Do you think religious people are criminals?'
 'No! I would no more condemn a religious person for believing that some supernatural being will save them, than I would condemn any criminal who believes that crime will save them. It is the concept of religion that I believe is a crime against humanity, not the followers of religion.'
'Go on.'
'The concept of the religions not *only* tries to kidnap, our natural pride in achieving good, but, after returning it as some guilt-smeared evidence, of so-called arrogance, it then has the *insolence,* to demand a rescuer's reward of becoming our lawmakers!'
Before continuing to address, what has turned out to be, his three best friends in life, David leans forward; and after looking at each of them in turn he emphasises, *'From the moment religion tried to pass itself off as the origin of morality, it began digging its own burial place in history.'*
Shrugging his shoulders, he continues, 'By using fear of after-life hell or greed for a ready-made heaven, and by installing a regime of addictive ritualization, the religions have recruited and conscripted generations of different societies into its ranks. The American Pie still has an almost seventy percent portion of religious followers in it. In one survey, nearly half of American Christians expressed a faith in the second coming of Jesus Christ.'
'Really!' Steven quips, 'How on earth are they going to muddle along 'til then?'
Raising his eyebrows in reply to Steven, then addressing Hanna and Rita, David continues, 'Nevertheless, like the War on Drugs, the conceptual battle against religion will not be won on physical, battlefields. It will be won in the minds and

hearts of a moral, re-generation, whose increasing membership align themselves to no religion whatsoever, yet who have risen to become the third highest *faith* in the world. The rise of re-claiming our personal responsibility for our moral future, is inevitable.'
Sitting back David adds, 'Because the religions haven't anything new to offer, either physically or morally, all they can really do is kick, claw and scream until history finally buries them.'
Looking at Steven, David informs him, 'The Hindu faith comes fourth.'
'Why look at me,' Steven replies, 'I'm not a Hindu.'
'No, but I presumed you were curious.'
'Unless of course, the second coming manages to come before the final burial does!' Steven offers.
Leaning forward to David, Rita asks, 'And what if that happens, my darling?'
Smiling at Rita, David replies, 'Then should that happen, then I will start digging my way to my inevitable place in hell, of course!'
'And I will mop your increasingly sweaty brow as you dig.' Rita answers.
With that said, the four friends continue with their game of choosing their favourite things.

Chapter 36 - The Garden

Even before the "Four Placardeers," as they called themselves, had left Verona and were on the train to Rome; their reputation had long sped before them, and had reached the inner powers of the Vatican, including the small group of three men, who took overall responsibility for the Pope's wellbeing.

Although most tourist will naturally associate the (quaintly dressed) Swiss Guard, as being the front line of security for the Pope; it is the more powerful the, Corpo della Gendarmeria dello Stato della Città del Vaticano, who are responsible for overall security. The Gendarmerie Corps duties provide; security, criminal investigations, and they also ensure public order at the audiences, meetings, and ceremonies at which the Pope is present. The Vatican Gendarmerie includes two special units, the Rapid Intervention Group, the Italian: Gruppo Intervento Rapido and an anti-sabotage unit, Unità Antisabotaggio.

The chief executive and leader of the corps is Inspector General, Ambrogio Servino, an Italian and Roman Catholic by birth and who in spite of his name, is a man of optimistic nature; and it is he that meets the Dean of the college of cardinals, Cardinal Tivo, and the Pontifical Swiss Guard Commandant, Chaplin Lieutenant Colonel Abategiovann.

It is a hot day, and after some formal and genuine pleasantries, the group of three stroll through one of the gardens of the Vatican. Cardinal Tivo invites his companions to sit beneath the shade beneath a corridor of vine-entangled bamboo, which also contains an 18th century, ironwork and marble table and chairs.

It is Cardinal Tivo who starts the main proceedings off by stating, 'After this double outrage on the two churches in Verona, may the blessings of Saint Michael the Archangel be upon you, and your comrade in arms, my dear Ambrogio.' Having bowed his appreciation, Inspector General Ambrogio Servino replies, 'Perhaps our gracious saint has already bestowed his blessing, by guiding us to, having already contacted our friends in Europol and the British police, in this matter.'

Speaking in a quiet voice, Cardinal Tivo suggests, 'This is good news to hear, particularly as there is now a probability that this Curch of Free-Heroes next assault will take place here, in Rome, and even within the sacredness of the Vatican itself. I of course, presume that your own authorities have predicted this too, my good Servino.'

Inspector General Ambrogio Servino nods and then says, 'We think that they may try and use one of the days when his holiness the Pope is celebrating a public event or mass, possibly the forthcoming one. We also predict … that the safety of the Pope himself may be at risk.'

When the Cardinal looks taken aback, the Chaplin Lieutenant Colonel, Abategiovann, leans back and states, 'They have already physically assaulted a Muslim Cleric.'

Servino nods again, then adds, 'The attack on the Cleric seems to have been unplanned. There is little doubt they went there to leave one of their posters. But after being discovered by chance, they then dealt with the situation by force. Nevertheless, we shall be providing extra protection, in addition to your own security at any occasion that we or your office thinks appropriate. What with the other protests and the various church sit-ins, we are, like yourselves, somewhat stretched? Nevertheless, we shall be stepping up both visible patrols of all churches in our area, and permanent undercover watches on the likely ones at which there might be an attempt to placard.

'What about copycats?

'Since the second attack, their emails sent to the office of Chief of Police, have contained a number and letter combination code. The code can be used as future verification of any placarding or communication. Plus of course, they have their website to confirm or deny anything they wish. There have been several posters and graffiti left at various religious sites, including several dozen posts to the Vatican website, but none have been verified as coming from the original Curch.'

'Original Curch?' Cardinal Tivo cautioned, 'You make it sound like it has been established for centuries, not weeks.'

'From the original offenders,' Ambrogio Servino qualifies and then continues, 'thank you for your correction. However, after many inquiries, we have had some interesting and yet disturbing news whilst researching into David Bell, the man whose DNA was found on the strawberry stained tissue near the church.'

'What news?'

'Bell has not been seen in his local village since the time of the second placarding. Now I will admit that I am not an expert in the use of computers. But I know enough to know that their ability to trace connections that would otherwise be practically impossible to do by leg work alone, is phenomenal. However, it still takes good detective work to put all that information to good use. Fortunately, we are not without such detectives.'

Waiting for and receiving acknowledgments from the other two men, Ambrogio Servino continues, 'When we searched David Bell's home, we conducted a fingerprint search too. Several prints belonging to various people came up. But one of these people included a known criminal … who shot a British policeman and several members of the public, who were employees of Crimetest.'

'But that is David Bell's organization!' the Cardinal exclaims.

'Apparently, this man was trying to sabotage the crime prevention service. David Bell's crime prevention service.'

'But you haven't revealed his name yet, Ambrogio.'

Bowing his head to the Cardinal, Ambrogio replies, 'His name is … Steven Chadwick. He also became a lot more significant when, as our detective uncovered, on further

investigation, that there is an arrest warrant for this man, for recently escaping from prison, in England!'
'But surely this Chadwick is an enemy of Bell, not ally?'
'So, it would seem at first. However, we have found out that Bell visited him in prison on a number of occasions.'
'I see!'
'Out of routine, our detective contacted the English police responsible for the recapture of Chadwick. As a matter of their routine, the English police had already looked into his prison record, including all correspondence. There were number of visits and letters between the two. The officer also came across two language correspondence courses, one for Portuguese and the other for ... *Italian*.'
'I see your point.'
Leaning forward, Ambrogio then emphasises, 'What is more to the point, is on further investigation, our officer found out that when Chadwick escaped, he used a *hypodermic* to inject a fast reacting *sedative* into two prison guards.'
Leaning back, Ambrogio then emphasises, 'Clearly, the method of using a knockout sedative in his escape from prison, and in the attack on the Muslim Cleric, makes a very strong case that this Steven Chadwick is in Italy *and* it is he who is working with David Bell.'
The look on the other men's faces told that they had already been convinced, so the Inspector General continued, 'As a matter of prudent precaution, I have also spoken at some length, with Superintendent Miles Rupert, the Detective who lead the original pursuit and capture Chadwick, in England.'
'What did he say?'
'Superintendent Rupert says that Chadwick is a very dangerous and unpredictable psychopath, both clever and devious. He also said that Chadwick *may* also be responsible for a series of murders in Britain, which the British press named as the Body Part Murders,'
At that point, the Inspector General laid two copies of Steven Chadwick's police and prison records onto the ornate wrought

iron garden table, and continued. 'The evidence is purely circumstantial and was thought not worthwhile in pursuing any formal charges. But one further thing that the Superintendent also revealed, and that was, that *before* the arrest of Chadwick by the police, at which David Bell was present, Bell offered him a safe passage, in return for the release of his hostage, a Crimetest employee.'
'This is not as unlikely as I first thought,' the Cardinal admits, 'But then that is why you are one of our nation's finest detectives, and I am but a humble servant of our great Lord.' Dismissing the compliment with a wave of his hand, Ambrogio continues, 'Since this information, the two detectives who located, followed and then sadly lost Bell and three companions. Never he less, they have been shown a passport photograph of Steven Chadwick. Both detectives confirmed he was in Bell's company. Unfortunately, we haven't been able to identify the two women who were there also. As a matter of prudent precaution, we have increased the priority for finding this man, if he should be found within our borders. We have also issued the proviso that should he be detected, no action should be taken, other than observation, without further instruction from myself or my deputy.'
Returning the Cardinal's grateful smile, Ambrogio adds, 'And as an even humbler servant of our Lord, I will keep you both personally informed of any worthwhile developments as soon as they come to me.'
At 8.37 that night, the Cardinal's personal mobile phone rang. It was Ambrogio.
Speaking quickly, but assuredly, the Inspector related, 'Something has just been brought to my attention by one of my investigating officers. Although we located and then lost Bell's whereabouts, there was also another incident at that town, on the same day.
'Please go on.'
'The body of a Muslim man, with known connections to extremist's organizations, was found covered up in a boat on

the beach. He had been killed by being hit on the head with a blunt instrument. A photo of the same man, pointing a gun and short sword was sent to several media companies, along with the whereabouts of his body. The photo and details were sent anonymously.'

After pausing to recover, the Cardinal said, 'It would seem too much of a coincidence, if Bell and his company weren't involved in this further … terrible escalation, my good friend.'

'As yet there has been no forensic, or witness evidence of who was responsible. But if Muslim extremists are involved too, then it can complicate things, on many fronts. We think that they may have been tipped off about Bell's whereabouts. It is difficult to keep our own investigations secret. As to why such a man was there, and armed as he was, is not open to much speculation.'

'Of course, I understand, my dear friend. So how do suggest we procced.'

'Essentially … as before. With Chadwick, we can and will arrest him on sight. We can bring David Bell in for questioning on suspicion of assisting an escaped fugitive. But there is no request from the British authoritics for any arrest warrant for Bell. But I would remind you, we still do not have *any* irrefutable proof of either's man's involvement in the Curch activities.'

'If we can observe them before arresting them,' the Cardinal suggests, 'it may prove beneficial, particularly if we can discover any leads to any more members of his organization.'

'I agree. We still think that the next attack will be in Rome, possibly at the Vatican. I know that Chaplin Abategiovann is an early to bed man, so I'll inform him in the morning of the latest news. Until then we will rely on our increased visible patrols and undercover surveillances, on all the likely targets.'

'I am sure that His Excellency the Pope, will be thankful for your work and advice, as I am Ambrogio.' With that concluded, the Cardinal switches his phone off.

Chapter 37 - Hanna goes to church
The methodical planning of the next placarding had been
carefully completed and rehearsed, twice, the day before.
Now, as she anxiously waits, at the edge of the bustling
crowd, Hanna sees her target-church, nestling in the far
corner of the crowded piazza.
She is already feeling even more nervous than when she was
about to take her first holy communion, more anxious than
when, at the age of 16, she was about to lose her virginity to
her first lover and she is also even feeling more panicky, than
when she began confessing to Father Padovesi, that she had
indeed, already lost her virginity.
Adjusting her hat and veil, so that they sit more comfortably
on her perspiring brow, and looking to her left and upwards,
she feels comforted to see a heavily disguised, David Bell
looking down at her; whilst he casually leans on the running
balcony wall of a 1st floor tier of shops.
Suddenly, as she enters the piazza crowd, Hanna stops dead;
as a voice in her loudly announces, '*You are doing fine!*'
As she recognises that the loud voice belongs to Rita, Hanna
looks down and remotely watches; as her own black lace
gloved, trembling hand, seems to glide itself to the inside
pocket of her black mourning jacket, and then lowers the
volume in her earpiece. Hanna then continues to "glide"
toward the church once again.
Sitting in the café, 30 metres to the left of the church and
three tables away from a disguised and seated Steven, a veiled
Rita nervously watches Hanna criss-crossing her way through
the crowd.
As Hanna stops to let an escorted group of school children
pass in front of her, she feels the rolled-up silk placard; no
bigger than a page from a magazine, is still safely hidden up
inside her sleeve. As several children wait for her to pass
through, Hanna remotely thinks, "It is not too late to turn
back." Then thanking the children, she presses on for another
minute until finally; with her pulse pounding in her ears so

loudly - that she fears that she might not hear any message coming in from Rita, clearly enough - she passes beneath the arched and elaborately carved stone entrance of the church. Eight seconds after Hanna enters the church, Rita follows her in; curtsies in the direction of the altar, makes the sign of the crucifix, and then sits along the second row of benches inside from the entrance - and seven seating spaces to the left of the unobtrusive, plain clothed female police officer; who has already spent over two hours of her shift, watching out for any sign, of any Curch of Free-Heroes' activities.
Looking through her black lace veil, Rita watches nervously as Hanna turns left before the altar, and then turns right as she pulls open a door and disappears into the area containing the public washrooms, cleaning cupboards … and vestry room.
In the vestry room, the priest is donning the last of his priestly attire for the forthcoming service. After checking that no one else is in the washroom, Hanna holds the door ajar, and seeing that vestry door is still closed, she takes out the rolled-up banner, and waits. Within 10 seconds, Hanna hears Steven's voice in her ear, calmly asking, 'Are you in the vestments area, I can't see any pictures yet, have you taken the flower away?'
Looking down to the phone, concealed behind her jacket lapel, Hanna removes the flower from the buttonhole; so the camera lens is uncovered, and the camera is faithfully recording and transmitting everything in front of her. She then asks, 'Can you see?'
A view showing the close-up and part image of a door and a hallway beyond, appears on Steven's screen, and he answers, 'Yes, we can see, now. You are doing well, we are all here for you.'
Unfurling the silken banner, Hanna removes the protective covering from the sticky-tab; placed at the centre of the banner's chord, and holds the banner at the ready, then she continues to wait.

As she waits she suddenly remembers the day when she and three friends sneaked into the cinema to see a film; although the film was not pornographic, it was meant for adults. Hanna could remember feeling quite shocked at seeing her first glimpse of, on film, pubic hair - then suddenly, the sound of a door opening and the sight of the priest coming out of the vestry - wrenches Hanna back into the now or never.

Fully opening the washroom door, she takes several quick, quiet and deft paces; until she is behind the priest and then, stretching her arm out she … *gently* … attaches the silk banner onto the back of the priest's loose-fitting outer garment.

As the priest keeps moving toward the door, a horrified Hanna sees that the banner is hanging straight - but the printed side is the wrong way around - and is facing the priest's back.

Quickly moving forward and squeezing her way past the priest - whilst deftly turning the Quest bearing banner the right way around - Hanna states, rather than asks, in Italian, *'Let me get the door for you Father!'*

Pushing and holding the door open, Hanna curtsies, as the surprised, yet smiling priest, thanks her and then proceeds out into the church and along toward the alter gate.

As Rita, (and the unobtrusive policewoman) sit watching the priest (followed by Hanna) walking toward the gate leading to the altar, neither woman is astonished to see the priest turning left through the gate, then making his reverent way along the red altar carpet; whilst Hanna also turns left but stops before the altar gate, where she makes a hurried sign of the crucifix, curtsies, then turning around she makes her way (just a little too quickly) toward and out of the main doors.

It is at this moment, that Abrielle, the undercover policewoman, notices the silken banner hanging from the priest's back. Although the writing on the banner is too far away to be read, she just about recognises the Curch of Free Heroes logo. Looking from the banner to the exiting Hanna, and back again, Abrielle rapidly moves toward the central isle, whilst announcing into her police issue mobile phone, *'Marcel! Pronto!'*

Presuming that the previously unobtrusive woman is going to arrest Hanna, Rita quickly kneels forward as if to pray, and blocks Abrielle's exit. Abrielle swivels her legs over the bench, reaches the central isle, then answering the unseen Marcel, she orders, 'The woman in black carrying a small black handbag, coming out now, hold on to her!' Abrielle then almost sprints toward the adorned priest, who is performing the usual bows and rituals in front of the altar - until Abrielle shouts out, *'Your Grace!'*

When Detective Marcel Macari receives Abrielle's call to stop the woman in black carrying a black handbag; he springs out of the unmarked police car, runs across the pavement, up the steps, and shouts out to Hanna, *'Stop where you are, Poli* –'*before* he runs straight into Steven's sweeping, outstretched arm. Pushing himself off the pavement Marcel manages to get halfway onto his feet - before Steven knocks him down and out.

As Abrielle removes the Curch of Free Heroes banner from the back of astonished priest, she looks back toward the main doors; by the time she reaches them, there are no signs of the woman who had blocked her path, the woman with the small black handbag, or the assailant who had assaulted her slowly recovering partner, Marcel. Even David had departed the balcony; whilst shaking his head and apparently talking to himself.

Although the silk banner with the printed 9th Quest, had been removed by detective Abrielle; before any of those assembled in the church had hardly noticed it, let alone recognised it as coming from the Curch of Free-Heroes, the close-up sequence of the events had been faithfully and clearly recorded by Hanna's hidden phone.

When the four companions were safe and sound, they watched the recording through several times, and each time they did, Hanna's three friends wholeheartedly congratulated her on her marvellous quick thinking and actions. When Hanna said that she wanted no more congratulations, her friends immediately congratulated her again, and then - David uploaded the recording to their website and several media outlets.

The 9th Quest stated:
The Curch of Free-Heroes
The 9th Quest
Ever increasing lifespan and goodness.
A Free-Hero's pursuit of an ever-increasing life span,
eventually limited, only by our abilities and free choice, can
be furthered valued by pursuing an ever-increasing
humanness.
The 9th Question:
Has the disregard of the ABC of verifiable proof, by religion,
led to the miss-spelling of religion?
www.curchoffreeheroes.info

Chapter 38 -The walk

Whenever Steven had a problem to solve, he liked to take it for a walk. As he passed a café/bar, he realised that he needed to go to a toilet, so he popped into the bar and used their facilities; however, as he exited the bar he suddenly found that he had solved the first part of the problem. He had found a way of obtaining a suitable guise for getting into, and even beyond the medium-security areas of Saint Peter's - after all, when nature demands, then even the devout have to obey. When he returned to the hotel, David, Hanna, and Rita were having a heated debate as to whether, let alone how, the group could placard the Vatican. David was proposing that the women should not be a part of the actual placarding, or even be in Rome at the time. The women were arguing that they should be part of the whole plan from planning, to its enactment.'

After listening to the debate for some time, Steven summarized, 'Ok! So far then, the plans are, one, to get some remotely controlled device to unfurl the placard. Two, steering a remotely controlled mini-drone that is carrying the placard slung underneath, and have it hover over the Pope and his procession. Three, buy and use some app' to hack into and highjack the online broadcast of the procession, and superimpose our placard.'

Respectfully addressing his fellow plotters, Steven suggested, 'All these plans are possible. But a drone is not that easy to control that precisely, without a fair bit of experience, particularly when it comes to guiding it through narrow or low spaces. It can be pulled down or even shot down by the police before it gets halfway to the Pope's procession. They are not to know that the drone isn't carrying some sort of explosive device.'

When his companions had finished looking at each other, Steven continued, 'High-jacking an entire TV network is no easy task either, even with the right hacking software. Placing a scroll of some kind, near or above the altar, and remotely

unfurling it after whoever places it has made their escape, is more feasible. But it should be placed in a position of some prominence, without it being discovered beforehand. It will mean going into Saint Peters, which is always crowded even on a quiet day, and not being caught red handed.'
Looking at his three friends, in turn, Steven then suggested, 'However, I think that there will be nothing that carries as much significance, as physically placing a placard of the tenth Quest, in Saint Peters, on the day of the Pope's visit.'
'How so?' Hanna asked.
'I've been studying online recordings and TV broadcast of the Pope's procession and service on the day, and there is a way.'
'How so? Saint Peters will be packed full on such a day, and the security will be very high,'
'As part of the main service, either the Pope or someone of high standing always reads out the prayers from a prayer book that is pre-placed, on a stand or pedestal. The appropriate page to be read out, is pre-designated by a piece of cloth or ribbon, so the prayer book opens automatically at that page.'
Seeing that his friends were following him so far, Steven continued, 'I suggest that some time before the Pope arrives, we insert and fix a copy of the tenth quest, in-between leaves of the prayer book. So that when the reader turns the pre-assigned prayer page, in order to read it out, he sees our copy of the tenth quest instead.'
Hanna asked, 'But he will ignore it, yes?'
'He will try his best to, yes. But whoever the reader is, be it the Pope or some high-ranking church official, he will be unable to completely hide his confusion or even shock, and is that look of shock, that we post on our website and the internet, alongside the question. Why was the reader so taken aback?'
Seeing that his friends are still with him, he concludes, 'Then we post the answer, by showing the inserted page of the tenth quest. We must, of course, use the button hole camera to

video the quest being inserted inside the prayer book beforehand.'

As his three friends thought about his plan, he added, 'It will require one of us to insert the tenth quest into the prayer book, roughly at the same time as the Pope's procession begins its journey to Saint Peters. I suggest that we plan it step by step together, and we plan it for one person to carry it out. I also suggest that I carry it out alone. I also suggest that on the day, all of you are well out of Rome.'

'We do not need martyrdom.' David stated.

Steven looked as if David had just insulted him, then he told everyone, 'This is not *martyrdom,* it is an act of protection. Protecting and furthering the successes that we have gained so far. And I don't intend to get caught. If the situation looks impossible or too dodgy, then we'll abandon the plan and choose a safer option later.'

Looking at Rita, Steven carried on, 'I take your point about my past reputation muddying the reputation of the Curch campaign, *but* if we don't succeed in the tenth placarding, as expected by the police, the Vatican and the people then our reputation will be diminished anyway. So, if any of you possess the experience and nerve to carry this out, or can do a better job than me, or hold up under the police interrogations if you are caught, then say so.'

When no one answered, he said 'Well I have the nerve, and because I have nothing to gain from any deal any police can offer to me, I am immune to such threats. And you don't have to unnecessarily risk yourselves or the rest of the quest.'

Steven's companions thought for some while, but when David held his hands up in surrender, Hanna and Rita agreed, and the planning began. However, it was decided that with Steven's lack of fluent Italian, any possible language barrier would at least hamper the plan; therefore at least one person would have to be near him, or at least in available phone contact with him. At which point the argument about who would be his minder broke out. It was eventually resolved by agreeing that all of the group would stay in Rome.

Chapter 39 - The procession

It is perfectly easy, if you book in advance, for any member of the public to attend some of the Papal events. However, anyone getting into Basilica and close to the Pope would require random luck, or an invited guest-only inner pass, to one of the invited guest-only, Papal calendar events. As far as any of the four companions were concerned, obtaining an inner-pass would require getting one from someone who already had one.

Looking at the various Vatican inner-pass holders' exiting the main railway station's gent's lavatory, Steven notes the holders of inner sanctum passes, which bear a red and green stripe; mostly have their pass either pinned to their chest or hung around their neck, and that each inner pass has the bearer's photo and ID details on its front.

The first and most prolific inner pass holders are the police. Then there are the Bishops, cardinals, and other dignitaries. There are also the physically and mentally disabled pilgrims, some of whom have helpers.

Perhaps, Steven thought, "I could pose as a sympathy-evoking wheelchair bound devotee, hoping for a miraculous cure." For the briefest of moments, he had the vivid memory of wheeling Lizzie around the Highgate Cemetery Catacomb. After seeing about a sixty or so potential pass "donators," Steven sees a group of eight hooded monks enter the public lavatory. Following them in, he watches one of them enter a cubical.

Waiting outside the cubical; and barging in as the monk opens the door to come out, Steven jabs the sedative loaded hypodermic into the shocked monk's neck, puts his gloved hand over the monk's mouth, closes the cubical door behind him, and gently lowers the monk back onto the toilet seat … all before the filling flush cistern had enough time to fully refill. Steven then begins listening for any sign of alarm from anyone outside.

Within the space of the cubical, and five minutes, Steven has transferred the Vatican inner-pass, and all other of the monk's personal ID, onto or about his own person or pockets. He also dismantled the monk's phone. Knowing that the induced stupor would last for about another four to five hours, he splashes the monk with the contents of a miniature bottle of whisky and waits.

Just over three minutes later, one of the colleagues of the monk raps on the cubical door. Using an American accent, Steven loudly answers, *'It's in use, can't you see the sign, you want to wait on out there, Buddy?'* Using his best English, the inquiring monk apologises, calls out his lost college's name, twice, and then leaves to tell his assembled brethren that there was no sign of their missing colleague; after which they all disperse into small search parties to search the railway station for him.

After a fruitless search, the monks reform and head off, in line, with their hoods up, for Saint Peters; where they presumed that they would meet up again with their lost colleague. Meanwhile, Steven, carrying the missing monk's outer clothing in a shopping bag, begins to discreetly follow the monks.

Thirty or so minutes later, the monks assemble at the pre-designated spot, situated several kilometres from Saint Peters, and reserved for those who would be part of the official procession through the streets of Rome; and which would eventually enter Saint Peter's Church.

Having now dressed in the outer garments of a monk, the hooded Steven looks like the genuine article. After joining the holy procession, some fifteen minutes behind the monks, Steven slowly makes his way through the surrounding streets and throng.

Feeling the passions and ardour of the pilgrims, devotees, and tourists; the nearest of which were within easy touching distance and smelling the wafts of perfumed necks and garlic breath, Steven becomes strangely moved by the surround-sound-dirge of praise and penitence.

As the procession begins to weave through the oldest parts of the city, it begins to wrap Steven in such a time warp of medieval history and pageantry that he suddenly begins to feel … *"The Call."*

The Call was not from God; for that would take a truly "Road to Damascus" event to achieve. Yet the call does begin to beckon Steven to the priesthood, or more truthfully ... the *power* that the priesthood could harness and bestow. As he and the procession shuffles along, Steven begins realising; that all he would have to do, to become all-powerful to these already converted, faithful, worshipers, would be to stroke, tease and flog them with their very own faith. Not since his time as a psychopath in England, had he felt such a potential source of power – but this religious power - would be totally legal.

"No prison sentence for abusing this lot!" Steven thought to himself, "And I could walk away at any time. But then, once taken up … would such a power be that easy to throw away?" Keeping pace with the procession, Steven plays around with the idea of even permanently hiding under a religious camouflage. What is more, donning the sacred identity of a priest would be ideal in many ways, especially for manipulating the faithful into doing his bidding. Although, Hanna might have objections, of course.

As the awed faces of the crowd beseech him, Steven tastes the power of being a religious leader, for a while. But in the end, he decides that the power from manipulating the gullible, had always smacked of petty power. It would be far more personally satisfying, to be a leader in the fight to take the Church's undeserved-power away from them. However, before he could achieve that, he knew that he, and he alone, would have to stand against the powers that protected the Vatican, Saint Peters, and the Pope.

Nevertheless, as he shuffles along; he no longer secretly mocks his fellow "brethren," for it would feel too much like mocking those who have gone to a place where, as he has to admit, "There but for the grace of good taste … go I."
Keeping his head down, Steven peels away from the procession; so that he could let the genuine monks get well ahead before they were stopped and checked at the barriers, at which point they declare one of them is missing, or they might even see him in the distance.
Clearing the main throng, Steven enters an alleyway that leads into the inner communal square, belonging to some five-story flats - and he immediately alarmed when he is confronted by a uniformed policeman; who had wanted to escape the crowds, to have a cigarette.
Speaking in Italian, the slightly embarrassed policeman asks, 'Can I help you, Father?'
Masking his alarm by looking embarrassment and turning to see that no one else was looking on, Steven grabs his crutch as if he needs to urgently pee, and pleadingly points to the stairwell no more than two metres away. At that point, the policeman gets the message, and gestures that not only should Steven answer the urgent call of nature, but he will keep a lookout for anyone coming along.
As he pretends to relieve himself and whilst looking at the back of the helpful policeman, Steven has an idea. So, whilst the policeman has his back turned toward him, he calmly reaches into his pocket beneath his monk's garb, brings out the box containing the final, pre-loaded hypodermic, opens the box; then smiling, whilst taking the five paces that lay between them, and before the policeman could prevent him, he jabs the sedative into his neck.
 Bringing his alarmed, angry and struggling victim to the cobbled ground and trying to muffle his protest was difficult for Steven - until the sedative rapidly took charge. Hauling the policeman beneath a stairwell of the flats, and stepping out into the open, Steven becomes calm and pleased that even

after the cries and muffled shouts of the policeman, all now seems quiet.

The policeman could not be seen from the stairwell entrance, without going to look under the stairwell itself, and he would probably remain where he was for some time to come; yet as Steven was about to move off, he pauses, ponders and then quickly returns to his serendipitous find.

Chapter 40 - The arrest of the 3

When the Cardinal recognised the call number belongs to the Inspector General, he excuses himself from the committee meeting and answers the call on his way out of the room.

'Inspector General, How good of you to call, have you some news?'

'I have very good news. We have located the whereabouts of David Bell.'

'Really! That is good news indeed Ambrogio. Where is he?'

'An off-duty officer recognised him waiting in a hotel lobby, in Rome. At this moment, Bell is the hotel's restaurant with two Italian-speaking women, one of them seems to be a very close friend of Bell, and all three seem to be waiting for someone. They are about four kilometres away from the Saint Peter's Square. We've spoken with the hotel manager and staff. Bell is booked under the false name of J K Davis, into a single room. The women have a shared double room. Both women seem to be using their real names, and neither has any criminal record. The rooms were booked using a Pay Pal account, in the name of J K Davis. However, we have viewed the security footage of the reception desk at the time Bell and the women's arrival, there was no one else with them. But ten minutes later the CCTV shows a man looking like Steven Chadwick booking into a separate room. Twenty minutes later, all four of them are seen together. The last sighting of Chadwick was when he left the hotel alone, he has not returned.'

'What would you advise?'

'At this moment, there we are keeping a close eye on Bell and the two women. But if he or the women leave the hotel, what with the crowds for the Pope's appearance, there is no guarantee that we will not lose them. The ceremony is due to take place in a little over four hours. It is too much of a coincidence that they are innocent tourists. And, there is also the very recent matter of an assault of a uniform policeman, in the area.

'A police officer?'

'He was found hidden underneath a stairwell, by a dog belonging to one of the people in the flats. The dog owner recognised him as the local patrol officer. The officer was stripped of his uniform, police radio … and revolver.'

'Then he is posing as a policeman.'

'No! We conducted a search of the surrounding area. The uniform, the empty gun, and radio were recovered in a rubbish bin, less than two hundred metres from where the officer was found. I think that the policeman recognised Chadwick, then challenged him and was overcome. The medical people think he has been heavily sedated, he is still unconscious.'

'Can he be brought round, he could give a description of what Chadwick looks like now, such as if he is in disguise and what he is wearing.'

'The doctors say that unless they know what drug has been used to sedate him, it could prove hazardous to bring him round too soon. I have no wish to go against their advice.'

'Of course not, of course not.'

'Nevertheless, the use of drugs to overpower his victims, fits with Chadwick's previous M.O. If he is responsible, then he probably stole the uniform and gun and dumped them shortly afterward. He had no or little intention of using the uniform or revolver, apart from using their disappearance to get our people to mistrust each other and confuse the whole picture.'

'If this is true then this man is a complete maniac.'

For a few seconds, the Inspector General pondered then he said, 'And that may be his undoing.'

'I agree, but you speak as if you have something specific in mind.'

'I have. Are you at your offices?'

'Yes.'

'Good. I am less than five minutes from your office, if you would care, I could pick you up and perhaps we could discuss this in more detail.'

15 minutes later, The Cardinal, sat in the back of a limousine, listening to the General Inspector's plan.

'The point about Chadwick's past criminality and his increasingly criminal behaviour, is that both can be used to our advantage.'

'In what way, Ambrogio?'

I suggest that we arrest Bell and the two women. We hold and question all three. That way we will have at least one of the possible offenders in safe keeping until at least the ceremony is over. Once Chadwick's criminal record is made known, particularly to the two women, and it is made clear how this man's behaviour is escalating … and that he may have his own, *maniacal* reasons for getting near to the Pope … the women or even Bell may crack.'

'Let me understand, are you suggesting that this man really wishes to physically harm His Excellency, or that we use that as a manoeuvre against Bell and the women? I only ask this, because if you believe His Excellency is in immediate danger, then I must inform him.'

'I am suggesting both possibilities. Even if the women aren't involved in the Curch activities, we may still get them to tell us about Bell's and Chadwick's recent movements. As far as this Curch business is concerned, then Bell is probably the General, and Chadwick the soldier, but even Bell may see the wisdom of dumping such a complete maniac. We need to find Steven Chadwick.'

'Then you must do as you think best, Ambrogio.'

When David spotted the four plain-clothed detectives entering the hotel restaurant and approaching his table, he immediately sensed they are policemen and that they had come for him. Looking at the sudden haggard expression on his face, Hanna asked, 'What's wrong David, are you not well?'

Twenty minutes later, all three companions were separated and being asked routine questions by detectives. In addition to the arresting detective of David Bell, the Inspector General sat in the same room and mainly listened and watched; as did

Cardinal by viewing the ongoing CCTV two rooms away. By the time the first round of questioning had ended, the question that Steven had previously posed to his three friends; as to whether they would be able to stand up under police interrogation had been answered, and so far, all three were holding up.

During a break for refreshments, the Inspector General addressed both his colleagues and the Cardinal, 'We have the most recent phone calls of all three suspects' phones. Bell was in possession of an unregistered phone. The phone has not been used until today, and has only one communication, and it was with another unregistered mobile phone. We believe that phone may be in the possession of Steven Chadwick. Both Bell's and Chadwick's phones are linked to an encrypted darknet server. Even if we could begin a trace of Chadwick's whereabouts during a phone call, he could be long gone by the time we plotted and arrived at his position.' Picking at a stray hair on his sleeve, the Cardinal asked, 'Have you a suggestion?'

'This man is suspected by the British police, of being this Body Part Murderer, and murdering and dismembering at least four or more people in cold blood. He has a known criminal record for using firearms, including the shooting of a policeman and two civilians. He is amongst a crowd of several hundred thousand of innocent civilians. We must consider all options very carefully before we act. However, on further conversations with Chief Inspector Rupert of the British police, I learned something more.'

'And?'

'We both agreed, that when he first sought out David Bell, in Italy, Chadwick's intentions were probably to use him as a convenient, cover or a safe house as it were, until he could move on. Nevertheless, Bell would know how dangerous a man Chadwick is, and he may have felt threatened. But, somehow, the two of them formed a pact. Bell used Chadwick to do his dirty work, and Chadwick went along with it to keep the peace. But Inspector Rupert says that Chadwick has a taste of taking calculated high risks. He added that he also has a taste for notoriety. However, Bell would know that. He would also know that harming anyone, would do far more harm to the Curch campaign than any possible good, so he would not consider it as an option. If Chadwick is spooked, and believes something has gone wrong, and that his cover and identity may be at great risk of being traded, in a deal with us, he will also presume that we will put every effort into capturing him. In that scenario, then Rupert believes, that if Chadwick feels cornered with no way out, his desire for notoriety would overcome his desire for survival. Bell may think he has Chadwick on a leash, but he is wrong. If cornered, Chadwick will attack anyone who is unfortunate enough to be within striking distance.'

'And you believe if Bell or the women, are told that this maniac is motivated by his own warped desire for notoriety, they would start to co-operate.'

'We are about to find out.'

Chapter 41 - The interrogations
Rita
Before the Cardinal entered the interview room in which Rita
was "voluntary assisting in police inquiries," The Inspector
General warned, 'So far, she has refused to answer any
questions. I doubt if things will change for the better.
Nevertheless, any information that we can get from her, may
be useful when it comes to questioning the other two.'
By the end of the interview, the prediction of non-
improvement proved to be true. The only response to any
question was to The Cardinal's one of whether she believed in
God; to which Rita's reply was, 'Do you?' after that she just
stared straight ahead and said nothing.
The interrogation of Hanna
Before entering the room in which Hanna was being held, the
Inspector General primed the Cardinal, 'The procedure of
questioning that you will observe, will be the same for the
other two suspects. Though the exception being, that any,
spiritual help, you might give to Hanna, could be significant.'
'Am I to take the role of the good cop?'
Giving the Cardinal a brief smile, Ambrogio answered, 'Each
police interrogator has their own personality, which is as
changeable as the weather, and is best not hidden or hindered
by taking on an unnatural character. Interrogations are
conducted not so much on the good cop bad cop
characterisation, but more of the lines of goods news bad
news. The threat of what will happen if the accused does not
cooperate, and then, the good news of what will happen if
they do cooperate can be just as effective, coming from a
"bad cop as a good one. If I may offer any advice, it would be
to just be yourself.'
Even at the age of 78, when the Cardinal first met Hanna, he
was struck by her sensual beauty, which seemed to be
heightened by her natural acceptance of it.
However, once the Inspector General had made sure that she
didn't require any water or other comforts, he wasted no time,

'Before you try to deny or admit any involvement with the recent Curch of Free-Heroes activities, at that point he pushed a green folder toward Hanna, 'This is an Italian language copy, of the British police's report on Steven Chadwick. You will see that it includes his criminal record, which states that amongst other things he has shot a policeman, kidnapped a woman, and shot two innocent people, who were trying to help criminals give up crime. The British police *also* strongly suspect that he was involved in a series of murders and mutilations.'

As he watched Hanna read through the last part of the document, The Cardinal saw that her face began to visibly pale, and a look of fear … or was it a sense of betrayal, seemed to be draining even her casual beauty.

Seeing the change also, the Inspector General nods to the Cardinal, who in turn says,' Hanna … my child… you cannot be blamed for being deceived by this man, or by any false promises and affections he might have … forced or tricked you into.'

Pausing to move closer to Hanna, the Cardinal continues, 'I have come from the Vatican itself, Hanna. And I am authorised to offer you forgiveness of our Father in Heaven, in the form of the personal forgiveness of the Pope. Please consider carefully how this will not only change what happens to you for the rest of your life, but what will happen to you in the life-after, which neither the highest nor lowest of his children can avoid.'

For a moment or two, as her colour and life resurges, Hanna remains thoughtful. Then looking straight into the eyes of the Cardinal, she states, 'You can take your promises of *your* paradise, and your threats of eternal hell, and peddle them someplace else. I will take my chances with Life and try to build a paradise on *here* on Earth. And if Life or God condemns me to an eternity in hell for trying, then at least I will have plenty of time to try and build a paradise there too!'

The look of astonishment on the Cardinals face is a clear enough cue, for the Inspector General to retrieve the folder, look at his watch, and pronounce that the interview had ended; he then nods to Hanna, and leaves the room with the Cardinal in tow.

As the two men stand outside the interview room The Inspector General offers the Cardinal, some words of attempted absolution as well as comfort, 'Even to an experienced interviewer, the role of a good cop is not always as easy as it may seem. But we will return to both women after they have time to think.'

The interrogation of David Bell

To The surprise and relief of the Cardinal, the interview with David Bell went a great deal smoother than the ones with Rita or Hanna. The interview began in earnest when The Inspector General pointed out certain facts.

'We have forensic evidence that you were present at the village where the church was placarded and desecrated with a strawberry and cream flan. I would also think that once a photograph of you is shown amongst the residents of the village, and the other places where churches have been desecrated, people will recall that you were present in the area on the day when these vandalisms against our sacred Italian churches took place.'

At first, David does not reply, he just simply smiles.

'There is also the future evidence, obtained from Hanna and Rita to be considered. And of course, there is the matter of harbouring and assisting the flight of a known fugitive from British justice. I speak of Steven Chadwick of course. His fingerprints have been found all over your home. No doubt when his photograph is shown to the same people who can place you in the areas of these desecrations, it will be remembered that the two of you were together.'

A frown now appears on David Bell's forehead, as the policeman continues, 'I am also equally confident that the same outcome will occur in the town in which a Muslim

Cleric was assaulted, inside his own mosque. I also have the evidence of two decorated and respected detectives, that you, Steven Chadwick, and Hanna and Rita, were all present in the same town, and on the day, when a man was brutally killed by having his head smashed in.'
Looking at David Bell's face and body language, it is apparent that he is far from confident when he replies, 'You seem to have circumstantial evidence, but little else.'
Holding his hand up, the Inspector General states, 'There is also the very *high* probability that, within the last hours, Chadwick has assaulted and drugged a uniformed policeman, and stolen his uniform and *gun*. You know this man more than I do, but such criminal behaviour seems excessive beyond sane reason, if he is just to trying to hang a protest placard somewhere, don't you think, David?'
In an attitude of informing, rather that accusation, the Inspector General then proceeds to tell an increasingly worried-looking David Bell about the prospect; that Steven Chadwick has his own agenda for coming to Rome and the Vatican - and being *very* near the Pope. By the time the explanation is over, David Bell seems very worried and out of his depth.
'All in all, Mr. Bell, even if this Chadwick causes no more harm, you are facing a very lengthy time in an Italian prison. So, I suggest that you stop playing games and consider, very seriously, about helping us catch this maniac before it is too late for us … to help you avoid any prison … at all!'
It was clear to all in the room that David Bell could be seen to be seriously considering the possibilities. But it was the Cardinal's next approach, which further weakened Bell's resolve to not cooperate. The Cardinal started off by stating, 'The Inspector General tells me that in your role as the head Crime Adviser for the Crimetest organisation, you were highly successful in turning many criminals away from crime, David.'

Leaning forward and opening his arms out, the Cardinal then asks, 'Tell me, David, what your advice would be to somebody who finds himself in the position you find yourself in. What would you genuinely advise him to do?'
After a pause, David Bell replies, 'The same as I have been telling myself since Chadwick turned up on my doorstep.'
'And that would be?'
'To do all that I could to prevent more crimes from happening.'
Seeing that the possibility that Steven Chadwick had formed his own dangerous agenda, had struck a note of clarity with David Bell; the Cardinal decides that it is the moment for him to take charge. Turning to the Inspector General, he asks, 'Would it be possible that David and I, could have a moment or two to consider a proposal that has come from the Vatican?'
Two minutes later, all recording devices had been turned off, and David and the Cardinal are alone.
David looks, with some surprise, at the Cardinal, then asks, 'So, is this the moment you bring out the holy thumb screws?'
Smiling at David Bell's small joke, the Cardinal answers, 'No of course not. But I thought that we might take a break in the proceedings, so that we could perhaps clear up a possible … misunderstanding … that may have occurred, some time ago.'
 'Misunderstanding?'
'An understandable, misunderstanding. But perhaps it would be better for all concerned that we reach a present understanding.'
'Which is?'
'Can we agree, that although we are not in a church confessional or a session of the Crimetest's advice line, what is said between us as we try to reach an understanding, remains as confidential as if we were?'
'I agree.'

'I mention the subject of confidentiality, because it seems to me that this situation before us revolves around the role of confidentiality, and its part in preventing crime.'
'Please go on.'
'And could we agree, that just as one of our priests will be faced with the dilemma of keeping a confidentiality, in a matter of grave concern, whilst still trying to persuade any sinner from carrying on with his wrongful acts, then so would one of your Crimetest Crime Advisers, or indeed your good self, be equally placed to keep a moral confidentiality, whilst trying to dissuade any wrongdoer from doing further wrong.'
'Yes, without splitting hairs, I can agree on that.'
'I only mention such things, in the light, that my intentions in meeting you privately, is that we can help each other stop a crime being committed, by firstly clearing up any sort of misunderstanding, that would otherwise block the decision to … allow the creation of the Crimetest Advice Service, into Italian law?'
'Please continue, Cardinal.'
Pausing just long enough for David Bell to see clearly where the conversation might be heading to, the Cardinal continues, 'As a member of the council, I have a first-hand knowledge of the matters which brought about our cautious and early decision, to oppose the Crimetest's proposals. And of course, I am also aware of any objections, such as, that it may be seen to undermine our own highly valued service of the confessional. However, David, I am sure you will understand our *initial* concerns, that if any future legal confidentiality of a Crimetest's advice session, were to be *later* overruled in some judicial appeal, then that in turn, may set a legal precedence for a legal challenge to our own confidentiality, in matters of the church confessional?'
'I understand.'
'However, since those times, I have very recently been in contact with the highest authority in this matter, and after careful considerations and legal advice, I can assure you, that

the church may well look more favourably on the possibility
of an Italian based Crimetest's crime advice service, in the
future.'

At that point, the Cardinal brought out a two-page document,
then passing it to David, he adds, 'As you will read, we are
now more than open to such a possibility. In, essence, this is a
signed agreement that the church will look more favourably
on the introduction of Crimetest's Crime Advice service, in
Italy.'

David studies and then re-studies the document, and then
points out, 'You seem to have been busy Cardinal, and I must
admit that such an understanding would be much appreciated.
But what is to stop you and you and your council from
changing their minds once again?'

'Leaving aside the fact that, without a substantial reason for
changing our mind, then such a turnaround would look very
unprofessional, bordering on the unethical? I can assure you
David, the Pope himself, who has seen this document, would
not look upon such a turnaround as being of any benefit the
Roman Catholic Church. So confident is my belief that this
assurance is all but binding, I would ask that you take this
copy away with you and show it to whoever you wish.'

'In return for?'

'In return for your understanding, that the matter of total
confidentiality in matters of preventing a crime, can be a
precarious business, for all concerned. Indeed, this ongoing
situation with this Chadwick can be said to be an example of
the dilemma we all face.'

'Please go on.'

'But now the situation has come to a climax that I am sure
you did not perceive and would never want to happen. This
maniac, this Steven Chadwick, with his own ego inflated,
highly dangerous and personal agenda for notoriety, is more
than an academic speculation. I believe that unless Chadwick
is stopped, then the outcome will be catastrophic for us all. Of
course, I'm sure that you realise, if such a catastrophe should

happen under the watch of a Crimetest's confidentiality code, then I fear that it would not only do long lasting harm to Crimetest, but also to any prospect of a Crimetest's ever being possible in Italy, or indeed many other nations.'

After David re-reads the document that he had been given, he hands it back to the Cardinal, and replies, 'If this is worth any more than the paper it is written on, then so be it. Then after a few second more thought he states, 'I will not hand him over to you or tell you his target. Nevertheless I will phone him and try to persuade into giving up the task and leave Italy as soon as possible.'

After returning to rest of the company and going over a plan of action, The Inspector General hands David Bell his previously confiscated phone, and then sits down and waits as the number is dialed.

When Steven answers his phone, he is still amongst the crowds flocking toward Saint Peters.

Within five seconds, David starts to speak.

'It's David. Hanna may have gone to the police!'

'What?'

'The three of us were at the hotel, I left for a moment, when I came back Rita was in a panic. She told me that Hanna had told her that the placarding must be stopped. Then she, Hanna, fled the hotel. Rita told me that she feared Hanna would go to the police. The next thing that happened was Rita said that she must try to find her, and she left the hotel too!'

'Did you follow her?'

'No, I thought it best to wait and see if Hanna came back. But if the police know about you, they will be looking for you. You must get out of there quick, you must call it off, get out altogether.'

'Have you phoned Hanna?'

For a moment David falters, then replies, 'Yes, but there is no answer. I called as soon as Rita told me what happened … Rita called too.'

'Even if what you say is true, they may as well be looking for a needle in a haystack.'
'But Hanna has her own photos of you, if she …'
'I'll call Rita and find out exactly what happened.'
'She not answering.'
'If Hanna wanted to try and stop me, she could have phoned me. At worst, she left to try and find me. None of this makes sense David, what's wrong?'
'Of course, she might be trying to find you, I hadn't thought of that, but you must call it off, then get out, leave altogether … if Hanna calls me …'
'That is the second time you've insisted I get out, David.'
'I just wanted to make sure you were safe … have you left the placard yet?'
'No, where are you now?'
'At the hotel.'
'Good, show me.'
'What?'
'Use the camera app' to show me where you are.'
'Where I am?'
'After all, if Hanna has gone to the police, then the police may be spying on you right now. So, why don't you turn the video app on your phone, on, right now and then pan it around, so I can get a *full* picture of your situation, David.'
Raising a hand in the air as he looks at the Inspector General for an answer, David Bell replies, 'Ok, hold on a minute'
'I'll hold on David … for three seconds'.
'Listen, I'm all confused, we don't have time for this, forget the plan, you must leave …'
'The plan is fine, at this very moment I'm dressed as a policeman.'
'A policeman!'
'A policeman, David. And I seriously doubt if Hanna intends going to the police. Rita probably misread the situation. Nevertheless, make sure that you keep the information about the police uniform to yourself. If you get any further news,

text me, do not call me. If necessary, I will call you back,'
Steven then disconnects the call.
Back in the interview room, the Inspector General allows
David Bell to switch the mobile phone off, then he explains,
'As you know, we already knew of the attack on the
policeman and the stealing of his firearm and uniform. What
we did not tell you, is that the uniform has been found. It was
dumped by Chadwick shortly after he stole it. He had no or
little intention of using it, apart from in getting our people to
mistrust each other, and confuse the whole picture. The fact
that he told you that he is still wearing it, strongly suggests
that he believes that you are helping us, and that you can no
longer be trusted.'
Turning to the Cardinal, the Inspector General states, 'There
is only one other reasonable option open to us. We deal with
Chadwick directly, by phoning his phone and offering him the
best deal that we can offer.'
'Which is?' the Cardinal asks.
'That if he hands himself in, without any further harm to
anyone, we will have to hand him over to the English police.
But as far as any business with this Curch affair is concerned,
then we will not press charges against him, nor Mr Bell here,
or the two women, nor will we investigate any further.'
Turning to David Bell, he asks, 'Unless of course, there are
more serious crimes that have not come to our attention yet?
What about the dead Muslim man on the beach?'
David thinks for about five seconds, then answers, 'There are
no serious crimes that I know of.'

Chapter 42 - The Inspector General and Steven
When Steven feels his phone vibrating in his pocket, he takes
it out and pressing connect, he listens.
 'Steven, this is Inspector General Inspector General,
Ambrogio Servino.'
Silence.
'Steven?'
'Yes, Ambrogio, how can I help you?'
'We have all of your forged passports and identifications,
from the hotel. Having seen your conviction for shooting a
British police officer and two civilians, I have told my men to
shoot you if you look as if you are intending to harm …
anybody.'
After taking in the bad news, and quickly dismissing his
regret about not bringing his forged passports with him,
Steven waits a while and then answers, 'How very frank of
you to tell me, Ambrogio. I presume that David has spilt the
beans … or should I say, the pasta?'
'Apart from contacting you to try and persuade you to give up
this … placarding business, Mr. Bell has not volunteered any
further help to us. Steven, I can assure you that if you turn
yourself in, then higher powers than I, will ensure that any
possible prosecution against you, David, Hanna, and Rita, for
any nonviolent act in furthering the Curch campaign, will not
see the light of a courtroom. As for any violent act against
any other person, of a different faith, then it is the opinion of
our prosecution services, that without any hard evidence, it
will remain on record as being too difficult to be prosecuted.'
'How reassuring that is for me to know, and for you to inform
me, Inspector General. Naturally Rita and David have booked
themselves onto a flight to some far away tropical paradise
island. And as a token of her repentance, and in view of that
those same powers which are not only leading you astray, but
who believe that she was led astray by me, namely Hanna.
Has volunteered to attend a year-long sabbatical in a secluded
nunnery, just outside Rome. Where the Pope himself will

keep one of his sacred eyes on her wellbeing …and everyone will live happily ever after.'
'Nevertheless, Steven,' the Inspector General continues, 'if you try to escape or harm anyone, those same powers will have to seriously look at everyone's situation again.'
 Looking around at the crowds, Steven considers his options, then replies, 'We appear to be pinned between the horns of a dilemma, Ambrogio. Behind one horn there is my moral compulsion to take away the rewards from those that do not deserve rewards. And let us face it, religion has more undeserved rewards than most. And behind the other horn there is your moral compulsion to take my freedom away, because you believe that I do not deserve it. So, the dilemma for me is … do I let my desire for justice die in the bullring, or do I let you and the church tether it to the confines of some British prison exercise yard, until all that is left … is a pile of bullshit!'
 For a moment or two, Steven pauses, as he remembers a conversion between his old nemesis Sandra Lott and himself, then he replies, 'She was right ... being the hero of the story is … very scary.'
'Who was right?'
'It doesn't matter.' Steven answers, and disconnects the call. There is a place, on some journeys, where the purpose of the trekker's original destination becomes diverted or side-tracked by new possibilities on the horizon. Sometimes, those glittering horizons indicate the very borders of a more wholesome land. At other times they are mere illusions, rather than any practical possibilities. Steven has experienced both such glittering horizons when he had first taken up the challenge to Crimetest, so many years ago.
Presently glistening on the horizon of Steven's mind, is an idea. It is such an audacious idea that Steven is now encountering; his jaw drops open with the sheer audacity of it. But first he needs to steal, beg, borrow or buy something. Twenty minutes later he has what he wants.

As soon as the call to Steven had been disconnected, the Inspector General orders a police officer, 'Get me a helicopter to the roof, we can land on the helipad near Saint Peters.' Then he orders another officer to get all three suspects together.

When the three friends arrive, the Inspector General tells them, 'We have issued a phone-photograph of Steven Chadwick to every uniformed and plain clothed officer in Italy. It will also be issued in a press conference. We also have his passports and identifications. If he tries to get out of Rome the chances of him being recognised are very high. If that happens, there is no telling what he will do, or what the arresting officers will do when faced with a fugitive who has already shot a policeman and two civilians in England. If we can detain him in Rome, then I will have some control over the situation and my officers. And I will do my utmost to bring a result in which no one, including Steven, is hurt … or dies.'

At that moment, an officer enters to the room and informs, 'Heli-transport will arrive within ten minutes Inspector General.'

Turning back to the three companions, the Inspector General explains, 'We are all being helicoptered to Saint Peter's. We go inside where the service is to take place. You will have a view of the whole of the proceedings.'

Confronting Rita and Hanna, the Inspector General emphasises, 'We believe Mr. Chadwick will attempt some sort of personal confrontation with the Pope. This man has already been convicted of shooting a police officer and two innocent people in England. He has also admitted to Mr. Bell, that he has assaulted and stolen an Italian police officer's firearm. He is *far* more dangerous than you can possibly know, or quite frankly could be expected to know. He is completely out of control, and, he has not come here to play. We believe he has come here to harm or even assassinate the Pope himself.'

Looking at Rita and Hanna in turn, the Inspector General advises, 'We have his photo, but he will almost certainly be in some sort of disguise. But you can recognise his manner, his way holding himself, and his way of walking. If you recognise him at Saint Peters, then you can save him, and many, many others from a great distress and harm!'

Chapter 43 - The Insolence

Dressed in the clothes of the monk, and with the monk's inner pass hanging around his neck and assisting an elderly nun in pushing her severely handicapped charge; Steven passes through the security searching area of Saint Peter's Church without too much undue attention.

However, upon entering the church; he glances toward the altar and notices (with a calm almost bordering on approval), that the pedestal that is supposed to be holding the prayer book, is bereft of any prayer book. Presuming that the curch authorities may have changed their routine, or David Bell has told the police of the full plan, Steven decides to fully commit to his own, *grand plan* of action, instead.

The most immediate problem would be in how to wait in the church, without being seen by the other monks of the same order who were already inside, and who would undoubtedly raise some sort of attention if they saw him. So, as soon as he has departed from the nun and her charge, Steven makes for the men's washroom.

Whilst waiting in one of the washroom cubicles, Steven does his best to ignore the various noises and smells of the environment. However, there is little choice but to wait, so, using his spare phone, he watches a muted, live broadcast, of the Pope's procession.

As Steven watches and patiently waits, Hanna, Rita and David Bell also wait, with the Inspector General, the Cardinal, the head of the police armed response unit, and three police marksmen (spaced out at intervals), at their respective places along the railed walkway beneath the massive dome of Saint Peters. Across the way on the same level, two more police marksman wait with their telescopic-sighted rifles held loosely at their side.

When the Pope's procession begins to cross Saint Peters Square, the washrooms begin to empty as people hurry to take their allotted seat and places. Watching the live TV coverage of the Pope crossing Saint Peter's Square, Steven finally decides to move.

No longer worrying about the possibility that monks might see him, Steven exits the washrooms and heads towards the rear far side of the assembled guests and dignitaries. Standing to the left of the rear row of dignitaries, he sees that the Pope and his entourage are approaching the end of their journey and are now passing beneath and are proceeding along the grand entrance of Saint Peter's itself.

With the rising chords of the strident choir in full voice, echoing around Saint Peter's, Steven is reverently moving toward the front aisle of dignitaries and guest. To his right, he sees that the Papal procession is glistening and glowing; with the radiant reds, sacred whites and deep rich purples of their undeserved rewards - whilst bringing the glittering horizon of his *grand-plan* ... nearer and nearer.

Hardly anyone takes much notice of the hooded Steven's movements; for they are all too focused and fascinated with watching the Pope and the procession. Certainly, the Inspector General does not notice Steven; but then he is not looking at the crowd below - he is watching the three companions of Steven.

When Hanna involuntary jerks her head, the Inspector General instantly follows her gaze and sees a hooded monk approaching the central aisle. Speaking urgently but quietly into his police radio, he gives orders to his plain clothed the officers on the ground floor.

'Move in and stop the hooded monk in the brown cloak at the front. If he makes any sudden moves, hold and arrest him. Block him from the Pope and the procession, *everyone else keep alert!*'

Reaching the rope barrier, the hooded monk partially pulls his hood back; to get an unobstructed view of the steadily advancing procession of the Pope - and the Inspector General at last sees the face of Steven Chadwick in the flesh.

Hearing a clear message of, 'Report when ready!' from the officer in charge of the police marksmen, the Inspector General turns to see the riflemen have already shouldered their rifles, and are drawing a bead on their target; as their leader further instructs, 'Report when you have a clear line of shot, do not, I repeat, do *not* open fire until you hear my express order to shoot.'

Within three seconds, all four marksmen report that they have a clear line of fire.

Moving closer to railings, Hanna feels the hand of the Inspector General pull her firmly back, as he warns, 'If you shout any warning, he may panic. The marksman will interpret the moves as an act of aggression, and they *will* shoot him!'

Down at the rope barrier, Steven notices the earnest movements of the plain clothed detectives, as they head towards his position, and he immediately realises that if he is to … *succeed* ... then he will have to act – *now!*

Up in the balcony, the leader of the police marksmen sees Steven reaching with both hands, beneath his cloak, and performing a sharp, upward pulling motion with his right hand and arm.

'He's just primed a pump-shotgun or drawn a sword under his cloak!'

Smoothly ducking beneath the waist-high barrier, Steven casually walks toward the mildly surprised Pope; who becomes instantly alarmed when he sees Steven, now only ten … nine … eight … seven … paces away … drawing his monk's gown aside – *as the sudden thunder-clap of the single rifle shot echoes off every unforgiving wall and arches every raised eyebrow within the church* - prompting, the final chorister's voice to falter and stop in mid-note; as Steven's weapon of choice loudly clatters across the resplendent and ornately tiled floor, until it slides to a halt at the feet of the dumfounded Pope, and his huddled entourage.

Even from high up, the Inspector General can see that the weapon of Steven's choice, is neither a primed pump-shotgun, nor an unsheathed sword; but an extended selfie-rod, attached to the mobile phone, with which Steven had intended to capture the *perfect shot* of a selfie image of the Pope, and himself wearing the placard, bearing the 10th Quest.
Five paces away from Steven, the kneeling Pope begins praying for the soul of Steven; who lays on his blood-soaked back with the placard slung around his neck. Kneeling beside Steven, a concerned bishop is conveying to him that the Pope is praying for his soul.
Lifting his head, and glancing at the Pope; Steven half smiles, half sneers, and then rests his head back, whilst giving his opinion on the Pope's efforts.
'Insolent bastard!'

The Tenth Quest stated:

The Curch of Free Heroes
The 10th Quest: Freedom of Self:
A Free-Hero's quest for the freedom of self; is valued by accepting that the totality of his or her, *self,* is by far the most precious thing that s/he can ever own. As such, the quests of a Free-Hero can be used to free her or his self; by choosing to discard the following limiting demands, choices, and actions known as:
The DISCARDING's of a Free-Hero:
Disliking our likenesses. Interpreting the miss-spelling of faith as the ABC of truth. Stealing the common-sense goodness of humanity, by claiming it for your own purposes. Covering up or practicing gender, race or ethnic abuse. Abdicating self-responsibility for the rewarding numbness of addiction or ritualization. Religion. Denying that honesty is the centre of anything worthwhile. Insolence. Numbing humanity's pursuit of truth, freedom, and justice, by using truthless bites and leech-pooh promises. Giving up on the 10 Quests of a Free-Hero.

The 10th Question:
How many ways can you discover; by which religious and non-religious supporters, can yet be respectful for each other's struggles?

www.thecurchoffreeheroes.info

Chapter 44 -Laying to rest

It is a terrible day for a funeral; particularly for a secular style funeral. There is no prospect of re-incarnation as a mouse, elephant or world-famous super-rock -star. No glorious afterlife to look forward to (or even a Hellish one). No check-in to a five-star, everlasting shiny Paradise; and due to the steady downpour of English rain - there isn't even a rainbow for miles around.

The private funeral for Steven is being held in England and is attended by David Bell, Rita and Hanna. Amongst the other mourners, Sandra and Andy had flown over from America with their baby son. There is also small, selected group of guests, and some invited members from the press. Although the ceremony is non-religious; for the eulogy, David uses the same "feel the lack" eulogy that Steven had used for the English man whose funeral they happened to chance upon, in Italy.

As the mourners move out of the graveyard, and whilst walking beside David, Sandra comments, 'That was a moving eulogy, David, I'm sure Steven would have appreciated it.'

'He should. It was one that he used for a total stranger, whose funeral we happened come across.'

Looking back to the graveyard, and then back to Sandra, David ponders for a moment, until Sandra asks, 'So, David what will you do now? Are there any more dragons to ride?'

Smiling at Rita and taking her hand, David answers, 'No. I think we'll try keeping out feet on the ground for a while.'

....

The End

Chapter - Works by the same author:
Same room – different doors
Promises to a Monster
The Crimetest's trilogy

. . . .

Synopsis for Same room – different doors
This is first part of the "Crimetest's" trilogy: After the drugs' related death of their daughter Lucy, David and Claire Bell, search for a common-sense justice; that will also be linked to their deep desire for the most powerful and sweetest revenge of all – turning revenge into reform.
The Bell's increasingly outrageous attempts to gain at least some sort of justice, engages them in a highly dangerous and escalating battle against; the egomaniacal drugs baron Lenny (the Hun) Bean, his cunning sidekick Ricky Ainsworth, a corrupt police Inspector, and last but far from least, with the failing strategies of the establishment's "War on Drugs."

. . . .

Promises to a Monster
Promises to Monster is a crime thriller/human interest story surrounding "Crimetest," and its legally confidential, advice-line for criminals; who may wish to give up crime - it's like "Victim Support" except it's for the potential victimisers.
The humane interest of the story revolves around the Crimetest's Adviser/Negotiators, Andy, and Sandra (*who add a touch of romance*), and their respective dealings with, George, a wannabe-rapist, Trish-trash-Trisha, a drug-addicted prostitute, and Steven.
Steven, who is already a full-blown serial killer, provides the pivotal and intriguing drama of the story; by threatening the very existence of Crimetest. In a fit of vanity ("*It is my most loyal trait in this disloyal life!*") Steven threatens that unless Sandra (or someone at Crimetest), breaks their code of absolute-confidentiality for all callers, by giving *his* details to the police; who can then trace and track and arrest him - then he will trace, track and kill Sandra's co-workers.

The relationships between the Advisors and their clients, and the questioning of the intended crimes, also poses a question to the reader and society. In that, if such a (legally protected) crime advice service is not allowed to be created; then society may well be refusing any potential criminal a last wish to say anything before, he or she has self-condemned them self (and their victim/s) to the crime.

....

The Crimetest's Trilogy:
All three novels; *Same Room – Different Doors, Promises to a Monster, and The Insolence and the Free-heroes* ...
Adapted into one novel

....

Forthcoming novel:
Aletheia's truth.
A novel about the truth, nothing but the truth and so help the truth.